FORBIDDEN SIN

REJECTED FATE BOOK TWO

ALEXIS CALDER

Cover Artwork by Melody Simmons
Editing by Court of Spice

CHAPTER
ONE

MY HEAD THROBBED and everything ached. With a groan, I opened my eyes, causing me to squint against the light. The events of the last few days flooded my memory; an overwhelming sensation that sent a rush of emotions.

"Madoc." His name came out in a whisper. The last thing I remembered was feeling his pain as clearly as if it had been my own.

I sat up, and had to squeeze my eyes closed against the rush of dizziness.

"You keep calling for him. Over and over."

Dax's voice made my eyes snap open. It took a moment to adjust to the dim light, but I saw his form sitting in a chair in the corner of my bedroom. I didn't even get a chance to figure out how I'd gotten here before Dax crossed the room to my bed.

Towering above me, he gazed down. His expression was cold and calculated. All of the previous affection for me was gone. "What happened between you and Madoc Umbra?"

The threat in his tone made my muscles tense. This was old Dax. The one I knew had been lurking under the nice guy act the whole time. This was the Dax I knew how to handle.

He'd thrown me off for a while, and I'd nearly lost myself to the desire to fit in. But I was never going to conform. Especially if what Dax said about my father was true. "You better not be insinuating that something happened between me and my captor."

"You've been calling his name in your sleep." He didn't mask the accusation in his tone.

"Maybe because I just got back from a traumatic experience at his hands," I snapped.

Dax's eyes narrowed as he stared at me. I held his gaze, determined not to back down. Nothing had happened between Madoc and myself, even if he was my mate. Anxiety might be swirling in my head as I worried about his well-being, but it wasn't going to last forever. Madoc was going to break the bond between us and we'd be nothing. A lump filled my throat at the thought. I hated that I was already mourning the loss of a bond I hadn't even explored, but that was the nature of mating bonds. Things were complicated enough as it was. I couldn't let myself linger on Madoc. Even if it felt like I was betraying part of myself by ignoring the pull between us.

"If you have something to say, you better say it," I demanded.

His expression softened and his shoulders sagged a bit as he released some of the tension he'd been holding. Dax ran a hand through his hair and blew out a breath. "I'm sorry. I got jealous."

"Of an Umbra wolf?" I asked.

He dropped to his knees in front of me, the gesture catching me off guard. "I told you how I feel about you. I won't have someone else moving in on my territory."

Your territory? My mind was still groggy with sleep and I knew I wasn't as alert as usual. But I managed to catch the fact that I was referred to with the same amount of affection as an object. I couldn't afford to drop my guard with Dax again. I'd been played, sucked in by his act, but the illusion was shattered the moment I found out he'd killed his own father.

That didn't mean I was free, though. It meant I had to be smarter about how I played his game. "How did I get here, Dax? What happened after the meeting with the elders?"

His brow furrowed, this time, I could almost say it was genuine concern. But I knew better. "You don't remember?"

I shook my head.

Dax took hold of one of my hands. "You had some kind of episode. You were screaming and you kept calling *his* name. Then you passed out. I brought you here."

"How long was in bed?" I asked.

"Almost twenty-four hours," he said.

I swallowed hard. Whatever had hit me when I'd felt

Madoc's pain had affected me. Was the soreness I was feeling from my own unhealed injuries or from whatever he suffered? I didn't know enough about mating bonds to understand all the details. My chest felt tight as I thought about him. I hoped he was okay.

Quickly, I shook the thoughts away. There wasn't anything I could do about Madoc right now. Especially not with Dax standing vigil over me. A few days ago, that had been sort of sweet. Now, I was kicking myself for not seeing the red flag. I had to turn this so I was in control. Dax was dangerous, but I needed him on my side until I figured out what I was going to do next.

How had I let myself get sucked into anything with Dax Carver? It was like a nightmare that made no sense. As if something else had driven me. I couldn't begin to explain the odd sensation rushing through me. As much as I needed to be free of Dax, there was a pull there that I wanted nothing to do with.

But this wasn't the time to say my truth to Dax. I needed time to figure out what all this meant. I couldn't let the questions about why I'd let myself fall for him cloud the real problems. I had to find out about my past while I waited for Madoc to break our bond. I had to play the part Dax had chosen for me, at least for a little while longer.

"Did you mean what you said outside the Hall of Records?" I had to move forward.

"Every word." He seemed even more at ease than he

had been a moment ago. This was what he wanted to talk about. He got off on the possibility of my untapped power.

"Tell me what you know," I said.

"Not yet. It's not the right time. You're still recovering. Still healing," he said.

"Dax, you don't drop that kind of information on someone and not deliver," I said.

"My sweet Ivy. Everything will make sense soon." He reached for my face and brushed his thumb across my cheek. I had to resit the urge to pull away. "Patience. There's a plan at work. Something bigger than both of us. And you have a starring role."

Something roared deep within me and it was as if my wolf was finally waking after a long absence. *Now you show up?* Where was she when I was trying to flee capture? I tamped the rising anger down. Now wasn't the time to lose control. I didn't know how to manage my wolf side yet. I got the sense that the only reason I wasn't locked in a cell somewhere was because Dax thought I was weak enough to control. He was keeping me from knowing what I was until he could use me.

How long had he been planning his seduction to gain my trust? And how had I fallen for it so spectacularly? I felt like an absolute fool.

I wasn't going to let him get his way with me ever again. I was going to have to turn his game against him. "I've never been the patient type."

He stood, then leaned down and planted a kiss on the

top of my head. "I'll be back soon. You should rest. You've been through a lot and I have big things planned for you."

Something inside me seemed to roar in frustration. I balled my hands into fists. "No."

Dax cocked a brow. "No?"

"I'm not playing your games until you explain this to me." I glared at him, determined to get this out of him.

He growled, his expression darkening in a way that was very clearly a warning. I had to force myself not to recoil away from him. I'd seen the dangerous side of Dax before, but there was power here he hadn't had when we were kids. Instinctively, I knew he'd out match me. Especially while I was still recovering.

"You're not the one calling the shots, little flower," he said.

I changed tactics. "Darling, please you're scaring me. This whole thing is scaring me. It's a lot to take in. Can't you give me something?"

Dax smirked. "Nice try, but I know the false bond between us is wearing off. I thought I'd have until your next shift, but it's fading since you were away from me."

"What are you talking about?" I dropped the act.

"You'll begin your training today with Xander and you will learn how to use your powers to help this pack," he said.

"What if I don't want to?" I did want to learn how to use my supposed powers, but I didn't want to help Dax.

"I knew you'd make this difficult, which is why I took out some insurance," he said.

My brow furrowed. "What insurance?"

"Here's the rules, Ivy. You will go to training and you'll go home. You will not leave this apartment for anything. If you cross me, I will kill your best friend."

His words slammed into me like a punch to the gut and it felt like all the air was knocked from my lungs. "What? Where's Kate? What did you do?"

"Nothing yet. She's safe. For now. It's up to you if she stays that way," he said.

I launched myself at him and he grabbed my arms, easily restraining me. How was I so weak all the sudden? Dax was stronger than me, but I should have some ability to fight back. I tried to yank my arms out of his grip, but he held fast.

"You forgot that when my dad died, his Alpha strength passed to me. When you learn to harness your powers, you'll be stronger than me. But for now, I've got the advantage. You want to beat me? Do your training and fall into line," he snapped.

"What happens when I'm stronger than you and I come for the pack?" I hissed.

"Then I guess I kill your best friend and meet you in the ring for a rematch." He pulled me closer so our bodies touched.

Disgust and desire warred within me. How was I still drawn to him after everything he'd done to me? What was wrong with me? "Let me go."

Dax grinned. "I'm going to miss playing with you, little flower. It wasn't all bad, was it?"

"I wish I'd never kissed you," I said.

"You should be thanking me. Without me, you'd still be the sad, pathetic foundling girl working at a bar," he said. "You will be by my side publicly. You will help me reach my goals. And maybe if you're lucky, I'll fuck you when you beg me."

"That is never going to happen." There was a part of me that wanted him but I could tell how wrong it was. He wasn't who I wanted. Even without Madoc's face filling my mind, I'd know to resist Dax. Whatever was pulling me to him felt strange and artificial. Why couldn't I break its hold on me?

"Dax? Ivy?"

I glanced toward my open bedroom door and caught sight of Xander. He locked eyes with me then quickly turned away. "I didn't mean to interrupt."

Dax released his grip on my arms and I resisted the urge to rub the sore area where he'd been squeezing me. "We were just discussing Ivy's training with you."

Xander turned back to us. "I'm not early am I?"

"Right on time." Dax turned to me. "Get dressed. And you know what happens if you try anything stupid."

CHAPTER
TWO

I STARED AT DAX, my nostrils flaring as I held back the anger. How dare he do this to me? I was used to him being a sadistic asshole, but I never saw this coming. At least not recently. I'd been too busy doing naughty things with him. My stomach rolled and I had to swallow down the vomit threatening. I'd hard core fucked up when I opened up to him. I couldn't risk doing that again. Not for anything.

Dax walked away, then closed the door behind him, leaving me alone in my room. I wanted to learn about whatever power I had so I could protect myself better but I never intended to be Dax's weapon. How was I going to get Kate and myself out of this?

It was one thing for me to consider leaving the Shadows. It was different for Kate. She had roots here. Her family fled here before she was born. They had status and belonging. Kate's parents were respected, and so was she.

I straightened as the thought struck me. I might not be

able to get Kate out, but what if the elders found out about this? Or the other higher ranking shifters? There was no way they'd be okay with one of their own being used this way by their alpha.

"Hurry it up, Ivy," Dax called.

Fuck. Quickly, I pulled on jeans and a tee as my mind whirred with possibility. Getting Kate out might not be as hard as I thought. I felt a little better knowing I had a direction I could go to help her. Then, it was a waiting game for Madoc to break our bond. I was tempted to leave now to avoid Dax. Going feral had always been a fear, but now it was staring to sound like the better option. If not for Kate, and the questions about my past, I might consider it. But I knew if I was really going to leave the pack, I needed whatever power I could wield to help me survive on my own.

After lacing up a pair of combat boots, I opened my bedroom door and walked into my living room. Dax held out a little pouch. "Kate insisted I bring this for you to use after training."

I wrinkled my nose. Even as a prisoner, she managed to send her herbs.

"Take it," Dax insisted.

I reached for the packet. "Tell me she's safe."

"She is. She's got all the comforts of home and I swear to you, I will not harm her as long as you behave," he said.

I glanced over at Xander. "And you're fine with this? What if he turns on someone you care about next."

Xander's expression was impassive and his eyes

flicked over to Dax, then returned to me. "He's the alpha. He makes the calls."

"Right. Until it's someone you care about, who gives a shit," I said.

"Time to go." Dax moved to my front door and swung it open. "Out."

I glared at him as I walked by and he smirked at me. It was unsettling. He was even more messed up than I ever knew. What kind of psycho kills his own father? And don't forget about his whole agenda with me. Shadow Wolves had a bad rap. We were considered ruthless and lawless and vile. But it was usually retaliation. Tit for tat. There was reason, cause, motive. Typically business deals gone wrong. And family meant something. There were lines even the worst Shadow Wolves didn't cross.

Sure, Dax's motive was to rule the pack, but he was going to get that anyway. And what the fuck did he need me for? He was already alpha. Wasn't that enough? Dax was the personification of all the evil things outsiders thought we were.

I stepped outside into fading sunlight and shivered as a cold breeze cut through my clothes. I hadn't grabbed a jacket but Dax was already locking my door. Of course he had my keys.

"My car's over here," Xander said.

"Try not to let her die on you," Dax said. "She needs to master her wolf side before we can move her to what we really need."

"Nobody's died on my watch yet," Xander said as he

walked toward the parking lot.

I followed him only because it was a way to get me away from Dax. At this point, that was the only thing I cared about. I needed some space from him to clear my head and figure out where to go next. Besides, I wanted to talk to Xander alone. I was pretty sure he was Dax's guy through and through, but he had to feel something about Dax taking Kate. It wasn't right.

As soon as I closed the door behind me, I turned to face him. "You know this is wrong, Xander. Even you have to see it."

He started the car and kept his eyes facing forward.

"Kate is respected. She's full pack. Dax went too far," I said.

He glanced over at me, then returned his gaze to the road. "You don't know how far he's gone."

"What is that supposed to mean? Is that some kind of a threat?" I asked. "Look, I'm here doing whatever stupid thing he wants me to do."

"It's bigger than you realize," Xander said.

"So challenge him or leave or something. Don't act like you're some kind of a martyr when you're his right hand lackey."

Xander growled, a low warning tone that made my wolf respond. I could feel her restlessness, her desire to get away from this enclosed space. *That makes two of us,* I thought.

"You've known this whole time that he was playing me. You're just as bad as him," I said.

"Just try not to get yourself killed while we're doing this training. He'll be pissed at me if I break you," Xander said. "Now stop talking. I'm not in the mood."

"You're not in the mood?" I snapped. "My best friend was taken and I'm living a nightmare."

"Everything would have been better if you'd just stayed with the Umbras," he muttered.

"Excuse me?" I asked.

"Nothing," he said.

I shoved him and he veered a little. "Hey!"

"Tell me what you're talking about. Tell me what really happened. You know."

He sighed.

"Xander, tell me. Most of my crew died and I don't even know if the others made it home. I was captured. Well, except Patrick, but I'd guess he's dead by now," I said. "What did he send us for that was worth so many lives?"

"It was about you," he said, glancing over at me. "It was always about you."

"What does that mean?" I felt nauseous. A whole team of people dead because of me?

"Dax found out about what you were and he needed to test you," he said.

"How is sending me in to steal something a test?" I demanded.

"You should have been killed by the Umbras," he said.

"I didn't get out of there based on strength or power. It was pure luck," I said.

"Dax doesn't see it that way," he said.

"This is insane. What power does he even think I have?" I asked.

"That's not my place," he said.

"Yet, you're the one who is training me? For what? Something you can't even tell me about? Make it make sense, Xander," I demanded.

"It's just your wolf for now. That's all I'm supposed to do," he said.

"You're kidding, right?" I asked.

"Look, maybe just be happy you're alive. None of us thought you'd make it back," he said.

I clenched my jaw in frustration. If not for the mating bond, I would be dead, but I couldn't tell him that. Nobody could know that. I wasn't sure what Dax would do if he knew but I was certain he'd want to exploit it at the very least, or maybe even kill Madoc. Fear made my chest tighten. I couldn't let that happen. I couldn't let anything happen to him.

My mind took me back to the break in with the team of shifters who was likely all dead by now. Then I recalled Willow's comments. "They turned me in that night, didn't they? They tipped off the Umbras."

"Dax doesn't want you to know this," Xander said.

"Give me something, please," I said.

Xander glanced over at me. "Dax wanted to test you. He never needed any documents but he needed the elders' approval. You were the decoy and to truly test you, he wanted to ensure you'd get caught."

"So the others turned me in?" I already knew it but it hurt more getting it confirmed.

"They tried to take out the Umbra alpha. You were the distraction. They called in a tip about a break in. You never stood a chance. At least that's what I thought," he said.

A weight settled in my stomach. It hurt to know members of my own pack would go along with a plan like this. How had I been so stupid? I'd abandoned everything I'd worked so hard for and went against all of my instincts when I blindly got involved with Dax. Was I that desperate for a connection?

A twisting guilty sensation rolled through me. I had a mate out there, someone who was destined to be mine, and I walked away. How could I walk away from a mating bond but fall so easily into Dax's arms?

I hated myself and I hated what I'd become.

Rage burned, making my face hot. "Asshole."

"It's a warning, Ivy," Xander said. "Look how far he's willing to go to get what he wants."

"What exactly does he want?"

"Power," Xander said. "And we're all part of the game."

"You're actively helping him," I reminded Xander.

"And so are you," he said.

I balled my hands into fists. I needed a way out of this. "Where is he keeping Kate?"

"I'm not sure," he said.

"She is safe, though, right?" I asked.

"You said it yourself, she's respected. He'll keep her safe as long as he gets what he wants from you," he said.

"And if I can't do what he wants?" I asked.

"We both know what he'll do," Xander said darkly.

We were quiet after that as the feeling of defeat weighed heavily on me. I never wanted this for me or for Kate. She was the only person in the world who cared about me and I was going to get her out of there safely.

"We'll be working on shifting today. I assume you remember how to call your wolf?" he asked.

"I've only done it once," I admitted. "Surely Dax told you that. He was pretty insistant on not letting me shift again before I left. Probably another way to make sure I was captured."

"That had nothing to do with the capture," Xander said. "You sure you haven't shifted again? I thought maybe when you were with the Umbras."

"No, I haven't." I felt like I was shrinking in my seat. As if I didn't already feel bad enough about my poor choices lately, rub in the fact that I was a late bloomer in the shifting department.

"You didn't look too enamored with Dax today," Xander said, a note of accusation in his tone.

"Was I supposed to continue a romantic relationship with him after all this?" I asked.

Xander looked surprised.

"You're kidding, right? He's alpha, but he killed his own father." As soon as the words came out I slapped my hand over my mouth. Then I stared at Xander, waiting for him to flinch. He didn't so much as turn to look at me.

Lowering my hand slowly, I stared at the man driving

the car. "You knew. You knew about what he did to his dad, and you watched him take Kate and yet, you stand by him?"

"You fucked him," he said.

I punched him in the arm.

"Ow." Xander rubbed his bicep. "If it makes you feel any better, you didn't have much of a choice."

"That's not true." I said, darkly. "I wish I could blame someone else for my actions with Dax, but he didn't force me."

"But he did, in his own way," Xander said. "And for what it's worth, I am sorry you got involved in all this."

Xander pulled the car into the lot near the woods. It was the same place I'd gone for the full moon party. He killed the engine but I remained in my seat.

"You better spill, Xander."

He turned in his seat so the two of us were facing each other. "You ran with him on the night of your first shift, right? Just the two of you."

"Yeah, so?" I asked.

"You've heard that first shifts are usually done in a group, right? When you have that shift, others join in and your run together," he said.

"Yeah, like a party. The kind I'm never invited to," I reminded him.

"There's a reason we run in packs. You ever heard of a *false bond*?" he asked.

I shook my head.

"This might be hard to believe, Ivy, but I'm on your

side," Xander said. "We all have our roles to play and we all have things at stake."

My brow furrowed and I noticed the sadness in Xander's eyes. Was it possible he was just as much a prisoner as I was?

He sighed. "You didn't hear this from me."

I nodded. "Just tell me, please."

"There's a phenomenon that happens between wolves on a first shift under a full moon. It's rare, and you have to have all the correct conditions. Dax made sure he hit them all. You had to shift on your own, but then you had to spend your time as a wolf on your first shift just with him. Nobody else. It creates a false bond. A feeling like a mating bond between those two shifters."

I sucked in a breath and my eyes widened. "Oh, fuck. So that's why..."

"It's why you felt things for him," Xander explained.

"Tell me how to break it," I said.

"I think you've mostly already broken it, but I'm surprised you've done it on your own. Usually it fades as soon as you have your next shift. So it's not a huge deal since most shifters have another shift quickly after the first," he said.

I didn't need to be told twice. Quickly, I removed the seat belt and opened the car door. "We're doing this, right? Shifting?" I felt frantic and overwhelmed. If shifting would get me back to having full control over my emotions when it came to Dax, I needed to shift right now.

CHAPTER
THREE

THE WORLD WAS CAST in a warm glow from the setting sun. It was chilly and getting colder by the minute. I followed Xander into the woods, the trees swallowing most of the light. Our footsteps through the underbrush were the only sound.

The conversation with him had been the first time I'd felt like anyone opened up to me. I realized that maybe I could get more from him. "Before we do this, what else can you tell me? I want to know everything you know."

"You really don't want to dwell on this or it's going to make you crazy," he warned.

"How would you feel?" I asked. "He forced a relationship between us. He took advantage of me." I shivered. "I had sex with him and I thought it meant something."

"The best thing you can do now is shift. It'll clear your head and you'll be able to concentrate better," he said.

I narrowed my eyes. "Why did you even bother to tell

me all this? It doesn't sound like something Dax would want getting out."

"He didn't tell me not to. Besides, as soon as you shift, you'll feel the break between you. Things will be as they were. I honestly already thought you had. I'm surprised how much you were able to defy him without a shift," he said. "But then again, I've never seen a false bond in real life. Most shifters make sure they run in a group the first shift."

"Well, nobody exactly prepared me or taught me how to do this shifter stuff." My tone was moodier than I expected. It took me right back to how unwelcome and different I felt growing up.

"Even more reason to do it now." He ducked under a low hanging branch. "Come on."

As I followed, a thrill of excitement raced through me, but it wasn't coming from me. I could tell it was my wolf, dying to get out. The thought should make me happy, but I still a little pissed she'd been a no-show when I needed her. "How do I make my wolf come when I want to shift?"

"Practice," Xander said. "You and your wolf are one, but your wolf is the animal side that doesn't follow orders as easily. Emotions drive our wolves."

You'd think she'd have wanted to shift and run away when we were captured if it was based on emotions. I'd been terrified, yet she'd been away. Then I realized I'd also been around my mate. I felt a grim flicker of acknowledgment. My wolf wasn't happy that I'd walked away from Madoc. *What else was I supposed to do?*

I didn't get to linger on my own inner turmoil long because Xander pulled off his shirt and tossed it on the ground. The guy looked good with his shirt off, that was for sure. Like most of the shifters I knew, he was strong and muscular. I wondered if he ever got in the ring to fight like Dax had.

Without a word, he stepped out of his jeans, throwing them on top of his abandoned tee.

I had to make myself look away. There was no emotional attachment when I looked at Xander, but I could appreciate a gorgeous male when I saw one and I didn't want him to know I'd been staring.

"So what do I do to make the shift happen?" I wanted to be prepared so I spent less time naked in front of him. It felt weird to undress in front of Dax's right hand man. It was like giving more of myself to Dax even though he wasn't here.

"There's not much of a science to it. I'll shift first, which should help remind your wolf to do the same. When you feel your wolf, don't resist. Lean into the emotions and follow her lead. We'll run for a bit, then change back. I'll have you shift a few times to get the feeling down before we move on to the next steps." He doubled over, his body breaking and reforming. Fur sprouted and my eyes widened as the change took him quickly.

A large light gray wolf stared up at me with Xander's bright blue eyes. He growled and nodded. My wolf responded instantly. I could feel her clawing inside my chest, desperate for release.

Quickly, I removed my clothes and then I gave in to my wolf. To my surprise, she took the lead and my body began to change on its own accord. It was instinct, but that didn't mean it wasn't painful. I winced as my bones broke and I doubled over, breathing through the change. For a moment, the pain was so intense it made my vision blur, then it suddenly stopped.

My senses overwhelmed me. The sounds of creatures running through branches, the smell of the pine and dirt. I even caught the musky scent of another animal that I knew must be Xander.

I turned my sight on him and noticed that he seemed clearer and sharper than he had a moment ago. When I peered into the distance, I could definitely see farther than usual. My heart fluttered in excitement. Everything was amplified. I forgot just how incredible being in wolf form was.

Xander's wolf made a grunting sound and I turned my attention back to him. With an inclination of his head, I knew he was asking me to follow. I nodded, the movement feeling oddly like my own and someone else's. Being in this form was both foreign and familiar. I wondered how it would feel after I got more used to it.

As soon as Xander took off, my wolf followed. I didn't recall making the decision to move. My animal side was gladly taking over to give us the opportunity to run. I leaned into it, trying to observe and learn rather than control. It felt so right to race through the woods. My paws sunk into the soft pine needle strewn ground for only a heartbeat before launching off to keep the momentum. I was fast, easily keeping up with Xander as we weaved through the trees.

This run felt similar to my first one, but I felt more in control. I wasn't calling the shots, my wolf was, but I was far more aware. The animal side of me wasn't taking over. I wasn't sure if that was normal, but I knew that if I wanted to stop running, I could. That first night, I'd felt compelled by something beyond myself. This was different.

With that thought weighing heavily on me, I stopped. Panting, I took a moment to look around. It was dark now, the sun fully gone from sight. I knew the woods were getting cold and that I was safer and better off in wolf form, but I had to test my abilities.

Xander's wolf turned around and headed back to me. He stood a few feet away, watching me silently. I didn't feel any pressure to follow him and there wasn't any connection between us. I wondered if I'd feel compelled to shift back if he did as I had with Dax.

I didn't want to give him that opportunity. I needed to know if I could do it on my own. Though we'd only been running a few minutes, I headed back toward my clothes. To my surprise, I caught the scent of something floral and sweet. Curious, I followed it and ended up at my clothes. So that was what I smelled like. Unlike Xander's masculine and very shifter musk, I had a unique scent that I hadn't ever noticed before. Was that part of my unknown heritage?

Xander's wolf called to me, then turned his head toward the woods. He wanted to run more. I resisted. He said he wanted me to shift a few times. I wanted to see if I could do it on my own without him shifting first.

Turning away from him, I closed my eyes and focused on my human form. My wolf whined internally. She wasn't ready to change back. *We can run again soon. I have to know how to control this so we can change if we're not safe.* It felt strange to talk to myself, and I had been warned not to try to control my animal side, but there was more there than just an emotional response. My wolf seemed to understand and relate to my desires. There was something else there, too. Something more. It had to be that other side to me. I needed to know the truth before I took this further.

After a few more deep breaths, I cleared my mind and visualized being back in my human form. Finally, I felt my body begin the change. The discomfort was short lived and I soon found myself on all fours, naked.

I grabbed my clothes and changed while resisting the urge to look back at Xander. When I turned to him, he was back in human form.

"What was all that about?" he asked. "We weren't done yet."

"I was. I need some answers. My wolf doesn't feel like an animal. I need to know what I'm working with here. I can't fully explore this part of me without knowing what else there is inside me."

"You know I can't tell you that," he said.

"How are you supposed to help me when I don't even know what I am?" I insisted.

He opened his mouth as if he was going to say something, then closed it. His jaw tightened and his whole body tensed. He turned away from me, his brow furrowing.

"What is it?" I asked.

"Something's wrong. Come on, we gotta go," he said. "Now."

CHAPTER
FOUR

XANDER SPED down the road to town and I braced myself against the fast turns.

"What is going on?" I demanded.

"I told you, something's wrong," he said.

"How do you know?" I asked.

He glanced over at me, then returned his eyes to the road. "You really can't sense it?"

"Should I?" I asked.

"Yeah, you should. The pack is connected. Once you're full pack, you can feel the others. Flashes of emotions, the more intense, the more clear they are."

I swallowed hard, recalling the feelings I'd had about Madoc. "How do you know it's real?"

"You just know," he said. "It's pretty obvious once you start paying attention."

"How do you turn it on? Can you use it to check in on people?" I kept trying to push Madoc from my thoughts, but it would help if I could know that he was safe.

"It doesn't work like that for most of us. It might in wolf form, but not in human form," he said. "We have more connection to our pack when we're shifted. Especially if the others are shifted too. How do you not know any of this?"

"I wasn't allowed at any of the events, you know that," I said.

He grunted in a tone that conveyed frustration. I wasn't sure if he was frustrated by me or by my lack of experience at the hands of our pack.

"So what did you sense?" I asked. "What did it feel like?"

"I got a vision. I could see Dax and I felt fear and anger. It was quick, a flash, but it was powerful. Something is very wrong," he said.

I squirmed uncomfortably in my seat. That was exactly how I'd experienced the feeling about Madoc. I wasn't part of his pack, yet I was connected to him. It had to be the mating bond. But I should be part of the Shadow Pack so why didn't I feel the warning from Dax?

"How does it choose who feels it?" I asked. Had someone else felt Madoc's pain or was it just me? The thought flooded me with concern. I didn't want to feel this way for him, but I couldn't get rid of it.

"The closer you are to the shifter, the more intense the feelings," Xander said. "So it's likely the inner circle felt it. I really thought you would too."

"I guess we know Dax doesn't think of me as inner circle," I said.

Xander didn't comment and I wasn't sure it was a bad thing. Honestly, I was relieved I wasn't going to get psychic messages about Dax. I didn't need him in my head.

We pulled up in front of Dax's house and Xander ran inside, leaving his car door open and not looking to see if I followed. I hesitated for a moment. I had no idea what was going on or what I was about to walk in on. After Xander disappeared into the house, I got out of the car and crept forward slowly. I listened for any sounds of distress, but there was nothing but silence. What if Xander's feelings were wrong?

As I approached the front door, a sinking feeling settled in my gut like a weight. I didn't want to see Dax or have anything to do with him. There wasn't even the slightest sense of loyalty or connection anymore. My shift had seemed to sever whatever lingered of the false bond between us. At least when I faced him, I wouldn't feel any more attraction.

Part of me wanted to flee. Dax was going to bring me nothing but harm, just as he always had. I looked back at Xander's car. The keys were still in the ignition. It would be so easy to get in and drive away.

Kate. I balled my hands into fists and continued forward. I couldn't run away from this and risk my best friend's life. Cautiously, I pushed the front door open and held my breath while I listened for any threats.

The house was a buzz of activity when I walked through the doors. It reminded me of when we were preparing for the heist. Only, this time, even I could feel the unease rolling off the gathered group in waves. I might not be connected the way Xander was, but I knew something bad went down.

I followed Xander to the dining room where we found the elders and Dax gathered. In the center of the table was a large wooden crate overflowing with shredded paper. Dax noticed our arrival and held his hand up to cease the conversation.

"What happened?" Xander asked.

"She should leave. She's not on the council," one of the elders said.

"No, she needs to know this," Dax said.

"Just because you're fucking her doesn't mean she gets to break protocol," he snapped back.

"Remind me who is in charge here, Benjamin? You might run the council, but this is still my pack." Dax's voice was like ice and it sent a chill down my spine. He'd kept that dark side hidden from me for a few weeks, but now it was on full display for all to see.

"Ivy, come in here," he ordered.

I could feel a tiny pull from the command, a note of his power as alpha. He hadn't used his full authority on me because I could have resisted if I wanted. So maybe there was a tiny part of him that wanted to be kind to me. I hated that possibility. I didn't want anything between us to be even the slightest bit real.

"Ivy." He inclined his head toward the table.

My curiosity won over my defiance and I stepped closer.

"You want to see why we need your help?" Dax asked.

I stared at him, my jaw clenched. I wanted the power he claimed I had but we both knew I didn't want to help him.

"Look in the box." He lifted his chin toward the crate.

"What is it?" I asked.

"You don't need to show her this," Benjamin objected again.

His desire to keep me from seeing it pushed me forward and I dug through the shredded paper. As soon as I started moving it around, I regretted my decision. Blood covered most of the shreds, and the deeper I dug into the box, the more bloody they got. My stomach lurched but I wasn't about to back down. Steeling myself, I moved away more of the bloody paper until I caught sight of something truly horrifying. With a gasp, I pulled my hands out of the box but I couldn't take my gaze off the glassy, dead eyes staring up at me.

"What the fuck?" I stepped away from the box and glanced down at my blood covered hands. Nausea rolled through my stomach and I swallowed it down. I couldn't let Dax know this got to me. That's what he wanted.

"They're all there. Patrick, Frankie, and Keith. You're officially the only survivor of your mission," Dax said.

"I thought they only captured Patrick," I said.

"They did. The others went back to break him out and they clearly didn't make it," he said.

"When?" My heart thundered. If they charged the Umbra estate, Madoc would have been there. Was that what I'd felt? Had they attacked him? If they were dead, he probably had survived. I tried to suppress the relief that rushed in. I shouldn't be feeling that way. Members of my own pack were dead, but all I could think about was if my mate was safe. This bond was so fucked up.

"I mean, was it after I was out?" I asked, hoping to salvage my strange question. I should care that they were dead but they'd sold me out. Sure, I would rather then were home with their families, but I was finding it difficult to mourn them while all of my emotional energy seemed tied up in Madoc.

"They weren't open to negotiations for Patrick so the team tried to get him out after you were out," he said.

Somehow, I knew that was what I'd felt with Madoc. It had to be connected.

"Now you know why we must eliminate the Umbra wolves. We've lived in their shadows for too long. They refuse us access to the other packs, keep us locked her in the Fringes, and prevent us from modernizing or growing. They must go," Dax said.

"I still think we should petition the other packs to let us become an official pack in the North American Alliance," Benjamin said. "We follow most pack law. We have a council and we can adapt our rules to meet the expectations."

"We shouldn't have to conform to them. They created us. We deserve to maintain our way of life," Dax said. "When we crush them, we'll take their place in the packs and nobody will be able to say anything. It's allowed under the old ways."

"Yes, but nobody follows those anymore," Benjamin pointed out. "The old ways are dead for good reason."

"Those rules are still in the books so they'll be forced to accept it," Dax said.

"Why not just challenge their alpha?" I asked.

"Because this was is better," he said.

"You're afraid you wouldn't win," I said. "That if you did win, one of the alpha's sons would take you down."

"He has four sons and I'm not a fool," Dax said. "You think they'd play fair? If I beat Erwin, what's to stop all four of them from charging at once? It would be war either way."

"The alpha challenge is the honorable way," Benjamin pointed out. "The elders would support you in that charge."

"No, they lost their chance at that when they sent us this package," Dax said.

"You won't do it because you know you'd lose." The words came out without my bidding. "Madoc, Cavan... they'd eat you alive."

Dax growled. "Xander, get her out of here."

CHAPTER
FIVE

I DIDN'T ARGUE with Dax because I wanted to get as far away as possible from those severed heads. My emotions were a mess. A rollercoaster of anger, fear, and frustration that I couldn't shake. They rolled through me one after the other, a confusing concoction of fleeting moments, none of them lasting long enough for me to feel one thing at one time. I was supposed to direct my anger at Madoc. At his pack. But I couldn't bring myself to do it. I knew he may have been the one who cut those heads off himself, yet the thing that upset me more was the fact that Dax wanted to use this as a way to justify his actions.

He'd sent me in to die. He sacrificed all of the members of the team for a goal he hadn't had the authority to do: assassinate the Umbra alpha. Then he's upset that they retaliated? He didn't give a shit about anyone in the pack. Not me, not the members of the team, nobody. If you weren't useful to him, he wouldn't waste his time with you.

Yet, how were the Umbras any better than the Shadows? The answer was, that they weren't. I had no business making Dax the sole bad guy in this situation. Fucking mating bond was getting in my head. It was impossible to make heads or tales of anything right now. It was a muddled mess in my mind.

The only thing that was clear was that I hated Dax. I had always hated Dax. He'd treated me like dirt my entire life and he'd gone too far this time. Forcing me into a false bond was unforgivable. Even the man who shared an actual mating bond with me had let me go.

Fuck. He had. His brother beat the shit out of me, but he'd tried to protect me. Traded me for another to get me out. How was it that my enemy showed me more kindness than my own alpha? The mating bond couldn't be the only reason. He could have had me killed. He chose not to.

I had to get away from Dax. I wasn't going to play his game which meant, he wasn't going to find use for me much longer. But I couldn't leave while he still had Kate. He knew she was my only tie to this place, the only thing that would keep me stuck here and semi listening to his orders.

I was standing next to Xander's car and for a moment, I hesitated. He was probably going to take me back to my guarded apartment. Part of me wanted to run; just escape now while Dax was distracted. Kate would probably be fine. But I couldn't. I could never betray her. She was counting on me. With a resigned sigh, I got into the car and slammed the door behind me. Then I turned to glare at Xander as he entered the driver seat.

"Don't give me that look," Xander said as he slammed his own door. "You took things too far in there and you know it. Saying their names like that? As if you're familiar with them? After just getting released from their clutches? It makes you look suspicious. It makes you look like you could be the one who has been..."

"The one who has been what? They already got Holden. We all know he was the one who was feeding information to the Umbras." I narrowed my eyes. "Unless there's something else. Someone else. What else am I missing, Xander?"

"Maybe if I explain some of this to you, you'll stop fighting this." Xander glanced at me then started the engine.

"If you're going to try to justify what Dax did to me, don't bother. If you have actual information for me, I'll take what I can get. Assuming it also helps me get my friend out of this predicament. Because you damn well know that none of this is okay."

"It's easy for you to say that while you've been blinded to everything going on in pack politics. You have no idea what we've been doing behind the scenes. You have no clue how close we've come to total collapse." Xander's hands were shaking and he tightened his fingers around the steering wheel.

A rush of sympathy rolled through me. What did I

know about Xander? He'd alluded to the fact that he was just as trapped as I was, another pawn in Dax's game.

If you would have asked me months ago if Dax was capable of half of the things I'd found out that he'd done, I would have laughed in your face. Dax always came across as the bully. The kid who was happy to take credit for other people's actions but never a leader. He was never the one to call the shots unless it involved humiliating or hurting someone else. Was that all this was? Another way for him to play like he was the kid with a magnifying glass above a group of ants?

The Shadow Pack deserved better. They had treated me like shit my whole life so I wasn't sure why I was defending them, but nobody deserved what I had been through. Except maybe Dax himself. *Asshole.* "If I'm forced to be a part of this, wouldn't it be easier if I knew what the fuck I was a part of?"

"Yeah. If you're willing to listen."

"Go ahead," I said.

Xander pulled into the parking lot at my apartment and killed the engine. Then he turned so he could face me better. "The first thing you should know, is that I don't blame Dax for what he did to his dad. Could there have been other ways to solve it? Maybe. But the way you see Dax act, that was all learned at home. I'm sure you heard the rumors about Preston and the way he treated people. That was nothing compared to how he treated Dax behind closed doors. He was good though, never left bruises anywhere anyone would see. There were a few times he went too far and Dax had to miss school until he recovered."

I remembered back to senior year of high school when there was an entire blissful week of Dax not being in classes. We've been told he had gone out of town to help a relative. Which made sense because shifters don't get sick and typically recover from injuries quickly. If Dax had missed a full week of school to recover from injuries when he was so close to having his first shift, he had been in bad shape. I didn't like the thought of him being hurt like that. But it didn't dismiss the fact that he inflicted the same kind of pain on me. "It still doesn't justify what he did. You don't kill your parents. Some of us don't even get parents."

"Just because they're blood doesn't mean they're worth the oxygen they breathe. Be careful putting your own insecurities on others. Family isn't everything it's always cracked up to be. You've seen that. You know. The ties, the things it makes us do, just from that title, that shared blood, what right does that give anyone to abuse or control someone else?"

"That doesn't give him a pass for what he did to his dad or to me. If he was treated badly you would think he would learn that it wasn't a pleasant experience. No, I'm not accepting that as an excuse for his behavior and if you are, you're stupider than I thought. Just because someone else hurts you doesn't mean you turn around and do it to others," I spat.

"I'm not excusing his behavior with you. That was over the line and I agree. But there's nothing I can do about it. But you seemed to take issue with the fact that he took out Preston. You should know it was an accident, it wasn't planned. Dax finally defended himself and Preston didn't back down. Dax kept going until he went too far. He called me that night, terrified."

"You helped him cover it up," I said. "And you let someone else take the fall."

"Holden was already on our radar as an Umbra spy. But he wasn't the only one. And he wasn't the worst offender," Xander said.

"Who else?" I asked.

"Preston was about to sell us all out. Holden was disgruntled and wanted back into his old pack. Preston was working against all of us."

"What do you mean?" I couldn't imagine how Preston would be involved with the Umbras.

"He'd been working with the Umbras for years. Funneling funds from the pack to pay protection or some shit. He was trying to buy his way in, to get rid of the Shadow Pack and make us part of the Umbras."

"But most of our pack is the shifters they didn't want," I pointed out. "How would that even work?"

"Anyone who wasn't good enough would be kicked to the curb. And all future outcasts would have nothing. Straight to feral. There'd be no buffer, no pack that would take in the outcasts or the unwanted. People like your friend Kate would have nowhere to go. They'd be alone out there packless, defenseless, driven mad by the lack of connection from any other wolf."

I swallowed against a lump in my throat. Currently, the only way out I could see was to go feral myself. But I'd forgotten some of the finer points of making that leap. If I left, I'd have no connection to any pack and there were cases where that could drive a wolf mad. I think I neglected that point because I had never had a connection to the Shadows anyway.

In theory, I would have once my debt was paid, but I still didn't even though the elders had said I was full pack. Xander had felt when Dax was in distress and I hadn't. There was no connection there and I wasn't sure there ever would be. Even if I stayed here, I felt like I was almost just as at risk of having that lack of connection as I would be as a feral wolf. But at least if I was feral, I could control my own life. Granted, I'd be lucky if I lived in a tent on the side of the road somewhere, but I wouldn't have to do Dax's bidding.

"All I've ever wanted was to be part of this pack. But I'm not. I'm not seen as anything other than some kind of commodity to help Dax achieve whatever bizarre power trip he's chasing down. So what if Preston wanted to join the Umbras? Dax can say no. Just keep us the way we are. Why does he have to go and take over the Umbras? Why not just take things back to the way they were before Preston?" I asked.

I was surprised that a little flicker of hope seemed to ignite deep in my gut. For a moment, I wondered if maybe

I could stay here as part of the Shadow Wolves and not have to leave. I had a comfortable life despite the fact that I wasn't welcome at pack events. In theory, that had changed for me now, but I wasn't sure if that mattered. I had a roof over my head, food, a car, warmth. Shit, I even had a friend. I didn't have a job or a way of making money, but I had enough to last at least a year if I was careful. Besides, I could find a new job. There had to be lots of things I was good at. Though, the only thing Dax seemed to care about was this power he was keeping me away from.

"It's too late for that," Xander said. "You saw what the Umbra wolves sent. It's one thing to execute prisoners. It's another thing entirely to giftwrap their heads and send them back to us. That's an act of war. If we don't retaliate, they're going to come for us."

"I don't think that's what they want. I think..." I pressed my lips together as I recalled one of the brief conversations I'd had with Madoc. He knew Holden wanted to take out Preston and it wasn't because Holden wanted to be alpha. The Umbra wolves really were at war with us but all I could do was try to think of a way to justify their actions. What was wrong with me? I'd grown up knowing the Umbras were bad news. I should be instantly defending my pack over them. I cursed internally. This mating bond was really getting in my head. How much longer was it going to be before Madoc severed it? I felt like I couldn't even trust my own thoughts.

I had one shot of saving myself and it was going to

involve me buying myself some time. "Never mind," I said. "I understand."

Xander raised a surprised brow. "You do?"

I nodded. "When is our next training session?"

"I'll come pick you up in the morning," he said.

I opened the car door and stepped out.

"Oh, Ivy?" Xander called.

I ducked inside the door. "Yeah?'

"Don't try to leave your apartment. Dax has guards all over. He'll know if you leave," he said.

I gave him a thumbs up.

"Don't forget your tea. Kate'll have a shit fit if she finds out you weren't taking care of yourself," he said.

I closed the door. There was no need for Kate's tea. I wasn't injured and I didn't like associating her kind actions of caring for me with Xander or Dax. As I walked to my door, the corners of my lips tilted up. While I'd been sitting in the car, a thought crossed my mind that made everything a little more bearable.

I was going to find that file and figure out my powers on my own. I might be guarded, but Dax was distracted and I could find a way to get into the hall of records. I wasn't going to change anyone's mind about the Umbras and if I was being honest, it wasn't my business. After the conversation with Xander I knew I wasn't connected with the Shadow Pack and that wasn't going to change. If I couldn't get Kate out by letting the elders know, I could get her out for good behavior. If Dax thought I was going along with him, he'd have no reason to keep her locked up.

I had money and I could learn to make myself stronger. At this point, the countdown was on. Knowing I was preparing to leave was going to make the next few days or weeks far easier. There was an end in sight, even if I wasn't sure exactly when it was. I was going to have my freedom. Real, actual freedom, very soon.

CHAPTER
SIX

MY APARTMENT FELT SMALLER and more claustrophobic than it ever had, despite the fact that I was the only person inside of it. I was hyper aware that Kate wasn't going to be returning anytime soon. There were plenty of nights when she would go out or spend the night with whoever her flavor of the month was, but this was different. I'd always felt alone in my pack, but I never felt this alone. It amplified all the thoughts in my mind, making me replay everything from the last few days over and over. I recalled the first time I saw Madoc in the ring and how my body nearly shut down at the sight of him. I saw flashes of his face constantly inundating me with thoughts of him. Madoc with his hand around my throat in the cell, the expression of indifference he wore as his brothers hauled me back to the cell, the hum of energy between us that rooted me in place until Kate broke the spell.

I picked up a pillow off the couch and threw it across

the room in frustration. If not for Kate, I might have asked to stay with Madoc. I'd either be an Umbra wolf or I'd be dead if not for her. The latter seeming far more likely. Madoc didn't have any interest in completing our bond. Agony ripped through me, sending a pulsing longing that was almost painful. I didn't want to be with him, so why did I have to go through this? I pushed the thoughts of Madoc down deep. I couldn't do this to myself. It wasn't real, anyway. He was a murderer. A monster. And as soon as he broke the bond, I'd be free of him.

Needing something to keep myself busy, I decided I should focus on my next steps. While I waited for a way to get Kate out, I was determined to break into the Hall of Records. I wasn't sure how long Xander and Dax were going to make me wait until they let me train in the power they wanted to use, but I wasn't going to wait for them. I needed to figure this out and gain the upper hand.

I peeked out the windows and easily spotted the various shifters that Dax had assigned to keep watch over me. There was one near my front door, one outside my bedroom window, and I was pretty sure there was at least one out back, but it was difficult to see from inside.

It was dark and I should feel tired, but my whole body vibrated with the unknown. There was so much at stake and so much I didn't understand yet. I made myself a cup of tea and carried it out onto the balcony. Movement caught my eye, and I was able to spot a shifter who was mostly hidden by a large pine tree. I kept my eyes off him and tried to pretend I was simply coming outside to enjoy a cup of tea. As I settled into a chair, I kept watch out of the corner of my eye. He was tense and partially exposed from his hiding space. The longer I sat there, the more he seemed to ease until he slipped back up against the tree. Now that I knew he was there, I could easily spot him. He'd made a mistake by revealing himself for no reason. I smirked as I took a sip of my tea. Maybe getting away from these guys wasn't going to be as difficult as I feared.

While I drank the tea, I scanned my surroundings, making sure I appeared to be just taking in a relaxing evening with my warm beverage. Eventually, I caught sight of two more shifters, in addition to the one not very well hidden by the tree. I frowned. There was probably a compliment in the fact that there were five men stationed around my house just to stop little old me from escaping. The thing was, Dax knew I wasn't going to take off while he had Kate in his clutches. Was he that concerned that I'd abandon Kate, or was he worried I'd try to do something else? Like break into the hall of records to read that folder.

While I'd been making my tea, I'd spent several minutes beating myself up for not instantly grabbing that folder earlier. But now I knew I'd been a little bit love drunk and not thinking as clearly as I should. That false bond gave me a little bit more confidence moving forward, the ability to forgive myself for some of my poor decisions. The one thing it did cast doubt on was my actual mating bond. The false bond had been bad enough. I knew a real bond would get stronger the longer it held, and if a false bond was enough to make me feel like I had fallen in love

45

with my mortal enemy, what would a true mating bond do?

Madoc's face flashed into my mind again and I blew out a breath of frustration. I needed another distraction. This one had lost its luster. Deciding I had enough information, I stood and stretched before heading back into my apartment. I set the teacup in the kitchen then turned off all the lights, hoping that the guards would assume I'd gone to bed.

Instead, I spent the next several hours observing them from the windows. They traded places every so often, and twice I saw guards replaced by others. That was interesting to note. They were working shifts, which meant Dax had quite a few people in on this. That surprised me. How had he convinced other members of the pack that they should be standing guard around a foundling who'd had one shift? What had he possibly told them to make them think I was worth protecting or worth imprisoning? I was curious as to what story he told them to keep them here.

As I watched, I made notes of the times my guards changed positions and when they were replaced. I had to see if there was a pattern or something that I could exploit so that I could get out of here a little easier. I also made note of any shifters I recognized. To my surprise, I only recognized about half of the shifters that came and went from my apartment that evening. Most of them looked like they were new, which could explain why they were so eager to impress the new alpha. But it also made me question their loyalty. What did they know about Dax? Or about me? If they were new here, they were probably still trying to earn points toward full pack status. And if they had been sent to the Shadow Pack, there was a good chance they had a history of dark deeds in their past. They weren't loyal because they felt an obligation to Dax. They just needed the boon. It might be possible to convince some of them that I was the better option to follow. Sure, I was planning on abandoning the pack, but maybe that would work to my advantage. What if they didn't want to risk being here when the shit hit the fan between us and the Umbras?

The sky had turned from black to blue and I saw the first signs of sunrise. I'd stayed up all night watching the movements of the guards, being too afraid that I would miss something instrumental in helping my plan progress. Not that I had an actual plan yet aside from biding my time, but I was feeling more confident that I was going to find a way out of this. I wasn't sure why, but I felt stronger than I had in years. There wasn't any reason I should, but I wasn't about to argue with the sudden optimism.

I stifled a yawn and glanced at the clock. With any luck, I'd be able to get an hour or two nap before Xander showed up. There probably wasn't much I could glean from studying the guards' movements at this point, especially since I'd want to return prior to sunrise. I hid my notebook with my notes under the couch, knowing that I couldn't trust anything or anyone that entered my apartment before sliding in between the covers in my bed.

. . .

I WAS BACK at the Night Howler, in the basement. A single bare bulb swung over the ring, casting odd shadows as it moved. For a moment, fear and confusion halted my movement. Then I realized there was no way this was real. The Howler was closed, and I was trapped in my apartment. Which meant this was a dream.

Squeezing my eyes shut, I held my breath, telling myself to wake. I'd always heard that if you were aware it was a dream, you'd wake. When I opened my eyes, I was still standing in the basement. *Fuck me.* This was now getting a little creepy. Why was I stuck here, of all places? You'd think my subconscious would send me somewhere else. I could use a break from my grim reality right now rather than a flashback to the past. When I'd been working at the Howler, all I wanted was out. It drove every decision I made, good and bad. Now, I wasn't sure it was the worst time of my life. A sinking feeling told me the worst was yet to come.

"Come on, Ivy, stop being so fucking melodramatic." My voice echoed through the large empty space.

"I'm pretty sure talking to yourself is a bad sign."

The voice made my heart swell until it felt like it would burst into a million tiny pieces. I winced. I hated that I reacted that way to anyone, let alone the Umbra shifter who had so recently ended the life of several of my pack. Sure, they were assholes who turned me over and didn't bat an eye, but all that meant was that they weren't any better than him. It didn't make Madoc in the right.

Spinning on my heels, I turned to face the hulking form that approached from the shadows. My heart was in my throat, my limbs on fire, my center already tingling in anticipation. *Down, girl.* It might be a dream, and I might have enjoyed our previous dream encounter, but that wasn't going to happen. I was aware that this was a dream, which meant, I should have some control. Silently, I tried to will him away. He continued walked toward me.

"What are you doing in my dream?" I asked.

"Maybe you're in my dream," he countered.

"Wait, is this real? Are you really *you*?" My pulse thrummed in excitement despite my best attempts to be angry about this situation.

"I think so," he said.

I blew out a relieved breath. If this was really him, and the fates had connected us in a dream, he must be safe. "Thank the gods you're alright."

His brow furrowed. "You were concerned about me?"

I crossed my arms over my chest. "Of course I was. We have a bond. It makes me feel things for you, remember?"

"How did you know anything happened?" he asked, not denying that he'd been in trouble.

"I felt you. You were attacked. It was bad. I was...." I couldn't make myself finish. I didn't want him to know how worried I'd been and how much effort it had taken for me to pretend that I didn't care.

"Your pack mates attacked me," he said. "They

49

couldn't get my father, so they thought they'd come for me. Four against one doesn't seem right, but I paid them back."

"By sending their heads to my alpha?" I shouted.

"Don't you mean your boyfriend?" He scoffed.

"Not my boyfriend. Not that it's any of your business."

He lifted a brow. "Not boyfriend? That's interesting news."

My heart was doing an annoying flipping thing and every part of me was fighting the urge to close the distance between us and complete the bond. It was insanity. I didn't know anything about him aside from the fact that he was willing to lop off heads and mail them to opposing alphas. I couldn't let the bond get to me. He was my enemy.

"Whatever. That's irrelevant, anyway. Unless you're here to tell me that the bond is broken, I have nothing to say to you." *But lots of things I want to do to you.* The thought came out of nowhere and I felt my cheeks heat.

"Slow down there, sugar. That's just the bond talking," he said.

"For the love of the gods, please tell me you can't hear my thoughts." I groaned. That would be just my luck. I couldn't connect with my pack, but I get paired up with this dangerous shifter just fine. I must have done something wrong in a past life to deserve this mess.

"Calm down, I can't hear your thoughts. But I can sense your emotions and I'm getting major *fuck me* vibes from you." He smirked.

"Don't flatter yourself," I said. "I was having a dream about someone else before you showed up." It was a lie, but it was the best I could do to try and cover the fact that the thought of Madoc naked was very much at the fore-front of my mind, and I couldn't push it aside.

Madoc growled, and his hands balled into fists. He moved closer until he was inches from me and I felt the unmistakable emotion of anger - and was that jealousy? It seemed to radiate from him, wrapping the two of us in a cloud of his feelings. My own emotions responded, making me feel remorse for causing him concern. I pressed my lips together into a line. I didn't like this. I felt wildly out of control. I hated feeling anything for him and I hated that my body was responding without my consent. It was wrong, but it also felt wrong to fight it. How did people deal with mating bonds? They were so volatile.

"What do want from me?" I asked.

"Even I don't have the power to hijack your dreams, sugar," he said. "I fell asleep and now I'm here."

"How do I wake up?" I looked up at the ceiling as if I'd get an answer from something external. Of course, there was no response.

"You know, we could find ways to kill time until we wake," he suggested.

"Aren't we trying to *break* the mating bond? Fucking you probably won't help that situation," I said.

"Right, that." He rubbed the back of his neck with his hand and looked away from me.

My brow furrowed. "What are you hiding?"

"It's proving harder than I thought," he said. "We're going to have to be together when we break it. So watch for my message."

"What message?" I asked.

Pounding made my brow furrow, and I turned away from Madoc. When I looked back, he was gone. The pounding increased and my eyes opened wide. I was awake and apparently Xander was here.

CHAPTER
SEVEN

XANDER STOOD naked in front of me, his eyebrows raised. "Any day now, princess."

I shot him a glare. "Not all shifters enjoy being naked in front of others."

"If you're worried about how you look, I can assure you, you have nothing to be concerned about," he said.

"That doesn't help," I snapped. Turning away from him, I quickly removed my shirt and shimmied out of my jeans. I glanced over my shoulder. "Why don't you shift and I'll join you?"

He shrugged. "I'll still see you naked, but if it helps speed this up, I'll shift. Just join me when you're ready."

I turned away and quickly removed my underwear and sports bra. I knew I'd have to do this, but every time I did it, I was more uncomfortable undressing in front of others. You'd think it would get easier, but it felt like the opposite. I was pretty sure I was more afraid of being naked now than I was when changing in gym class as a teenager. Maybe it was some kind of delayed trauma response or something. Whatever it was, I didn't think it was worth wasting too much time on.

Between Dax and Xander, I'd take my chances with Xander any day of the week. It was probably part of why I had convinced myself that I'd go along with this while I figured out how to get that folder. Add in the comment from dream-Madoc and I was stuck here no matter what. How was he supposed to get word to me anyway? That was if the dream had been real.

I wished there was someone I could ask, but bringing up mating bonds would cause unnecessary scrutiny. Especially since Dax was still masquerading as my boyfriend. Having a mating bond with him would explain his sudden interest to people who were likely questioning his choice.

A low rumbling growl sounded from behind me, and I knew Xander was getting impatient. Then I felt the tug of my inner wolf. She seemed ready and excited about the prospect of shifting again so quickly since our last try. Yesterday's shift had been quick and uneventful, and I got the feeling that my wolf was up for a longer run today. It was a good thing because that was exactly what Xander had in mind.

On the drive over, he explained how today was about stamina. He said it was rare for a shifter to stay in wolf form for too long, but it was sometimes necessary and could take time to get used to without feeling the urge to go back to human form. He also warned me it was harder to shift back when you were tired. So his entire plan for me today was to wear me out to the brink of exhaustion.

It probably wasn't the best night to stay up all night. By the time Xander had come, my guess was I had gotten two whole hours of sleep. But that wasn't totally unusual. There had been plenty of nights where I stayed up after a shift at the Howler only to get up and go open for the lunch crowd.

A tug of sadness came over me, reminding me again of what my life used to be like. I'd wanted nothing more than to get out, but looking back sent a rush of nostalgia tinted by rose-colored glasses. I suppose the grass isn't always is greener. I shook the cliches from my mind and tried not to think about Holden and my old life. It felt like so long ago, despite the fact that it had been a couple of weeks. How had everything changed so fast?

I wondered about Holden. Was he still alive? Had the Umbras welcomed him with open arms? Was he sitting around laughing about what he had accomplished? Or was he just as grumpy and moody as he always had been?

The low growl sounded again, and I gritted my teeth as I quickly removed the rest of my clothes and called to my wolf. She was ready, anticipation bubbling under my skin as if she'd been waiting this whole time. I took a deep breath, then called for the change. Surprisingly, it was faster than yesterday. My wolf had wanted this. It was like she'd simply been waiting for me to initiate.

As my body folded over, I noticed that the transition felt less intense. It was uncomfortable, but more seamless as my body broke and reformed into its new shape. It wasn't long before I was staring through those sharp, crystal-clear eyes, looking far into the distance and catching every single detail.

The sensation was still overwhelming. My senses fired on a level that wasn't possible in my human form. The forest was alive, the sounds of creatures skittering through the underbrush, wind rustling through branches, and from somewhere farther off, I could hear the sound of water.

Xander's wolf nudged me with his nose as if he knew how distracted I was. This was what happened when I didn't get enough sleep. My focus was shit. Xander took a few tentative steps forward, then glanced back at me to make sure I was following. I trotted ahead until I was level with him, then I took off at a run, blowing past him.

Absolute joy surged through me as wind ruffled my fur. I relished the sensation of my paws skimming over the soft ground. It was almost like flying at this speed. I still felt more free in this form than I ever had in human form. I suppose I couldn't be too upset if this was what I had to do the next few days as I was figuring out a plan. There were far worse ways to spend my time.

Getting used to my wolf and how she moved and how she experienced the world was useful. I knew I was faster in my wolf form in addition to all the heightened senses. Once I learned how to fight in this form, I'd be far deadlier than I had ever been in my human form. The thought sent my heart racing, and I pushed forward, picking up the pace. I needed to see just how hard I could run and just how far I could go before I reached the point of exhaustion.

I couldn't sense Xander behind me and I wasn't even sure where he was, but I didn't care. I was living through my wolf, and I was running on pure elation and adrenaline. The harder I ran, the harder my heart pumped, the less room there was in my brain to worry about anything else. The exertion silenced all the overthinking I'd been doing, giving me a sense of peace I hadn't felt in a long time.

Eventually, I slowed my pace and started to take in my surroundings more. The sound of running water roared in my ears and I headed toward it, breathing in a fresh damp scent that reminded me of rain on pavement. There were also other smells mingling with the clean smell of the water and I knew I was catching scents of different plant life, or possibly even the fish that lived in the stream. It was strange to have so many sensations all the time, and I was grateful that my senses weren't this enhanced when I was human. It would be rather distracting to have so much sensory information all the time.

I paused in front of the water and stared into the clear liquid. It tumbled over rocks as it raced through the landscape. Areas of white foam and ripples caused by the strong current made the water look ice cold. The streams around here were runoff from the melting snows and with the winter chill in the air, there was nothing warm about that water. We didn't get a lot of snow where we were, but higher up in the mountains there was plenty. It had been a mild winter, so the ground was still soft on the surface, but I wondered how my wolf would handle everything if it was covered in snow or ice. Would it be just as easy to navigate, or would it make running more difficult?

I heard footsteps approach and turned to catch sight of Xander as his wolf stopped next to me. For a moment we stood there in silence, then Xander's wolf made a grunting sort of sound and took off again. I knew he wanted me to follow, so I gave chase, this time staying right behind him as he navigated through the woods. He was fast, and my wolf started to struggle to keep up. What had once felt exhilarating was getting a little bit more difficult. But that was the point Xander was trying to make. He wanted to push me to my brink and exhaust my wolf. And that was what he did for the next several hours.

We weaved around trees and ducked under low-hanging branches. We crossed through streams, my paws getting soaked by the icy water. Thankfully, the fur kept me relatively warm, and I dried fairly quickly as we ran.

Eventually, my wolf started to resist. She didn't want to run anymore, and I didn't blame her. I was drained. I looked up, trying to catch a glimmer of the sun through the canopy of trees to gauge what time it might be. We've been running for what felt like hours and it had to at least be midday. At the thought, my stomach grumbled, reminding me that I hadn't eaten in quite a while.

Xander's wolf turned back to me, giving me an expectant look. While I couldn't understand what he was thinking or what he was feeling, his expression was clearly disappointed. He wasn't done with me yet. Unwilling to give him the satisfaction of giving up first, I raced forward, pushing through my fatigue, desperate for a second wind. *I could do this.* I could do whatever he needed me to do because I was going to get stronger, faster, better. And when I found out what my special power was and how to use it, no one was going to be able to control me anymore.

Finally, after another hour or so of running, Xander stopped. I halted next to him and sat back on my haunches, panting as I caught my breath. Overcome with a sudden urge to curl up in a little ball and go to sleep, I resisted. Xander had warned me that it was harder to shift back into human when you were tired. I wondered if I'd pushed too hard. I could have slowed down, but I'd been too determined to show my strength.

I caught the scent of something floral and sweet. Following the familiar scent, I took a few steps froward and stopped in front of my clothes. We came full circle, right back to where we had started. I had no idea where we'd been running or where we'd gone, but Xander's wolf knew. He kept us on track and returned us right back to our starting point. I needed to pay more attention to navigation next time. I also needed to notice scents better. Curious, I padded over to Xander and inhaled. His scent was musky and masculine, but there was a note of something uniquely him. Similar to me, he had floral undertones. I made a note to remember his smell, just in case.

Xander's wolf shuddered and bones cracked as he

began the transformation from wolf back into human. I stepped back, giving him space. Our time was up and I was looking forward to returning to human form.

My wolf protested, urging me to skip shifting and rest. I could tell that's what she wanted, but I knew I had to resist. I closed my eyes and willed myself to take control, trying to find that part of me that would trigger the shift back into human form. There was a little bit of conflict internally, but I fought through it until my own body began the change. A couple minutes later, I was on my knees in the dirt, uncaring of the fact that I was totally naked in front of Xander. I was far too tired to give a shit about who saw me naked right now.

Xander started tugging on his clothes, and then he picked mine up and tossed him to me. "Not as shy as you were before, huh?"

I gave him a dirty look and then got to work getting dressed. It was interesting how quickly I had gone from being shy about my body to being too tired to worry about it. Maybe that was why shifters didn't care. With enough practice shifting, and so many times of doing it, it became second nature. Besides, when you continuously saw everyone naked, you started to worry about yourself less. I suppose I needed to get to that point. Even in school, none of my classmates seemed concerned, but I hated being undressed in front of them. After I tugged my boots back on and laced them up, I stood and then stifled a yawn. I caught sight of the sun through the trees, noting that it was low in the sky. We've been out here awhile. My stomach growled again, and Xander laughed.

"I guess we did skip lunch," he said.

"I don't suppose you have a snack in the car that I don't know about?" I asked.

"I'm afraid I'm not that prepared," he said. "But we could grab some food on the way back to your place."

"Is that even allowed, or does my prison sentence forbid me from grabbing food in public places?"

"You know, the sooner you give into all of this, the sooner Dax will loosen his grip." Xander started walking back toward the parking lot.

I followed behind him. "I'm doing the training. I didn't try to escape. What else am I supposed to do to show that I'm going along with this?"

"Well, last night you weren't exactly on the same team. This is quite the change from the last conversation you had with him. How is he supposed to know you've had a change of heart?" Xander asked.

"I don't think I've had a change of heart so much as I've surrendered," I explained. "What choice do I have? Where would I even go? Even if he didn't have Kate, I don't have any other options."

"That's not true. You and I both know that."

My brow furrowed. "What's that supposed to mean?" My stomach tightened and for a moment I worried that he knew the truth about me and Madoc, but how could he? Nobody knew that. He had to guess that I was considering going feral.

"Nobody wants to talk about it, but going feral is always a choice. They make it sound like it's this terrible thing, like it's the end of the world and you'll be destitute. I don't think that's how it is. None of us get to leave here, so how do we know what it's really like?" Xander's eyes widened and he swallowed. "Never mind, that was a stupid thing to say. Forget I said anything."

"You sound like you've put some thought into this. Or like you know something." I opened the car door and slid into the passenger seat, closing the door behind me. When Xander got in, I turned to look at him and he was deliberately avoiding my gaze. "Xander?"

"I said forget about it." He started the engine.

EIGHT

THE MORE TIME I spent with Xander, the more I realized he was keeping things from me. That wasn't much of a surprise. People had kept things from me my whole life. Something about Xander felt different. I got the sense he wanted to say more, but held back. I wondered if Xander could be an ally eventually. I wasn't sure how far he would take things against Dax or if he was too far in to budge.

"How did you and Dax end up so close? I never saw you two together in high school." So many shifters gravitated toward the future alpha. Every time Dax's gang preyed on me, I made note of who was there. It was pure survival to know who I needed to avoid when I saw them walking down the halls. Xander was never one of those faces.

"I'd been working for Preston, so Dax and I got to know each other."

"How does one go from working for one alpha to working for that alpha's killer?" I asked.

"I'm loyal to the pack, and Dax knows that. Besides, I held no love for Preston. As I've told you, Dax learned everything he knows from his father, the good and the bad." Xander's grip tightened on the steering wheel, his knuckles going white.

"You don't want to work for Dax." I probably should have phrased it as a question, but I was damn sure my instincts were correct on this. "You've made comments before. That we're all doing what we must. So my question is, what does Dax have on you?" It all made sense now. Dax had my best friend, so I was going to play his game until I could see her returned safely. Xander seemed loyal to a fault, but I got the sense that his loyalty was just as manufactured as mine. Maybe he could be an ally.

"It doesn't matter. I'm loyal to the pack." His words sounded more for his benefit than mine.

"Dax must be very confident that whatever it is he's holding over your head is ironclad. Otherwise, he wouldn't put the two of us together. But what if that was a mistake? What if we could help each other to get what we really want?"

"I'm going to pretend you didn't just say that. My job is to train you to use your wolf. Once you have that under control, I'm to instruct you in other matters," he glanced at me, then looked back at the road.

"Are you going to tell me what this is anytime soon? How am I supposed to even train in something when I don't know what it is? You do realize it's maddening not knowing. You would think if Dax wanted my loyalty, he could throw me something." If Xander would just tell me, I could skip trying to break into the hall of records. Then I could simply focus on getting Kate out.

"You know I can't do that. I told you, there's some things I can't even say. Tomorrow, we're working on your fighting skills. Dax says you're good, but how are you as a wolf?" Xander asked, changing the subject like a pro.

I glared at him. I wasn't done with the other topics of conversation, but Xander had shut me down and I knew better than to press. It seemed like there was still a possibility that I could turn him, but I needed to tread lightly to keep it from backfiring.

"I'm a solid fighter. I had plenty of practice. But I've never fought as a wolf." I wasn't even sure what you were supposed to do for that. Did you just bite and claw? It seemed like there wouldn't be a whole lot of strategy fighting in that form, but I was sure I was missing something and I was eager to learn.

All through school, every member of the Shadow Pack learned how to fight. We started young, learning blocking and defense, then we had more formal training on fighting with our fists and our feet and basic weapons.

While there were plenty of kids who'd been better than me, I could hold my own just fine. But I was out of practice, despite how well I'd held up in the ring against Dax. I frowned, recalling that he'd said he held back. Nobody ever wants to hear that their opponent wasn't giving their all. I suppose I should be grateful because Dax was likely much stronger than me, especially now. I hated that his new role made him even more dangerous. It wasn't fair that the assholes got the power and the strength. I'd always been so much smaller than the other shifters, which meant I had to work harder.

I knew all too well the feeling of being helpless. I never wanted to feel that way again. I had to be able to hold my own and defend myself. "Wouldn't it make more sense to show me this power that Dax says I have? I'm small. There's only so much I can do in either human form or wolf form. If there's some other way that I can be more effective, shouldn't I be learning that?"

"Yes, but your stamina and endurance are not what they need to be. Once you start dealing with that, it's a whole other level. I'm not sure you could handle it yet."

Xander sure seemed to know a lot about the thing that nobody would tell me. How was he the expert? My eyes widened. "Holy shit. Why didn't I see it before? You have something. Whatever this thing is... You have it too, don't you? That's why you're the one training me. It's not just me, is it?"

Xander's jaw tensed, and a vein in his forehead looked like it was going to burst. I had hit a sensitive topic. Which meant I was right. How was it possible, though? And how had I never known about this before? Why wasn't it pack gossip? If Xander could do something special, we'd all know. Disappointment settled inside me and I wasn't as sure as I had been. Maybe he wasn't like me. Maybe I just hoped there was someone else.

"Or not. Maybe you're just the guy stuck with the job. I guess this whole thing is making me crazy." I shook my head.

Xander kept his eyes on the road, his jaw still locked and that vein still bulging, but he didn't speak. I balled my hands into fists in frustration, my nails cutting into my palms. Was he hiding something from me or not? "Say something, Xander. For fuck's sake, just say something."

"You know, one of the most interesting things I have discovered about the Shadow Pack since moving into the inner circle is that none of us really knows anything about anyone who's in our pack. This entire pack is built on secrets. Dark ones, things that would make you scream in terror; things that would change your entire perspective on life. Every single member of this pack is not what you think they are. All of them have something to hide."

"That's nothing new, Xander. Everyone in this pack has a past. We're all here because we don't belong anywhere else. Our pack is made up of murderers and conmen and thieves. But whatever it is that I have, that maybe you have too, you can't tell me that's not different."

He was most definitely hiding something from me. Why else would Dax keep him so close? Why else would he risk letting the two of us be alone when Dax kept me from everyone else? And why would he have Xander train me when we had seasoned veterans who had been training shifters to fight for the alpha for decades?

Xander pulled the car into the parking lot at my apartment complex. "Why don't you head on in and I'll drop off some food later."

"So now I'm being punished for asking questions?" I asked.

"The questions you're asking are the kind that could get us both killed. Just give me a few days and things will make a lot more sense, please. I know you don't know me very well, but I am begging you to trust me." He sounded so sincere, and I could almost feel his concern.

I wasn't sure why, but I closed my mouth and nodded. I could wait a couple of days because I had the sense that Xander and I weren't as different as I originally thought. I opened the door and stepped out of the car.

Xander was silent on the walk to my door. He unlocked the apartment and motioned for me to step inside. I entered and expected him to close the door behind me, leaving me alone again. Instead, he followed me in and closed the door behind him.

"I'm supposed to remind you to drink your tea. So Kate won't be upset or worry." His tone was odd, and his eyes darted around the apartment.

"I didn't get hurt today, though," I added. "It's really only for injuries."

"Still, it'll make Kate and Dax feel better to know you're taking care of yourself," he said, as he walked into my kitchen.

Brow furrowed in confusion, I followed him. Was he going to make tea and force me to drink it? What was everyone's obsession with Kate's tea lately? Sure, Kate could be intimidating, but how was she managing to give orders while she was in captivity?

Xander was holding the packet of herbs when I entered the kitchen, and I frowned. He could make it for me, but I wasn't going to drink it. He lifted a finger to his lips in the unmistakable signal for quiet. Automatically, I glanced around, looking for signs of company. We appeared to be alone.

Xander walked over to the sink and poured the contents of the bag down the drain. My eyes widened. "What are you?"

He closed the distance between us and pressed his finger to my lips. I got the hint and tightened my jaw, watching him turn on the sink and run the garbage disposal in silence. I had no idea what he was doing. He'd walked in here telling me to drink my tea, then proceeded to dump it all down the sink.

"Have a cup tonight and one in the morning to prepare," he said. "There's a good chance you'll end up with some bumps and bruises during our training." Xander set the empty bag down on the counter. "I'll see you in the morning."

My heart thundered in my chest. Xander was putting on a show for whoever was listening. Shifters had excellent hearing, but I knew a few had freakish hearing even by shifter standards. Based on Xander's actions, it was safe to say one of those skilled shifters was outside my apartment. A chill spread down my spine. I thought it was bad when they were just waiting to see if I left and now I know they were listening to everything. I really, really hoped I hadn't talked in my sleep.

Chest tight with worry, I tried not to overthink things that had already happened. I couldn't change anything I'd done last night, but I could be more cautious moving forward. Unless Madoc showed up in my dreams again. *Fuck.* I hadn't even warned him in the dream that I was surrounded. What if he came for me himself and ended up captured by my guards?

"You alright?" Xander asked. "You suddenly got very pale. Did you get enough sleep last night?"

"I'm fine," I said. "I think I'm tired. We had a big day. I'm going to have my tea and get some sleep."

"Good," Xander said. "I'll see you in the morning."

My heart was still racing after I locked the door behind Xander. But now it was less about self-preservation and more about concern for Madoc. How was I going to let him know I had a whole crew of people watching my every move?

CHAPTER
NINE

"ARE you going to explain now why you dumped all of Kate's herbs down the garbage disposal last night?" I snapped my seat belt in place and turned to watch Xander's response.

He started the car and backed out of the parking lot before taking a quick glance in my direction. "Sometimes you need to learn to let go of the past. And sometimes it's just better to see what your body can accomplish on its own."

"So you decided that the herbs that probably don't do anything anyway, but might actually help me recover from injuries, should be tossed down the drain the day before I learn new fighting techniques?" I rolled my eyes. "Two days ago you were telling me to drink those damn herbs, and I wasn't even injured. Now, the time that they might actually help, I don't have them as an option."

"Why do you even care if you don't think they help?"

Xander asked. "I think you can get by without them for a while."

I wasn't sure why I was so concerned about not getting to drink the awful concoction, but none of it made sense. While I'd hated every single time I've been given those herbs by Kate, it was something I had been drinking at least once a week for most of my life.

Kate and I have been friends for almost as long as I could remember. Dax and his friends had always picked on me, but it didn't turn physical until we were about twelve. One day, the pushing and rude comments escalated. I couldn't remember who threw the first punch, but I remembered fighting back. From that day forward, the bullying was so much worse than it had been. Kate had started bringing the herbs to school shortly after. She insisted I make it into tea at the foundling house and nagged me daily until I finally gave in. I recalled the first time I took a sip. It had always been awful, but Kate was the only person who cared about me, so I figured it was worth drinking.

None of the people who worked at the foundling house cared what any of us kids did. We basically lived in a free-for-all kind of situation. As long as we kept the huge dorm room all the girls shared clean and didn't make too much noise, they didn't have a whole lot to say. Us kids basically raised ourselves until, one by one, we moved out when we came of age.

I was fortunate that Kate and her parents were willing to cosign the apartment so the two of us could have a place of our own. I'd gotten a job while I was still living at the foundling house and I had saved enough for a deposit and to help purchase basic necessities, but I never would have qualified for the lease by myself. Kate and her parents were my ticket out. I didn't even want to think what my life would have been like if I hadn't had their support.

There were several kids at the foundling house that I'd grown up with who got into trouble shortly after leaving. At least two of them had vanished from town and one of them had died during a shady business deal gone wrong. I know four who shared a terrible one-bedroom apartment in the worst part of town. They might be working legit jobs at the pack grocery store, but few legit jobs paid well enough to survive. That's why I'd been so desperate to keep my position at the Howler, even if it was a shit hole. And now there wasn't even a Howler to go back to. I shuddered. My life could have been so much worse. I owed a lot to Kate, and I was going to make it up to her.

"Maybe it's less about the herbs and more about the fact that you're a hot mess," I said. "You are all over the place. You opened up to me yesterday, then you dumped the herbs, and now I'm getting the silent treatment?"

"I've told you before, there are certain things I can't say, but I've asked you to trust me." He kept his eyes ahead as if the road in front of him was the most interesting thing in the world. I suppose I should be grateful that he was such a careful driver except for the fact that I knew he wasn't so focused on the road because he was trying to be safe; he was trying to avoid making eye contact with me.

Xander was this strange puzzle piece that didn't quite fit in anywhere. He and I seemed so alike, as if we each had one foot in the pack and one foot out. I wanted it to be because he was like me, so that whenever I found out what I was, I wouldn't be alone. But maybe that wasn't the case. Maybe he was just someone doing his job for his alpha, even though he didn't want to.

"We're going to try some role play today in the woods," Xander said. "I'm going to be the bad guy and you're going to try to escape me."

"I thought I was supposed to learn how to fight in my wolf form?" I asked.

"It's not usually that straightforward unless you're in an alpha challenge. More likely, you'd be in a situation where you're in human form and your life is threatened. Unless you can guarantee that the person fighting you is another shifter, you're better off not shifting right in front of them. Your goal will be to evade me and then shift and then continue running. See if you can hide and outsmart me in that sort of way before we get to actual fighting. Especially given your experience as a wolf, which is limited, hiding and running might be your better bet."

"Hiding never benefits me. Every time I tried to run I ended up captured and if I could fight back maybe I'd have a shot," I protested.

"Were you running in human form?" he asked.

I pursed my lips. He had me there. When I was at the Umbra estate, I had tried to flee, but I wasn't able to shift. I had a feeling that any of those Umbra wolves could have caught up to me even if I was in my wolf form, especially since I'd been injured. But add in the mating bond, and I never stood a chance.

We were already at the parking lot near the woods, only this time there was another car here.

"Expecting company?"

"Stay here," Xander said. He killed the engine and quickly exited the car. I waited until he was a few steps away before I got out myself. Like I was going to sit in a car alone and wait for someone to jump out of nowhere while I was trapped. No thank you.

My feet crunched across the gravel and Xander glanced back over his shoulder. "You are terrible at listening to directions."

"You realize if this was a trap, you would have left me alone in there. Might be exactly what they wanted."

Xander grunted, a sound that almost sounded like he agreed with me. I wasn't quite paranoid enough to think that somebody was after me, but after what I'd been through the last couple of weeks, I wasn't about to take any chances or put myself in a situation that seemed dangerous for no reason.

I stayed right behind Xander as he approached the car and paused as he looked in the windows.

He turned to me. "Well, whoever drove this car here isn't still inside. They're probably in the woods, which means we may have to adjust our plans a little."

"Why would it matter? We're still on pack lands, aren't we? It's not like any humans could be here and anyone from our pack wouldn't be too surprised to see a shifter running through the woods."

Xander cocked a brow. "Aren't you the one who just told me this could be a trap and someone could leap in and snatch you from under me?"

I wrinkled my nose. "I didn't quite say it like that, but I may have said something similar."

"I'm sure it's just someone out for a run in the woods. If you see anything suspicious when we get in there, you head straight back to the car. Dax will kill me if anything happens to you."

"Yeah, I'm sure he'll be super heartbroken." I was glad I hadn't seen Dax in a couple days, but I didn't like the reminder that he was probably keeping tabs on me. I was certain that every day Xander gave him a play-by-play of what we had done together.

My jaw tightened and my face felt a little hot with anger. I hated how much power and control Dax had over me right now. If he didn't have Kate, there was so much more I could try.

"You know, it's not my place, but you and Dax aren't as different as you think. I know what he did to you was wrong, but if you gave him an actual chance, who knows what could happen?" Xander said.

"Did you seriously just suggest that I should give Dax a chance in a romantic relationship? Did you get hit in the head? If I'm not mistaken, you're not in a position to be giving me advice like that. You're not exactly working for him because you're best buds. I might not know what you're hiding from me, but I figured that part out at least."

Xander growled. "We should get started. If you come across another wolf, just go the other way. If anything gets weird, find your way back to the car. Do you think you can do that?"

"Probably," I said with a shrug. For a moment, I wondered what would happen if I ran and just kept running. What if I just went as far as I could until I ran out of space to run? Could Xander just tell Dax he lost me in the woods? Surely Dax wouldn't hurt Kate, would he? Maybe they would assume some animal got me or that I died of starvation or cold. Shit, maybe I would die of starvation or cold. That was a terrible idea. Running off with no sense of direction, no clothes, no food, no supplies, and no plan would be the worst possible thing I could do. I wasn't that desperate; at least not yet.

"I'll give you a three-minute lead. Starting now," Xander said.

"So we're playing hide and seek?" I clarified.

"Two minutes and forty-five seconds," he said.

I huffed in frustration. Fine. I guess I wasn't going to get anything new from Xander today. Grateful I could at least get out of sight before I stripped, I took off into the woods. I didn't make it very far before I ran into the owner of the car, knife in hand. He grinned. "How nice to see you again, Ivy."

Shit. I hoped Xander found me while I was still breathing.

CHAPTER
TEN

"Hey, Joe, long time no see," I said.

"Zip it," he hissed. "I don't understand why Holden didn't fire you that first night, and I certainly don't understand why he insists I keep you alive now. Especially after you blamed him for your boyfriend's crime."

"First of all, Dax is *not* my boyfriend," I snapped. That fucking forced bond was really starting to get to me. It was one thing that I had to live with it, it was almost worse that it continued to be shoved in my face.

"Well, that's interesting news, but I'm not here to ask about your love life," he said.

"Then why did you bring it up?" I lifted my hand up. "Never mind. I don't care and I don't want to talk about it, anyway. What are you doing hiding in the woods with a knife?" *Weirdo.* Thankfully, Joe was small, and I was pretty sure I could take him.

"I came with a message for you," he said.

"You did?" I lifted a surprised brow. He'd been working with Holden, and now I wasn't sure what he was doing. In fact, I knew nothing about him. Until that night at the Howler, I'd never seen him before.

Joe pulled out a folded piece of paper and handed it to me. "Try to read it when you're alone."

"Like I am now?" I asked.

A branch snapped, and my heart nearly leaped out of my throat. I spun to look behind me and could see signs of movement. *Shit.* Now I didn't want Xander to find me. Not until I could figure out what the hell was going on with Joe.

"Enough with the cryptic bullshit," I said, as I turned back to him. My shoulders slumped. He was already gone. I looked around for signs of him in the trees, but he was good. There were some advantages to being small.

Remembering that I was supposed to be playing hide and seek with Xander, I shoved the note into my pocket. I hoped whatever was on it wouldn't get me killed if Xander or someone else found it before I did.

Without waiting to see if I was alone, I pulled off my clothes and called to my wolf. She came even faster this time, shifting with more grace and ease than last time. I was pleased, and my happiness seemed to embolden my wolf. She took off, and my animal side was thrilled at the idea of a game.

Racing around trees and over roots, I tried to focus on my footfalls instead of the contents of that unknown note. There were a dozen questions swirling in my mind, topped

79

by who Joe was sending a message for and why he'd been waiting in the woods. How had he known I'd be here? And how long had he been waiting?

It was a little creepy. Even if he was a messenger. I hoped that note wasn't a personal message. I didn't have any room in my life right now for some weirdo with an interest in me.

As I ran, I remembered that Madoc had said he'd be in touch. I felt like an idiot for not jumping to that conclusion first. If Joe was in touch with Holden, and Holden was with Madoc, that was a perfect way to get to me. I'd been so focused on trying to keep Madoc out of my head that I hadn't even let myself recall his dream message.

My heart raced, and it wasn't from running. Suddenly, I was terrified of the contents of that message. Madoc said he'd be in touch when it was time to break the bond. I should be thrilled, but my chest was tight with terror. The idea of severing that bond was almost painful.

Get it together.

I didn't want Madoc. I wanted my freedom. A mating bond was the complete opposite of that. Since experiencing that false bond, I now had a first hand trial run to prove how stupid the bond could make you.

My paw caught on a root and I went down, tumbling to the ground. That was new. Usually, my wolf was far more surefooted than I was. I got back up on all fours and went down again as searing pain shot through my front right paw. Dammit. Leave it to me to sprain my wrist in wolf form. How was that even possible?

Limping, I continued on, determined to stay away from Xander for as long as possible. Every time I stepped on it, the pain intensified. I should heal quickly, especially in wolf form, but I didn't know how long that would be. A sprain could take weeks to heal for a human.

My ears twitched as the sound of someone approaching drew nearer. I growled, pissed that I'd let myself get caught by Xander so easily. This was Joe's fault. Couldn't he have just told me the message instead of being all sneaky about it?

A dark gray wolf emerged in front of me. This wasn't Xander. I'd know that scent anywhere. I growled, a low warning sound. I didn't care if he was the alpha. I was not going to play games with Dax.

Another creature joined us, his scent giving him away before I saw him. I looked over just as Xander came around a tree trunk. He stopped when he caught sight of Dax and the two wolves stared at each other in silence for a long moment.

Finally, Dax's wolf shook his head, then headed out into the woods. I narrowed my eyes, watching for any sign that he expected us to follow. He didn't look back for us, so I turned my attention to Xander.

His wolf growled, then leaned down, as if preparing to pounce. That's when I remembered we were still training and he was coming after me. My wolf limped forward, the injury preventing me from running at full speed. I winced as pain shot through my leg, making everything so much harder than it should be.

It wasn't a surprise when Xander brought me down. He pinned me quickly, his jaws snapping at my face. I rolled, trying to get away from his hold, but he was strong. My wolf seemed to protest my movements, as if she wanted to override what I was doing.

It took me a few seconds to remember that my wolf was going to be better at this than my human side. She knew how to fight in this form better than I did, even if she'd never practiced the skills.

I let go, easing into the animal instincts. It was harder than I thought it would be. My mind didn't want to move to the animal side. It was something I'd found difficult since my first shift. I never felt like I was two sides as strongly as other wolves did. When they talked about it, I got the sense that they lost control of their human side completely. My human side wouldn't shut the fuck up.

Leave it to me to overthink being a wolf.

Xander shifted his weight, and I took the opportunity to move so I could nip his shoulder. He flinched, and it was just enough for me to wiggle out of his grasp. I rolled to all fours and tried to run, but my leg wasn't going to get me far. What was it with me and injuring myself? I had to be the worst at this whole escaping thing.

Instead of running, I turned to face Xander. His wolf was huge. Definitely larger than me, but that wasn't anything new. I'd always been small. Which I'd been able to use to my advantage in regular fights. So many underestimated me or didn't see me coming when I'd go for less conventional tactics.

I charged forward, emboldened by those thoughts. Ducking down, I slid under Xander's legs, then lifted myself as tall as I could, throwing him off me. He landed on his side with a thud but was on his feet quickly.

With my weight on my good leg, I swiped at his face with my injured paw. Making contact with his muzzle didn't feel great, but I was able to keep him back.

Xander charged forward, a massive paw going right into my side. His claws bit into my skin, but not as deep as they could have. It hurt, but I knew he was holding back. We both were. What was the point of this if we weren't going to be able to practice properly?

I attacked him again, and he blocked me. We went back and forth for a while, with half-assed attacks and blocks, until I made the mistake of leaping off my injured paw. Instead of landing on top of Xander, I collapsed.

Defeat seemed to swirl around my head like a dark cloud, and without my command, my wolf retreated. I was naked in the dirt before I even realized what had happened. If there was a grade for this session today, I'd have failed everything.

CHAPTER
ELEVEN

"Are you going to tell me what happened here?" Xander didn't hide the disappointment in his tone.

"Well, for one, I seem to be a pro at hurting myself." I clutched my sprained wrist close to my body, afraid of injuring it further. I knew it should heal quickly, but all the running on it had probably made the initial injury worse. "What was Dax doing out here? Are you going to explain that part to me?"

"I keep forgetting you can't hear him," Xander rubbed his forehead and closed his eyes for a moment. He blew out a long breath as he dropped his arm to his side. "It makes everything so much harder since you're not connected. We're going to have to talk to the elders about that."

"I'm less concerned about that and more concerned about why he was here in the first place. Was he checking up on us? Does he not trust you?" That was *very* interesting. The thought sent a little thrill through me. Each time I interacted with Xander, it felt like some of his façade was chipped away and I got closer to the person underneath.

"He came because of the other car. Someone called it in as suspicious because it belonged to Holden," Xander explained. "Nobody had seen it for a while and suddenly it appeared in the same place you were going to be."

I tensed, thinking back to my brief interaction with Joe. He must have been driving Holden's car. The note in the pocket of my jeans felt like it might start to blare like a siren. If Dax hadn't already found it, Xander might when we returned to our clothes. I hadn't even had a chance to read it yet, and I needed to know what it said.

"You didn't run into anyone out here, did you?" Xander asked.

I wasn't sure which option would get me in less trouble. If they discovered the note, I could just say I didn't know how it got in my clothes. While Holden had been grumpy, rude, and mean, oh, and a murderer, he almost felt more predictable than the murderer I was currently dealing with. Dax was unstable. At least I felt like with Holden I was safe unless I crossed him.

I had to know what was on that note, especially since there was a good chance it came from Madoc and explained what we needed to do to sever our bond. *Please still be in my pocket.*

A swell of longing surged through me unexpectedly and I nearly toppled over as a vision of Madoc came out of nowhere. It was as if just thinking about him had summoned a full-on fantasy. I could almost feel his lips pressed against mine and his rough, calloused hands sliding over my skin. I shivered and pushed the thought away. *Holy shit*, where had that come from? I really needed to read that note and figure out how to end this bond. Getting random fantasies about Madoc wasn't going to work for me.

"Ivy, you with me?" Xander asked.

"Yeah, but I'm naked and freezing. Where are my clothes?" I quickly turned away and inhaled a deep breath, trying to catch my floral scent. While it wasn't strong, I thought I caught just a hint of it in the distance. Rather than waiting for Xander to explain what we were going to do next, I started walking toward my clothes. The training had been cut short. Good thing too, because I wasn't in the mood for more.

"We can't seem to get one complete training session in, can we?" Xander asked.

"Maybe if we could just move on to the real training, we wouldn't have such a problem." I'd been more than patient and I was getting beyond annoyed that all of this was being dragged out. I was no closer to figuring out what my power was and, with my new injury, I couldn't risk sneaking out tonight. I needed to figure this all out, and I needed to do something about the mating bond. I really hoped that note in my pocket was good news.

The walk back to our clothes was silent, which I was fine with. It took all my willpower not to stick my hand in my pocket and make sure the note was still there. I tried to casually brush across the front of my jeans to make sure that the paper stayed in place. I could feel it against my hip, but the stupid shallow pockets made me nervous, and I was worried it would fall out as we walked.

After we were both dressed, we started heading back toward Xander's car. "Is Dax still out here, or did he head back to town?" I wanted to be prepared in case he was waiting for us in the parking lot. On one hand, it wouldn't surprise me to see him, but then again, he'd been a lot less interested in me since the false bond was broken.

"I don't feel him out here anymore."

"Do the elders know he has Kate?" I wasn't sure why I hadn't just asked it sooner. Probably because I was still trying to figure Xander out and now, I knew there was only part of him that supported Dax. As he told me before, he was loyal to the pack and for right now, Dax was the pack.

"I'm not sure, but I don't think you'd get as far as you'd like by informing them of the situation."

"How long is this going to go on? He can't keep her forever," I said.

"Not too much longer now since you stopped drinking the tea," he said.

I stopped walking, "What does the tea have to do with anything? Xander, start talking."

"I told you, I can't say anything." He sighed and ran a hand through his hair. Then he glanced around as if checking to make sure we were alone. I found myself copying his movements, the hairs on the back of my neck standing on edge. Why was he suddenly being so cautious? We'd entered the woods with a strange car parked and he basically brushed that off. Was he working with Joe? A double agent that close to the alpha seemed unimaginable, but I wasn't sure what to believe anymore.

We were right inside the tree line, the car in sight, but still hidden by the trees. Our car was now the only car and if Xander couldn't sense Dax, there was a good chance we were truly alone.

"You gotta give me something. You're a walking anomaly, Xander."

"Can't you just –"

"Trust you?" I interrupted. "I'm going to start making up some crazy shit if you don't give me something else."

"You are never going to let this go, are you?" he asked.

"Would you?" I pressed.

He let out a frustrated breath. "You know we have witches that live on our lands? Some are half wolves, some are part of the pack, some are married to shifters, and some just live here because they have nowhere else to go."

"Yeah, so?" Of course I knew that. Kate was half-witch herself. Though, she'd gotten all the shifter blood, and was able to shift as a full wolf. She'd explained how hybrids got one gift or the other.

"Our pack has always employed their talents on the down low. There's a lot that can be done with their magic, but it's not talked about. Sometimes it *can't* be talked about," he said.

My brow furrowed. "Are you saying someone has

spelled you or used magic to prevent you from saying certain things?"

Xander didn't respond. Instead, he turned away from me and started walking toward the car again.

Brow furrowed, and irritation growing, I chased after him, still cradling my injured arm. "You don't just drop something like that on someone and then walk away." I should be used to it by now. Xander was excellent at giving me little hints and then shutting up.

"I'm amazed I was even able to say that much," he snapped.

"What does he have on you? Why are you doing all this?" I asked.

"There's something under the seat for you." Xander unlocked the car and stepped inside.

Even more confused, I got into the car and immediately reached under the seat. My heart felt like it fell into my stomach when I realized what I was holding. The folder I'd been after. The one that I saw in Dax's bedroom. The one that I was hoping to break into the hall of records to take. This was going to save me a lot of trouble. It felt heavy in my hands.

"How did you..." I shook my head. "Never mind. Thank you."

"I never told you anything." Xander started the car and pulled out of the parking lot. "Make sure it's hidden when you go into your place. Don't let anyone see it."

I nodded as I stared at the folder. Now that I had it, I

wasn't sure I wanted to know what was inside. "This is going to change things for me, isn't it?"

"Yes."

"Whatever is in here, are you going to show me how to use it?" I asked.

Xander nodded. "We'll start tomorrow."

Anticipation rolled through me, and my stomach twisted into nervous knots. This was why I stayed, well, aside from the fact that my best friend was being held hostage. But now that I was so close, I couldn't help but worry about where this was going.

What if it wasn't anything interesting? What if I couldn't do the things that Dax thought I could do? What if being half something else wasn't enough to give me control of whatever power Dax wanted to abuse? Kate didn't have any of the magic of her witch heritage. How were they so sure I would?

"What if I can't do it?" I asked.

"Only one way to find out," Xander said. "And if anyone asks, we're still working on shifting."

"Thank you." I had the feeling that if Dax found out what Xander was doing, he'd be in big trouble. I also knew Dax had something over Xander but I wasn't sure what it was. Xander was taking a huge risk by doing this, and I felt even more guilty about my intentions to leave the pack.

"Is there anything I can do to help you?" I asked. "I know you're facing similar problems."

"I don't think there's anything anyone can do for me.

I'm in too deep." He pulled into my apartment complex and exited the car.

Carefully, I shoved the folder under my shirt. It was bulky and not as well hidden as I'd like, but it would have to do. I hurried to catch up to Xander and followed him inside my apartment.

"I'll see you tomorrow." He was back outside, locking the door with my key before I could ask any questions.

CHAPTER
TWELVE

MY HANDS SHOOK as I pulled the folder out from under my shirt. In a daze, I somehow made it to my couch before I collapsed. Something sharp jabbed my hip, and I remembered the note. In my surprise about the folder, I'd forgotten about the note. Talk about too much anticipation at once.

I set the folder down on the coffee table and pulled the folded paper out of my pocket. It reminded me of the notes Kate and I used to pass in class and my heart hurt for her. I was failing at doing anything to get her out, and I felt like an asshole. Dax sniffing around today wasn't a great sign that he was trusting me enough to let her go.

The only thing that kept me going was that as long as Kate was truly safe, I knew she wouldn't want me to risk myself for her. I would in a heartbeat if she was in danger, but I believed Dax when he said he'd keep her safe. It was insane, but I did.

Carefully, I unfolded the note and scanned the writing. My heartbeat grew more rapid with each word.

As the moon finds her peak
As the sea's tides rise
All the stars are dimmed
Twin souls are free to fly

A CHILL RAN down my spine. What a way to deliver a message. I wondered who had written the poem or why they'd gone to such lengths. From what I could gather, I was supposed to meet Madoc on the full moon, which was at the end of the week. But where was I supposed to meet him? And how was I supposed to get there? Sure, I could sneak out, and I could probably get past the guards, but I had no idea where to go from there.

I read the poem a few more times, trying to figure out if there were clues in the verse. We didn't have a sea nearby. There was a river, but that wasn't very specific.

The folder sitting on the table caught my attention, and I set the poem down. I'd work on that more later. Right now, I wanted to finally figure out what Dax had been hiding from me.

Dozens of sheets of paper were stuffed inside the folder. Some were official looking forms, some were scribbled notes on torn pages, and a few were thick and glossy.

I skimmed through the documents, wincing at the mentions of the disciplinary actions I had received as a child. I'd forgotten about a lot of that, probably out of self preservation. Instead of focusing on how tough things had been for me as a kid, I'd often just generalized it in my head as just one giant shit show.

Seeing records of the times I was locked into the solitary room or disciplined for talking back was jarring. I had learned it was often easier to keep my mouth shut than to question things, which is probably why I was in this situation in the first place.

Upon first glance, there were no documents that had anything to do with my parents or my background. I wasn't sure what I expected, but I suppose I thought I'd see something with big bold letters that explained what I needed to know. Pushing away the feelings of defeat and frustration, I slowed down and went through each document one at a time. I found my intake form, where the lines for my parents' names were both blank. A box had been checked, verifying that I had been abandoned at the doorstep. In the comments section, someone wrote in tight cursive that a note had been left with me, simply stating that my name was Ivy.

My throat tightened, and my eyes burned. I hadn't been prepared for the emotional toll this would take on me. I should have thought that through better, but I'd been so focused on trying to find out what my heritage was that I forgot about the fact that I was going to have to relive my abandonment on a level I'd never done before.

Most of us kids at the foundling house never knew our parents. There were the occasional children whose parents died while they were older, but that was rare. In our pack, if you didn't want your kid or you couldn't take care of them, you simply dropped them at the foundling house. It was the only option for a child whose parents died or couldn't raise them for one reason or another. There were times when there was a new kid every week, but there were also long stretches of no new additions.

Most of the time, teenagers who were suddenly without parents just took to the streets. And some of the kids I grew up with dropped out of school to follow that route as well. I'd always been focused on becoming an official member of the pack, but I wasn't sure when that had started. Thinking back, I realized many of the kids I grew up with didn't care if they were a full member. I wasn't sure where that idea had come from or why it was so important to me. It seemed kind of silly now, because the only thing that it really prevented me from doing was participating in parties with people I didn't like anyway.

I hated that I'd been so fixated on that. I wouldn't be in this mess right now if I'd been satisfied with my place. And Kate would be home and safe. Anger and disappointment rolled through me. I missed Kate so much it hurt. It was even worse knowing I was the reason she wasn't here.

Hoping that the knowledge of what I was might give me some kind of upper hand, I forged ahead. I moved on to the next document, trying to skim through without forming any emotional attachment. I found papers with school records, doctor checkups, and even a birth certificate where they had listed a made up birthday for me because nobody knew my original birth date.

All of this was interesting, albeit depressing as shit, but none of it was the information that I needed. I flipped through the papers over and over, sure I had missed something. Why would Xander give me this if it didn't have the information I was looking for? He knew what I wanted. He wouldn't have handed this to me for no reason. Unless whatever documentation I was seeking had already been removed before Xander had swiped it.

I groaned and leaned back against the couch. Rubbing my temples, I took a deep breath. This was a lot more emotionally intense than I expected, and I really didn't want to have to think about all of this if there was no payoff. There had to be something of value in here. This was what Dax had used to learn about me.

Steeling myself, I leaned forward and decided to look through everything one more time. I set aside the disciplinary records and school grade reports. None of those would have what I was looking for, but maybe it would show up on medical records. I scanned those, but found nothing unusual. As a shifter, we rarely got sick and weren't subject to human maladies. We only went for a checkup every five years, but there was nothing of interest on any of those papers. I turned the page and caught a glimpse of a page of test results. How had I missed this before? Across the top of a rather intense looking form were the words *Magic Assessment*. The page had dozens of tiny boxes checked and a ton of small print.

I snatched the document back out of the pile and realized this wasn't a school test. This was something else. A memory crept in, something long repressed. I'd been young, maybe 5 or so, and I sat alone in a room until one of the elders walked in with somebody else, a woman. The woman held my hands and I remember feeling pain and heat and then I didn't remember anything else. I shook the strange memory away and focused on the form. It was odd and I couldn't remember if it had just been me, or if they did it with all of the foundlings.

Boxes were checked, indicating my hair color, eye color, sex, and age. Below that were 50 or so little boxes listing all kinds of supernatural creatures in a super small font. The first one on the list was wolf shifters, and that box was checked. Below it were a dozen other animal shifters, followed by witch, vampire, mage, and so on. I didn't even know most of these creatures still existed or were even on our radar anymore. My finger traced down the list to another checked box.

I froze, my hand shaking as my finger sat underneath a species that wasn't wolf shifter. I whispered the words aloud, "High Fae." Just saying it sent a chill down my spine.

There had to be a mistake. Fae didn't exist, at least not in our world. There were theories and speculation that once they had been here, or that they accessed our world through magic portals. But it was all ridiculous. The stuff of children's stories, things that were used to scare us into good behavior when we were young. We'd all heard stories of other supernatural creatures with powers more terrifying than anything any of us wolf shifters could do. The fae were in that category.

This had to be what Dax saw. He had to have seen this form and then decided that whatever test they did to me was accurate. But that was ridiculous. If I was fae, wouldn't I know? Wouldn't I have showed some sign of power or magic? If I had the strength or grace or abilities of a fae, I wouldn't have spent my whole life as a punching bag.

I stuffed the papers back into the folder and closed it up before leaning against the couch and closing my eyes. What I wouldn't give to be able to talk to Kate right now. She would know what to do; how to get through this. If I really was part fae, it explained why Dax wanted to try to tap into those powers. Of all the supernatural creatures I'd heard of, they had some of the most terrifying powers. There were stories of fae who could control elements or compel others to follow their commands.

Though, now that I knew what the other half of my heritage was, I wasn't so sure I wanted to go there. There were so many unanswered questions. What would I even do with that kind of power? If my father was fae, how had he even gotten here? And did my mom, whoever she was, know what he was? She must have, because Dax alluded to the fact that she got rid of me because she was worried about my powers. Did that mean my dad didn't even know I existed? I wouldn't be surprised if I was the product of a one-night stand rather than a love match.

An uncomfortable feeling settled into my stomach. It wasn't great to realize that you had never been wanted. I always sort of figured that, but it was easier to pretend that my mom was on her deathbed and couldn't care for me before finding all this out. Part of me wondered if my life would have been different if my father had known about me. Assuming he hadn't, which I had no proof of. But what if he had? Could I have been raised by him with the knowledge of what I was? Would there have been support and training for how to use my different abilities? What if I didn't even have any abilities? Kate didn't have any magic from being half witch. Even those herbs she gave me came from her mom or her grandma and not her.

I tensed as I thought about Xander's reaction to the herbs yesterday. First that, then he gave me the folder. I couldn't help but think that the two were somehow connected. Xander might not be totally on my side, and he was nothing like talking to my best friend, but if I couldn't have Kate, maybe I could talk to him. I'd been told I was stuck here, but there weren't any warnings about not having people over.

I walked into my bedroom before I remembered that I didn't have a cell phone anymore. Irritated, I walked back to my front door, opened it and stepped outside. Of course, one of Dax's goons stepped forward. He was a large man with a bushy salt and pepper beard and huge thick eyebrows. I'd never seen him before, but he was twice as wide as me and he towered at least a foot taller.

"Just where do you think you're going, Princess?" he asked.

"I need to get ahold of Xander. Can you call him for me?" I used my sweetest tone.

"I'm not your messenger." He scowled at me.

"Fine." I walked back into my apartment and grabbed my jacket and pulled it on. Then I walked back outside and closed the door behind me. "Do me a favor, make sure no one comes in since I don't have a key to my own place anymore."

The grumpy shifter stepped forward, blocking my path. "You're not going anywhere."

"I have a question about my training. If you won't contact Xander for me, I'll go to him myself. Dax is going to be pissed if he finds out that you prevented me from reaching my full potential. Isn't that what this is all about? Getting me all trained up and ready to fight?" I probably shouldn't have said any of that, but I was irritated.

"Lady, I was just told to protect the alpha's mate. I don't know what you are talking about."

I clenched my jaw. So that's what he had told everyone. Claiming we had a mating bond would explain why he was with me. It was infuriating, but it didn't bother me nearly as much as the fact that he was wasting pack resources to protect me. Why wasn't anyone questioning that? No other alpha stationed guards around their lovers' homes. He'd turned me into some pathetic damsel in distress who needed saving.

I took a deep breath as I considered my next words very carefully. "If you won't contact Xander, then get me Dax." It was a risk, because I sure as hell didn't want to see Dax, but I had to try.

"Alpha said he didn't want to be bothered," the shifter said with a grunt.

I started walking but only got a few steps before the huge shifter grabbed my arm. Heat surged through me as my anger simmered. "Let. Go. Of. Me."

"Get back inside," he demanded.

I had tried to play nice. I thought it was my only recourse with Kate locked away, but something inside me snapped. I was tired of being pushed around and treated like I was nothing. I went from being bullied to being used and I was done. It felt like a floodgate opened and all the years of anger and rage surged forward. I screamed, letting it all out.

A burst of white light exploded from me and both the guard and I were thrown into the air. I landed a few feet away on the pavement, cracking my jaw on the ground. Stars danced in my vision and I groaned as fresh pain made my eyes water.

I looked over at the man who had grabbed me. He was lying on the sidewalk, unmoving; his open eyes unblinking. Blood seeped out from under his head, staining the cement a dark crimson.

CHAPTER
THIRTEEN

THERE WAS NO MORE DENYING that there was more to me than just wolf shifter. Even reading the documents hadn't been enough to fully convince me that there was anything different about me. And I'd have convinced myself that even if there was, it wouldn't matter. Knowing that Kate had zero access to magic despite her mixed heritage had constantly been on my mind.

I stared at my hands, regret swirling inside me as I recalled the strange glowing sensation. I didn't know where it had come from. It just manifested and took over. I had no control. And someone was dead because of me. Nausea rolled through my stomach and my throat tightened. I'd killed someone. I hadn't meant to, and I didn't want to, but it happened.

My heart was breaking for this stranger despite his actions. He didn't deserve to die and I shouldn't have been put in this position. Anger replaced the sorrow as I realized this whole thing could have been prevented. This wasn't my fault. This was on Dax.

He'd kept this from me and then caged me like a wild animal. Nothing about my life was okay. He shouldn't have hidden my past from me and he shouldn't have trapped me. Those guards never should have been there. I never should have been here. Maybe Xander was right. Maybe everything would have been better if I would have just stayed with the Umbras. Though, in that situation he probably thought I would have ended up dead. Darkness settled around me. Is that what Xander thought? Was he saying he wished I never made it back in one piece? He knew what I was capable of, but had he expected this? How much of this could he have prevented?

"What happened here?" someone called.

I looked up to see a pair of shifters glaring at me. I wasn't sure what happened myself and I wasn't in the mood for their questions. "You might want to clean this mess up or people are going to start asking questions."

I didn't wait for their response before heading back inside my apartment.

I TURNED at the sound of my door opening and I jumped from the couch, ready to defend myself if needed. Xander held his hands up in front of him. "Whoa. Calm down. I'm not going to hurt you, I swear. You texted me, remember?"

Still gripping the cell phone I'd stolen from the dead shifter, I swallowed, then nodded. "Thanks for coming."

"Turn off the magic. I don't want to end up like that guard." He inclined his head.

My brow furrowed and out of the corner of my eye, I noticed that my hands were glowing again. Eyes wide, I clamped my hands into fists and then shoved them behind my back. "I don't even know what it is, let alone how to control it."

"I thought we'd have a couple more days before your magic would show," he said.

"Xander, please, what's going on?" Now that it was just the two of us, most of my anger was replaced with fear. What was happening to me? What if I couldn't control this power? What if I hurt innocent people? What if I hurt myself? My chest tightened with anxiety and my head was spinning. I'd never been this overwhelmed before in my life. I wanted the power to fight back. I wanted to be able to defend myself, but this felt like it was taking things too far.

"Just try to breathe and stay calm. It will prevent you from losing control. I'm going to help you through this." Xander lifted his hands and a soft glow emanated from them for just a moment and then he closed them, turning it off.

"Why didn't you just tell me?" I asked.

"I couldn't. I wanted to, but I told you there are ways to keep people quiet when you don't want them to speak." Xander walked into my living room.

I never would have imagined that magic would be

used to silence shifters. But now that I had seen bits and pieces of the behind the scenes, nothing surprised me.

"It dawned on me yesterday that I couldn't tell you, but I could show you. That's why I gave you the folder. I was hoping you'd know before you had an accident." Xander sat down on the couch and let out an exasperated breath.

I sat down next to him. "Well, I appreciate the gesture. What now?"

"I suppose we work on teaching you how to control it. It's always been the plan, but Dax wanted you weak for a few more weeks. He didn't want me to start so soon. He definitely didn't want you to know the truth." Xander grabbed the folder. "You need to hide this."

I grabbed it and carried it into the kitchen, then shoved it in the freezer. When I walked back, I found Xander reading the note from Madoc. *Shit.* How could I be so careless?

"That's mine." I ripped it out of his hands. I shouldn't have left that sitting out, but I'd been so overwhelmed when I read the contents of that folder, I forgot about the bond. Quickly, I shoved the paper in my pocket before sitting back on the couch.

"I never saw you as the type to write poetry," Xander said with a smirk.

"There are a lot of things you don't know about me," I snapped.

I jumped at the sound of the knock on my door, but

wasn't able to have a moment to consider who the intruder might be before Dax walked into the room.

I glared at Xander. "You called Dax?" I hissed.

"I didn't call him, but you took out one of your guards. What did you think was gonna happen?"

I stood and crossed my arms over my chest. "I really don't want to see you right now."

"But I come bearing gifts." He pulled the door the rest of the way open, and a rush of emotions exploded through me. Kate was standing in the doorway, looking no worse for wear, a huge smile on her face.

I raced forward, shoving Dax out of the way so I could embrace my best friend. "Oh my gods, I missed you so much! And I'm so sorry. This whole thing was my fault. I never wanted you to get involved." I stepped back but kept my hands on her shoulders so I could look at her for any signs of injuries or mistreatment. She appeared in good health, which was reassuring because I was half tempted to use the glowing power that I had discovered on Dax for kidnapping her.

"Are you alright?"

"I'm fine," she tossed a dirty look at Dax, then looked back at me, "I'm pissed at the whole situation, but I'm healthy and safe."

I dropped my hands from Kate's shoulders and turned my attention back to the alpha. "You realize you went too far, don't you? A false bond? Kidnapping? You're sick. And if you think I'm going to use my fae magic to help you win over the other packs, you've got another thing coming."

Dax smirked, the look a little unsettling. I wanted to step back, but I held my ground, not wanting to show him that his creepy expression was getting to me.

"She figured it out? And I assume that's why one of your guards is dead?" Dax looked way too excited about the prospect of someone being dead. "You're just as powerful as I was hoping, then."

"Wait, you did that?" Kate said. "And what do you mean, *fae*? What am I missing?"

"Apparently, my father was high fae. So I have scary magic that kills people," I said.

"Are you okay?" she asked.

"Is she okay? She killed someone. You're just as twisted as the rest of us, Kate," Dax said.

"I'm nothing like you, and neither is Ivy," she snapped. "You are lucky you're the alpha or I'd..."

"You'd what?" Dax sneered. "You want to challenge me, Kate? Try for my position? As if you could run this pack, you filthy half breed."

Kate lunged forward, and I pulled her back. "He's not worth it."

"You both know you're no match for my alpha strength," he said.

"You're a monster," Kate said.

I was seething, anger rising like heat. Quickly, I pulled my hands away from Kate just as the glow returned.

"Your roommate might be the bigger threat to you," Dax hissed. "Careful that she doesn't do to you what she did to that innocent shifter out there."

Guilt twisted my insides. Sure, that dude was on Dax's payroll and helping keep me prisoner, but he hadn't deserved to die for that. I didn't even know his name.

"I killed someone because of you. If you would have just been honest with me from the beginning, this never would have happened. And if you think I'm going to use any of my magic for any of your nefarious purposes, you're insane." I wanted to comment about how I'd only gone along with it because of Kate, but I wasn't about to risk him taking her away.

In fact, as soon as Dax left, I was hoping to convince her to get the fuck out of here. I was stuck until I figured out Madoc's riddle so that I could meet up with him and end this bond. But then maybe I could join her. Maybe Kate and I could go somewhere else. Maybe there was even another pack who would take us in.

Never mind, I knew that wasn't going to happen. Especially since we were both only half shifter. Half shifters weren't welcome anywhere. We had no options other than going feral and I was going to have to really convince Kate to leave her life behind if I expected her to do that. But maybe it could be temporary? Just until someone else could dethrone Dax.

With his behavior, it was probably a matter of time before someone challenged him again and beat him or before the Umbra wolves took him out. A little shiver went through me and I'd like to say it was a negative response to thinking about the Umbra wolves, but there was a little part of me that wanted them to be successful. If that happened, I knew they'd swallow up the Shadow Pack and kick anyone like Kate out. It wasn't really what I wanted.

It had to be that stupid mating bond again. Why would I want the Umbra wolves to have any sort of success or any power over the pack I grew up in? Though, now that I was seeing more clearly, there were very few redeeming qualities about my pack.

"You figured out your heritage and your power because of me. And you are going to help me, because there's only one person who can help you control that power. I know you don't want to go out and accidentally kill more people. But if you don't have this fae thing under control, that's exactly what's going to happen," Dax threatened.

"I won't use it. I never used it before tonight. I don't need this power," I said.

Dax scoffed. "Ask Xander what happened when he came into his powers. Ask him about his sister and his mom. Both gone in a flash of light. Hell of a coverup for my dad too. Xander's crimes should have cost him his life, but I saw the potential in having someone so powerful on our side. With some training and practice, Xander got it under control. But it took him years and a whole lot of accidents along the way."

"Xander?" I stared at the shifter who had almost become my friend over the last couple of days.

I'm sorry, he mouthed, then dropped his gaze to the floor. I could almost feel the anguish pouring from him. To have to relive the worst moment of his life, delivered almost gleefully by Dax, had to be torture.

Xander was the only one who seemed like he was looking out for me lately, especially since Kate was being held captive. I knew Dax had something on him, but I never imagined it would be this.

"I'm so sorry, Xander." It was the first thing that came to mind: sympathy and sorrow. So much power and so little control. In the brief moment I used my own power, I'd felt that, and I knew it had to be true. The magic had bubbled to the surface, unbidden. It was reactionary, emotional, and unstable. I had blood on my hands, but nothing compared to the blood that Xander must feel on his very soul.

"Why do you think I'm letting Kate come back here? She's honestly in more danger now with you than she was with me. You have two choices: learn how to control your powers so you don't hurt someone you love or stay locked up in here with your best friend until an accident happens."

"Dax, enough," Xander said as he stepped in front of the alpha. His hands were balled into fists. "If you want me to train her, she needs to get some rest. Using that magic takes a lot out of someone. She needs to recover so I can work with her in the morning."

I reached for Kate's hand, and she pulled away from me. "I love you, but if your touch is killing people, let's keep some space until you figure out how to control this thing."

"Smart girl," Dax said.

"Why are you even still here, asshole?" I spat.

"Yeah, time to go," Kate said.

I flashed her a smile. I missed her so much.

I was pretty sure Dax had brought her here so that I might kill her on accident, but I was determined not to let that happen. Xander's past was tragic, but he hadn't had any support or help. Unfortunately, I knew I needed at least some lessons from him. We were going to have a lot to talk about tomorrow.

"I was serious about what I said before. You will stand by my side in public as my mate, my partner."

"That's not necessary, Dax," I said. "You got what you wanted from me for now. Why fake a relationship on top of it?"

"I told you, I want you. And I always get what I want. Besides, once everyone sees the kind of power you have, they're not going to question me when you stand by my side." Dax crossed the room to the door and hesitated in front of it. "Figure out how to use that power. You don't have choices, you have orders. I know all of your weaknesses and I will exploit them as much as necessary to get what I want." He walked out the door, fading into the night.

Anger bubbled and seethed as I glared at the place where Dax had been standing. So much about what he did was wrong on so many levels. He was manipulating and conniving and I had to wonder what else he was doing behind closed doors to other members of this pack to get what he wanted. If he was willing to blackmail Xander and kidnap my best friend to get us to play ball, there was no telling what he was capable of.

"I'm still mad at you," I told Xander. Sure, I had sympathy for his past, but he'd kept this from me. He was part of the whole thing.

"I know," he said. "I'll see you in the morning."

A strange understanding seemed to settle between us and I wondered if the fact that he was part fae, just like me, was why the two of us seem to bond so quickly. I didn't feel like I fit in with my pack. I never had, and maybe this was why. Finally alone in our apartment, I turned to Kate.

"Please tell me we have some junk food, because we're going to be up all night going over everything that I've missed." Kate's smile was infectious, as if she hadn't been locked away the last few days. She was a hopeless optimist, constantly finding the best in every situation.

"And don't leave anything out. I want to hear it all," she said.

"I've got plenty to share," I assured her.

CHAPTER
FOURTEEN

"Weren't you just a prisoner?" I asked. "Shouldn't I be taking care of you or making you some soup or something?"

"I was locked in my parents' house. In my old high school bedroom. It sucked, but it was nothing compared to what you went through. My mom brought me three meals a day, and I got to look through old yearbooks. It was a bit of a torture in terms of nostalgia, but I'm fine. I'm safe. I was far more worried about you the whole time, and it seems like I've missed a lot. So you're not all shifter?"

"I guess that's something we have in common," I teased.

"Heck yes, us misfits have to stick together, don't we?" She grinned.

"Only you have no access to the witch half and my other half is apparently able to kill people," I said.

"You're going to figure it out. You always do. You're strong, and if anyone can figure out how to use this to their advantage, it's you."

"You know I'm not going to work for Dax, right?" I asked.

"I'd be disappointed if you did," she said. "About before. Look, I'm sorry I encouraged you to go after him. I didn't realize he was..."

"Deranged?" I offered.

"Yeah, something like that. I thought maybe he matured, people change," she said.

"Apparently, they don't change that much. You haven't even heard the worst of it," I said. "But you're right, we are in serious need of junk food."

Over pizza bites and chicken fingers dunked in ranch dressing, the two of us caught up over all the events of the last few days. When I told Kate about the false bond, she leaped from the couch and charged for the door. I had to grab her and pull her back down. She was probably more angry than I was about the whole situation, and I loved her for it. It was nice to have someone on my side.

She told me about her time trapped at her parents' house, which was frustrating, but thankfully not awful. It turned out her dad's business was in debt and the alpha wiped the balance of his loan in exchange for keeping Kate captive in their house for a few days. I wasn't sure I'd be able to forgive someone who did that to me, but Kate's parents were lovely people and I could see why she was conflicted.

After we'd finished our snacks, I was feeling a little bit better, though we hadn't broached the subject of what was coming next. It seemed like we danced around the topic, changing the direction of conversation every time it crossed into anything resembling what we would do after I figured out how to use these powers. There was also the weight of the huge news I hadn't told her. *Madoc.* Flutters filled my stomach at the thought of him and I couldn't help but wonder what he was up to now. Frustrated, I forced myself to stop picturing him.

I dusted crumbs off my fingers and turned to face her. "There's something I didn't tell you before, about my time with the Umbras. The real reason I got out of there alive."

"Did you use this magic? Glow your way out?" She chuckled, and it did lighten the mood a little bit.

I smiled, then shook my head. "I wish this would have appeared while I was there. It would have made things a lot easier if I could have just fought my way out. Gods know I tried, but I failed every time. There was no way I was getting out of there on my own. I'm lucky they even kept me alive as long as they did. I really should be dead." I looked down at my hands, then back up at her. Why was this so difficult to tell her? I sucked in a deep breath, steadying my nerves.

Kate rested her hand on my knee. "It's okay, whatever you have to tell me. I won't judge, I swear. Please tell me you hooked up with one of those Umbra boys. A really hot one."

My eyes widened because she was closer than she realized to the truth, despite her joking tone.

She pulled her hand away, then covered her mouth as she let out a squeal. "Oh my gods, you did!"

"No, but you're not too far off in a really weird way. So, you know how you've always talked about fated mates and how you hoped you would find yours?" I began.

"I'm not sure if I like where this is going," she said.

"Well, the idea of a fated mate is romantic and all, unless that mate happens to be an Umbra wolf," I said.

"Wait, you're telling me you found your fated mate, and he helped rescue you?" I swear she was going to swoon right there on the couch.

"Slow down," I said. "It's a little more complicated than that. Turns out, the fates decided I should be paired with Madoc Umbra. Future alpha of the Umbra Wolves."

Kate's eyes grew wider than I had ever seen them before. Her jaw dropped open, and she stared at me in absolute silence.

"Yeah, so he couldn't hurt me because of the bond, and I think that's why he agreed to the prisoner trade. Because even though he doesn't want to be with me and I don't want to be with him, the bond wouldn't let him willingly put me in harm's way."

"Holy fuck."

"Yeah, that's an understatement." I took a drink just to have something to do, then set the can of soda back on the table. "So, Dax thinks I got out because of these powers that I have. But I didn't. It was all some twisted bit of luck, fate getting in the way."

"Are you sure?" Kate asked. "You're sure there's a bond?"

"I'm sure." I surprised myself by how quickly I answered and by how certain I actually was. It should have startled me, but I knew it was the truth. I knew I had a bond with Madoc, even though I still slightly doubted the fact that I was part fae.

Okay, so maybe that was denial, but a girl can dream. The magic hands that kill people put a damper on any hopes that being half-fae was a mistake.

"So what does this mean? Are you leaving and joining the Umbra pack?" Kate asked.

"No, of course not. When it was just me as a Shadow Wolf, it was already a no-go. Can you imagine if he found out that I was half-fae?" A heavy weight of disappointment settled inside me.

"He's your mate. He'll want you no matter who you are or what you are," she said.

"He's the heir to the Umbra pack. Their next alpha. He can't be with someone like me." It was as if a knife cut through me. The agony of not being with Madoc was causing me physical pain. I let out a choked sound but tried to cover it up with a fake cough. It was so wrong to feel so intensely attached to someone I didn't know.

Someone who didn't even want me.

"You can't do this, Ivy. I know things are complicated, but you have to go to your mate." Kate's voice was laced with concern, which just amplified the pain I was already feeling.

"I can't."

"You don't have a choice," she said.

"Like shifter law matters here," I huffed.

"I'm not talking about the law. I'm talking about your life. This is already eating away at you, I can see it. The longer you go, the worse it's going to get. There's a reason they make you complete the bond. If you don't, you won't survive." Kate set her hand on my arm. "I want you to be here with me, I do. But I need you to be okay more."

"Wait, aren't you afraid I'm going to melt you or something?" I shrugged off her hand. "You keep touching me. You can't do that. It's not safe."

She chuckled. "No. I know you. I might be the only one who does. I'm not afraid of you, but I didn't want Dax to know that. I think the only reason he left me here was because he was hoping it would be a worse punishment than being at my parents' house."

I raised my brows. "I sort of wondered if he was hoping I'd have an accident so he could make me look bad. That, or he thinks I'll stress over not hurting you and that you'll sit here and cower."

"Look at me cowering," she deadpanned.

We both burst out laughing, then Kate pulled me into a tight hug. "Always, I'll have your back. Shifter, fae, Shadow or Umbra."

Tears stung my eyes, and I squeezed her. I had missed her so much. Dax had no idea what a gift he gave me when he brought her back. Sure, we were still surrounded by shifters watching the exits, but right now, I was so grateful to have Kate that I didn't care.

Kate released me, her expression suddenly serious. "Now, here's the big question. How are we going to get you out of here so you can sneak back to your mate?"

"Funny you should say that." I pulled the poem out of my pocket and passed it to her.

Her brow creased as she read, then she looked up at me. "What is this?"

"Instructions, I think. On where to meet him to break the bond," I said.

She blinked a few times. "You can't be serious. Is that even possible?"

I shrugged. "He says it is."

Kate's shoulders slumped and that same look she gave me when I got the shit beat out of me crossed over her face. "I'm so sorry, Ivy."

"For what?" My throat felt thick and my chest ached, but I wasn't about to tell her that the thought of breaking the bond hurt worse than all the beatings I took growing up. "It's the best possible solution."

"Are you sure? Even if it is possible, are you sure you'd want to ruin your one shot at finding the other half of your soul?"

I sighed. It was difficult to explain to her, but even if there was a part of me that wanted Madoc; she hadn't been there when he told me he was going to break the bond. He didn't want me, which was for the best. It would bring us nothing but ruin. "I'm sure. We can't be together. We're like oil and water. Two different worlds."

"The fates aren't supposed to make mistakes," she said quietly.

"That's not helping," I pointed out.

"I'm sorry. It's just so fucking sad. If anyone deserved a happily ever after, it was you," she said.

"I'm not sure I believe in happily ever afters," I said.

CHAPTER
FIFTEEN

KATE WAS STILL asleep and after how long we'd stayed up talking last night, I wasn't about to wake her. My stomach rolled with anxiety, and I knew I wasn't going to be able to get anymore sleep despite the early hour. I kept myself busy by taking a super long shower and drinking coffee while I watched the guards mill around outside my apartment. I wondered how they would react if I stepped foot outside after last night's incident. Would they be afraid of me? Did they know what had really happened or had Dax told them some other kind of excuse?

If I was calling the shots, I probably would have upped the ante and requested that the guards use more force than they had before. Knowing that Dax was even harsher than I was when it came to things like that, I wasn't sure I wanted to test the theory.

A strange feeling trickled down the back of my neck, making my hair stand on edge. It was as if a little jolt trickled over my skin. It felt like a warning. I set my coffee cup down, fully on edge. When I crossed to the door and looked out the peephole, I saw Xander approaching. It was as if I had felt him arrive. I couldn't plug in to the other wolves in my pack, but I'd sensed Xander. It wasn't the first time I felt a strange connection to him. Was this a fae thing? Could I sense Xander in the same way he could communicate with Dax? It was too weird. And I wasn't sure it mattered anyway, since I wasn't planning on sticking around.

I opened the door and faced Xander with a glare. I was conflicted about how I should feel about him. He had hidden things from me, but he also tried to show me in his own way. He'd been blackmailed the same way as I had, but it was a lot to process.

A cool breeze ruffled my hair, and I inhaled the fresh air. As much as I wanted to stay mad at Xander, the prospect of getting out of town and into the woods outweighed anything he'd done. There was freedom in the training sessions, even if they had been short-lived.

Grabbing my jacket, I stepped outside, closing the door behind me. "I'm not sure if I should be furious with you or thanking you."

"I know what you mean. But you know I couldn't say anything," he said. "There are still things I can't tell you."

"That sounds ominous," I said.

"Try not to overthink it. Your focus needs to be controlling that power now that it's out."

"A heads-up about that would have been nice," I mused.

"I wasn't sure how yours would show. And I really did think you had a few more days, at least, before the magic showed."

"How come it didn't come earlier?" I asked. "Are fae just late bloomers?"

"Mine came when I was very young. But there are things I can't say." He seemed almost as frustrated as I was.

"How do you break that hold? There has to be some way. I don't know how you live with that," I said.

"One of these days, I'll be able to explain everything to you," he promised. "But for now, we should get going."

"Why do you stay?" I asked. "I know what you did is horrible, and you have to feel the worst kind of pain imaginable, but it wasn't your fault. Take it from me, there was no control over anything I did last night. It just happened."

"I guess I stayed for my dad. Now, I stay because it's what I know. Though, sometimes I'm tempted. It's a lot more complicated than simply running away." He glanced at me. "You could do the same, yet you're still here."

I pressed my lips together to prevent myself from commenting. I understood his hesitation. I wanted to get out of here, but it was so complicated. I didn't have family keeping me here, but I had Kate. That was probably close enough. "I didn't realize your dad was still around. Do I know him? He must be high ranking."

"You've met my father, he's in charge of the whole council."

"Oh shit. That's why you stay. It's not just you. If word got out, he'd be ruined too." It made sense. If Xander was punished for murder, it would draw attention to his family. They must have covered it up as something tragic, but I didn't recall hearing anything about the sudden loss of a pair of shifters. Maybe I'd been too young to notice.

"Everything is always more complicated than it seems," Xander said.

"Wait, so your mom was fae?" I had so many questions. How can someone who is fae not train their own child with how to control and use the magic? If she was here now, would she be able to teach both of us?

"My dad had an affair, none of us knew until after the accident," he said. "He moved here with my mom when I was a baby. Everyone, including me though his mate was my mother."

"I can't believe he would hide that. Do you know who she is or where she is? Maybe we could ask her for help." I snapped my mouth shut. "I'm sorry, that was insensitive."

"Don't worry about it, it's the exact same thing I said. And I did find her. It's how I learned how to control this. She returned back to where she came from after she helped me, but I can teach you all the things she taught me."

"Do you think it's possible we're related then? There can't be very many fae running around. Dax seemed to think it was my father, but there was no information in that folder about my parents."

"That folder wasn't complete. Dax pulled some things out so he might know more than you and I know," he said.

I hummed. That sounded right. Of course there would be more secrets and information hidden from me. Part of me wanted to know who my parents were, but I wasn't sure if it would help or hurt. In the end, did it even matter?

The parking lot was empty when we pulled in, and I was grateful for the space and distance of being away from the pack. The cold wind bit my cheeks and cut right through my jacket. Normally I wasn't a fan of winter, but today I just wanted to be outside, away from town surrounded by nature. It didn't matter that there was a huge storm threatening, I was just grateful to have a tiny slice of freedom.

Surrounded by the cover of trees, the wind wasn't as harsh. My shoulders sagged as some of the tension escaped. Closing my eyes, I inhaled the scent of pine and the unmistakable scent of incoming snow. We only got a few large storms a year, and even I could feel this one in my bones.

"I'm still not sure if I'm mad at you," I told Xander.

"I get that." He looked skyward and narrowed his eyes. "I think we still have a couple hours before it starts snowing."

"Thank you for teaching me though," I said quietly. "I'm grateful I don't have to go through this alone. For what it's worth, I'm sorry for what you went through. I can't imagine how terrifying it must have been to have that power appear without any support. It comes on so suddenly, and there's no control. It must have been terrifying."

As scary as the events of last night were, at least I understood where it had come from within seconds of it happening. Grief rolled through me, a heavy weight deep inside that I wasn't ever going to be able to shake. I hadn't meant to kill that guard, but I had. It was something I was going to have to live with. The only thing that gave me some sense of peace was the fact that I was going to learn how to control this so it wouldn't happen again. There was a part of me that longed for the power, but another part of me that feared what I was capable of.

"Honestly, I blacked out that night. I only remember flashes, but most of it is locked away so deep inside I can't recall it."

"That doesn't mean it wasn't terrible," I said. "It must have been hell for your dad too," I said.

Xander knelt down and picked up a pine cone, then rose and launched it into the woods. "Fucker didn't give a shit about what happened to my mom or anyone else. His biggest concern was that the pack would find out about his infidelity. That's why he was willing to go along with covering it up rather than giving me the punishment I deserved."

Anger made my chest burn. No wonder Xander said the elders wouldn't do anything to help Kate. They were just as corrupt and misguided as Dax. They pushed back against Dax's plans for war, but probably not for any sort of ethical reason. It would probably disrupt their other plans or bring changes they didn't want.

Everything in the Shadow Pack was on the brink of destruction and I doubted anyone who lived here outside of the elders knew exactly how shaky our futures were right now.

"You know that wasn't your fault, right?" I asked. "And you know you don't owe your dad anything. Aren't you the one who told me something about blood not being everything?"

"I was young when it happened, and I was terrified. If it happened to me now, I'd probably go feral. But I'm in too deep, this is where I belong. You still have options, though some are better than others."

"Things can change," I said, even though I wasn't sure I believed it.

"You know that's not true. Things don't change for shifters like us. The fates looked down on us. They don't line up the way they do for everyone else. You want some free advice? Take the power you can get. I know you don't want to hear this, but being the right hand of a powerful alpha is going to get you a lot farther in life than trying to stake it out on your own. Sure, freedom sounds nice on paper. But it won't feed you when you're hungry and it won't put a roof over your head when it's raining. I have my moments too, where I fantasize about leaving it all. But in the end, we're meant to be in a pack. I wish that wasn't the case, but this is the lot we were given."

"You know I'm going to disagree with you on this one. You're not the one being asked to marry someone you don't want," I said. "It's one thing to go along with the support of the pack. It's another thing to give up my identity completely."

"And what identity is that? Foundling? Do you even know who you are, Ivy?" Xander took a step toward me. "All I've ever seen from you is the girl who keeps her head down. Sure, you can fight to defend yourself. But you don't fight for the things you want. I'm not sure you have it in you."

Anger and hurt swirled, blurring my vision. I never thought about it like that before, but he was right. I'd always been reactive. I had no plans, no dreams, nothing I could claim as truly mine. I didn't even know who the hell I was. I always thought that by becoming a Shadow Wolf fully, I could create an identity. But I wasn't even that, and I wasn't sure I wanted it anymore.

"I am not having this conversation with you. Are you going to teach me how to use this thing or not?" I was back to being mad at Xander. Though, if I was being honest, I was angrier at myself.

"That anger you're feeling right now? You're going to need to use it." Xander's hands began to glow.

CHAPTER
SIXTEEN

"You were trying to make me mad?" I narrowed my eyes.

"Much as emotions help drive a shift, emotions can help guide our magic," he explained. "You can use your emotions to get it going, but you have to maintain control. If you let the emotions drive the magic, bad things will happen."

"I think I get that." Emotions had clearly been at play last night.

"The fae my dad hooked up with told me that she's an elemental fae. Which means she can wield all four elements as magic." Xander cradled a warm sphere of light in his hands. "We aren't full fae, so our magic looks different."

"You think this is what I am? An elemental?" I stared at the glowing orb, transfixed by the beauty and his control. I knew how dangerous the magic was, but in his hands it took on a comforting, benign quality.

He released the light, his hands returning to normal. "I think so. Your powers manifested the same way as mine. So it would make sense that we're the same kind of fae."

"Well, that's lucky for me, I guess." I wasn't sure what kinds of fae were out there or if elemental fae were like wolf shifters. There were other types of shifters, but wolves were the most common. It wasn't like there were any fae around to ask, so having any information was going to help.

"Last night, I was angry and maybe a little scared. But I didn't summon any kind of power that I was aware of. How do you know when you're calling to it and when you don't want it to come? Will I be able to control that after some practice?" I asked.

"I'm mad at Dax almost every single day, and I have yet to accidentally kill him." Xander smirked.

"Bummer," I muttered.

"Most of it is about control. Keeping your emotions in check even when you don't feel like you can. Things that help me are visualization and breathing. You know, imagining something peaceful and calm even when I don't feel calm."

"Like meditation?" I asked.

Xander nodded. "I know it sounds a little weird, but when you feel an intense emotion, one of the fastest ways I've found to turn it off or slow it down is to imagine I'm somewhere else. Somewhere I actually want to be."

"You sure you want to stay here in this pack?" I elbowed him playfully. "If the way you calm yourself down is imagining you're someplace else, maybe you need to take a deeper look at your own life."

"We've talked about me enough. This is about you." Xander took a few steps away and extended his arms from his side, fingers splayed wide. After a deep breath, he closed his eyes then released the breath as he opened them. All of his movements looked so methodical, almost like a dance. He slowly began to lift his arms and muted white-gold light illuminated each of his fingertips.

It was far more controlled than what I had created and even more controlled than the orb he had demonstrated earlier. He swept his arms directly out in front of him, maintaining about a shoulder width gap between his outstretched hands. The light began to expand, little sparks that reminded me of lightning expanded from each of his fingertips, coming together in the center to form an arc of light. The orb was smooth and contained, but this was rougher, more intense. I could see tiny tendrils of light stretched between his fingers, connecting from one hand to the other in almost lightning like strands. The glow began to intensify, blurring those lines, so bright I had to squint as I stared. Suddenly, Xander closed his hands, cutting the light off and leaving us standing in the freezing woods as if nothing had happened.

My heart raced in anticipation. I *wanted* that. I wanted the power; I wanted the control. "Can you aim it at things? Use it as a tool or a weapon? Or can you just make fancy fireworks?"

Xander lifted one hand, and with a flick of his wrist

he held another orb of light. As if throwing a ball, he launched the light ahead of us. It slammed into a tree trunk with a sizzle. I ran toward it and once the smoke cleared, I could see a hole that traveled all the way through the tree trunk. My jaw dropped, and I blinked as I stared at the smoke curling up from the charred wood.

"How do you use this without others figuring out what you are?" I could see so many applications for this kind of magic. But wolf shifters liked to talk. For a pack full of secrets, it always seemed like it was a matter of time before the secrets got out. Sure, some things were able to stay hidden, but being able to launch light or create light out of thin air didn't seem like something that would stay hidden for long.

"I never use it on pack lands. Only when we've traveled to other locations and only in emergencies. While you can learn to control it, it's still volatile. The best thing you can learn is how to prevent it from coming when you're not ready for it. Until you're certain you can control it, it's not worth the risk."

"But you've used it. That's why Dax keeps you around and why he was interested in me once he found out I had the same background. If he didn't know about your magic, he might not have cared that one of my parents wasn't of this realm." My tone came out more accusing than I meant, but it was hard not to see just how connected the two of us were.

"That's true. But, because you have me, you'll get to

learn how to control this and you won't have to make my mistakes. Now, let's get started."

I had so many questions, but I sensed the shift in Xander's emotions. He was done talking. We'd gone too near his past. "Alright. Teach me what you know."

Xander moved so he was right in front of me, with only a few feet separating the two of us. "Keep your hands loose at your side, roll your shoulders, and take a deep breath. I'm going to have you call to your magic in just a moment, and it's important that your heart rate is as low as possible and that you are as calm as possible. I have no idea what our magic will do to each other and I don't think it's a good idea for us to test that out. So please, try not to lose control on me."

I closed my eyes and inhaled deeply, forcing myself to find calm. The chill in the air kept me alert. The sound of the wind in the trees and the scent of the pine helped keep me centered. This was a good location for calm. There was no way I would be able to find any level of peace if we were still in town.

"Reach inside yourself and try to find that place where your energy comes from."

I opened one eye and looked at Xander, skepticism clear in my expression.

"Just close your eyes and try it," he insisted.

Closing my eyes, I tried to work out what he meant by finding where my energy came from. Sometimes, I could feel my wolf rising inside me. I could feel when she was restless or eager. As I slowly focused on my breathing, I considered last night's accident and how I had felt a surge of power consuming me. It seemed impossible to pinpoint a specific location where that power had originated. It seemed more mental or emotional than physical. I thought about the light; it had been so intense and over-whelming that it had knocked me down. Yet Xander seemed confident that I could do this, which gave me a flicker of hope.

While he'd spent years honing this power, I wasn't trying to fully harness it as a weapon just yet. If I was being honest with myself, I wanted that. But for now, I would settle on not accidentally killing people.

As I considered the source of my magic, I thought about the fact that anger had been the driving force behind it. But not just anger, as I knew that would be a dangerous emotion to wield through magic. It was about protection. I felt the need to defend myself, and when I thought Kate was threatened, the power had returned.

Concentrating, I sent that to the forefront. The idea of defense, protection, a way to stand up for myself and those who might not be able to take care of themselves.

Memories zipped by, reminding me of times when I'd been smaller and less equipped to stand up to bullies. That sense of helplessness was what had driven me to pay attention to fighting classes and practice the skills in the alleyway behind the foundling house when no one was watching. Even these past two years, I had made sure I always spent some time with the punching bag Kate and I kept in our apartment. It wasn't perfect by any means, but it was important for me to have a chance. This magic didn't just level the playing field, it would help me dominate it.

Something warm simmered in my chest. It felt like liquid courage, confidence; something soothing yet vicious all rolled into one. My eyes popped open and instinctively I looked at my hands. Sure enough, the glow was there. The magic shimmered and sparkled along my fingertips just as Xander's had.

"You found it. That was faster than I expected. Now, watch carefully." Xander held his hands out in front of him, then slowly curled his fingers into fists. "You need to extinguish it like that. Close your hands and send it back."

There was a part of me that didn't want to release the magic. Part of me wanted to push further and explore what it could do. The possibilities of what this meant for my own protection were astronomical. Once I mastered this, I never needed to be afraid again.

"Turn it off, Ivy," Xander said. "You have to gain control before you can use it. Trust me. I've made the mistakes and I'm walking you through it so you don't have to make them. Learn from me instead of learning the hard way."

This much power surging through me was a heady feeling, and it was difficult to cut it off, but I recognized Xander's wisdom. He'd been through this, and whether it was a good idea or not, I trusted his judgment. A little disappointed, I closed my hands into fists and willed the magic to subside.

"That was good," Xander assured me. "Now we get to do it again."

I straightened, thrilled at the prospect of getting to work on bringing that magic forward faster and easier. I wanted to move on to other skills, but just as with learning how to fight, there was an order to things. I nodded, then closed my eyes and inhaled.

We went through the exercise over and over. Each time I called to the magic, it came quicker, stronger, more confident. It wasn't as stressful to close it off, either. The first few times, it felt like the magic almost had a mind of its own, wanting to be used in ways other than what Xander was demanding. But with more practice, I didn't feel that urge.

Snowflakes landed softly on my eyelashes and my cheeks, a reminder of how long we have been at this. The threatening storm was upon us and while the flakes were small and infrequent now, it wouldn't be long before they picked up into the promised blizzard.

I shook my hands out, exhaustion starting to set in. Quickly I brushed some snowflakes off of my face, then got to work calling the magic once again. It came forth with ease, and I capped it off, sending it away.

As the snow thickened, the flakes growing larger and fluffier and falling in clumps; the woods began to take on an almost magical quality. It was quiet and a fine layer of snow already dusted the pine trees.

I rolled my shoulders and took a moment to stretch before tilting my head back up to the sky. Fluffy, white flakes caught on my eyelashes and landed on my nose. I recalled a time when I would have stuck my tongue out to catch the flakes and it made me smile. Not all my past memories were bad. "Do you think we should head back?"

"It's probably time. You did good. The main thing is to remember to find that concentration so you can turn it off if it comes up on its own. Don't try to use it yet. I know it's tempting, but you're not ready."

I was disappointed that I was being restricted from exploring this magic further now that I finally knew what it was, but I understood the caution. "What else can it do? You blasted a hole through a tree and I killed someone without causing any physical damage. How can one power do both things?"

"I'm not entirely sure, to be honest," Xander said. "I haven't gotten to explore it as much as I'd really like, but I'm sure you can understand why. I'm almost afraid to see how far I could push it."

"I get that." We walked the rest of the way back to the car in silence, my mind busy replaying the sensations of calling my magic and sending it away. It was a strange force, part of me, but not. It reminded me of my wolf in that way. It was something I could control, yet there was an element of unpredictability that made it unstable and imperfect. Xander had always hid his power away, afraid to draw attention. But as we drove back to my apartment, I started to wonder what could someone with both of these gifts, wolf shifter and fae, accomplish? Especially if they didn't have to hide.

CHAPTER
SEVENTEEN

THE WIND KICKED UP, and snow swirled, making it difficult to see in front of us. I was surprised we managed to make it to my apartment in one piece. Inside, I didn't even have time to shake off the snow before Kate ambushed me.

"I figured it out!"

I shook the snow off my head and pulled my jacket off. "Figured what out?"

"The poem. I know when you're supposed to meet him."

I tugged my boots off and set them next to the door. "I already figured out it has to be the full moon. The problem is I don't know where I'm supposed to meet him."

"Oh, I thought that part was obvious," she said.

"But the full moon part wasn't?" I chuckled.

"Whatever. The point is that I found out that one of the hills nearby used to be called Starlight Hill. Nobody uses the names anymore, but they're all labeled on the old maps," she said.

"Wait, we have old maps sitting around our apartment?" How the hell was I supposed to have figured this out? Did Madoc think that I sat around and looked at old maps or that I had memorized the geographical names of all the places surrounding the Shadow Pack lands?

"It's in one of those books my dad gave me. You know, the ones he gives me every year for my birthday." Kate pointed to the stack of books on the coffee table.

Each year, her dad gave her a book about the natural world. Some years it was books about bugs or birds. Other years it was history or geography. He figured it was good for an artist to know random things. It was sweet, but I don't think she got much use out of them.

Kate picked up a thin paperback book with a black-and-white photo of a severe looking old woman on the cover. "It's a diary of one of the original settlers back when this place was still a mining town."

"I never would have thought to look in there," I said. "Good thing I have you around."

"How was training?" She tossed the book on back on the table.

"Good. I think I'm headed in the right direction to not accidentally kill you."

"Dax will be so disappointed," she said with a laugh.

"Get this, the hill wasn't named for a mine or anything. It was named after an ancient legend about a god and his mortal lover."

"Oh?" I headed toward the kitchen and got to work making myself a sandwich. Kate followed, explaining the story of a princess and a long dead God of the Stars. It was one of those tragically romantic stories, and it seemed a little too on the nose for what Madoc and I needed to do.

"Of course he had to choose the place with a history of star-crossed lovers," I grumbled.

"What was that?" She closed the pantry door behind her, emerging with a bag of pretzels.

"Do you want a sandwich?" I asked, hoping she didn't hear what I said. I didn't want Kate to know, but thinking about seeing Madoc and then ending everything hurt more than I could put into words.

"No, I'm good with the bag of salt and carbs. Did you know my parents fed me nothing but meat and cheese all week? I guess they're doing the keto thing. If I never see another bacon-wrapped piece of meat in my life, I will die happy."

"I thought your parents were vegan?" I asked.

"Must be their mid-life crisis. I hope it's short lived," she said through a mouth full of pretzels. "Hey, you must be so excited that we know where you need to go. One step closer to no more bond."

"Yeah, sure." Other than the fact that it felt like I was going to have to tear out half of my heart. I aggressively sliced my sandwich in half, cutting through the paper plate. I hated this whole thing. I hated the mating bond. I hated that I was dreading breaking it. And I hated the hold that it had over me. I was sure things would feel better when it was done and over with, but until then, each passing day, the ache to be with my mate grew more intense. There were times I could ignore it completely, but when it was quiet and I was alone, he was the only thing I could think of.

"You look fine, by the way. No injuries at all." Kate said. "I guess I'm not useful anymore. All I could do to help in the past was make you tea."

I tensed, recalling the night Xander had tossed the rest of the stash. "Kate, do you know much about what's in that tea?"

"Not really. You miss the taste now that you don't have it anymore, don't you?" she teased. "I knew it would grow on you. I can ask my mom to make more if you want."

"I'm good, thanks." I forced a smile, trying to cover the feeling of unease. "You sure it was just for healing?"

"That's what my mom said." Her brow furrowed. "Am I missing something?"

I shook my head and took a bite of my sandwich. "Nope. Just hoping I won't need it again now that I have badass powers."

Kate laughed. "This is going to go to your head, isn't it?"

I shrugged. "It might. But it's not going to help me solve the Madoc issue." Internally, I cursed. So much for trying to keep my thoughts away from him. No matter what I did, Madoc seemed to be at the forefront of my thoughts, just waiting for me to drop my guard.

"There are two guards in the back, one outside each

window, and two near our front door." Kate crossed her arms over her chest and leaned against the counter. "We need to think of a way to get ourselves out of here so you can make that meeting."

I hadn't even noticed the guards outside my front door on my way in today, but I didn't doubt Kate's reconnaissance. The surprising part was that she seemed to want to join me. "Is this just because you want to see what he looks like?" I teased.

"I can't lie, that's a big part of it. There wasn't enough light at the prisoner exchange to get a good look. If I knew he was your mate, I would have pushed my way to the front."

"Are they going to let you leave? Did they say anything about you being a prisoner, or just me?" I asked.

"I'm not sure. I didn't ask. Honestly, I was grateful to be away from my parents and back with you." She frowned. "But I don't think it matters. As much as I want to see this big, bad Umbra Wolf up close, I don't think I'm going to get to go."

It was clear Kate had an idea, but I wasn't following yet. "You have a plan."

She nodded. "Play along the next few days and by the full moon, I'll get you out. If I can play the part of the distraction, you should be able to get out without issue."

"You really think I can pull this off?" I asked.

"No problem. The bigger issue is going to be what we do next. You're going to have to figure out something about the whole Dax thing," she said.

"Have you ever thought about leaving here?" I asked.

"Is that what you're thinking?" Her tone was quiet and I couldn't tell if she was surprised by my question.

"It might be what's safest for both of us while Dax is on this power trip. He's going to tear the pack apart one way or another and I'm not sure I want to be stuck in the middle," I said.

She sighed. "It does feel like there's a big change coming. And I have to admit, I would like to see the world beyond this town. But, it's home."

"I know, but what do you do when your home isn't safe?" I asked.

"I think it's going to get better. It has to. The elders won't let Dax run amok. That's what they're there for."

"I'm pretty sure he doesn't care. And I don't think the elders do, either," I said.

"I'll think about it," she said. "But promise me something?"

"Sure," I said.

"If you're going to take off, I respect that. But don't go without saying goodbye," she said.

"Never," I promised.

CHAPTER
EIGHTEEN

XANDER ALMOST CANCELED MAGIC TRAINING. But between the nearing full moon driving my wolf to feel more restless, and the upcoming expectation of meeting with Madoc, I needed some kind of physical release. Working on my magic was a good distraction. Plus, I desperately wanted to be able to control it and to be able to use it. The snowstorm had left us with several feet of drifting snow in our usual practice place, but at my suggestion, Xander had gotten a hold of the keys to the Howler.

The dingy basement was just as I had remembered it, cold and damp and dimly lit. When I looked at the ring, bathed in the light of a few naked light bulbs, my mind went straight to that dream of me with Madoc. I quickly shoved the thought away, but not before a rush of heat went straight to my core.

I was afraid to believe it, but it felt like the mating bond was getting stronger by the day. I wondered if it had something to do with the full moon. The wolf side of me had to be the part driving the bond, at least that's what we'd all been told about bonds. Though, I was only half wolf. So what if it was the fae side? Did fae form mating bonds? Should I even be able to form a mating bond with a wolf since I was only half wolf?

When I let my mind wander, it took me to places full of questions and no answers.

I blew out a frustrated breath, trying to send the pointless thoughts away. It didn't matter why the fates had put us together, it just mattered that it needed to stop. He was a distraction, a speed bump in my plans for moving forward. I felt like I couldn't even get my head straight on what I was going to do after we broke the bond because anytime I tried to picture what came next; I saw his face. The fates certainly didn't want to me to imagine my life without him. At this point, I would settle for just imagining a future by myself where I could call the shots in my own life.

Xander tossed his jacket on the floor, the sound knocking me from my reverie. "This was a good idea, Ivy. We've got a lot of space here."

I glanced around again, catching sight of the bar in the corner where I'd worked a few shifts. The time spent working down here had been too good to be true. It had been too much money for too little work. I should have known it was all going to crumble.

"You knew about what they did down here, didn't you?" I asked. "Did you ever get in the ring?"

"No way," Xander said. "I knew what was going on down here, but I never came to see it for myself."

"How come?" I asked.

"You know why," he said. "I couldn't risk getting called into that ring."

"Of course. Magic hands. I guess I'm lucky that didn't show up the day Dax dragged me into the ring."

"Luck had nothing to do with it," Xander said.

I knew Xander wanted to say more. I was starting to get a sense of it from his tone and the way he said certain things. I also knew he was probably still prevented from speaking freely. It had to drive him crazy. "Is there anything I can do to fix that? A cure or antidote? Nobody should be silenced the way you are. It's just another way of being a prisoner in Dax's bullshit games."

"Everything is so much more complicated than you realize. But we're not here to talk about me. We're here to help you control that magic. Let's get started with opening and closing it off to warm up."

We went through the exercises; me practicing turning on and turning off my magic. It was so much easier today, coming far more naturally than I expected. After a while, we moved on to other ways to control it. By the end of our session, I had managed to create that glowing ball of light that Xander had shown me yesterday. It wasn't going to hurt anybody in this form and I wasn't sure what would happen if I tried to release it, but it felt like progress.

Using magic was exhausting. As much as I wanted to

press forward, I gladly donned my coat and followed Xander out a few hours later.

When I got home, Kate and I discussed our plans for how to sneak out. The next several days blended together in a series of working on magic with Xander and getting things ready with Kate.

I was exhausted all the time, and Kate said it was the magic taking my energy. She said her mom talked about how magic was like exercise. The more you used, the more tired you got. But you could build it up just as you could get stronger or faster when you worked out, but you would never get to a point where there would be no repercussions for the magic used. Just as an athlete could work their way up to running miles, magic could get stronger and less taxing, but I would still need time to rest in between.

It made sense, and it was the best information I could get since there weren't any fae around for me to talk to. Every night I collapsed into my bed, and every night I dreamed about *him*. It was embarrassing to wake up in the morning and recall the dirty things he'd done to me in my dreams. The worst part was how I missed him when I woke. Too often, I reached across my bed, waking in surprise to find it empty. The only blessing was that none of my dreams linked us the way it once had. All of it was in my head, though sometimes I wasn't sure if that really made it any better.

As the hours ticked closer to the full moon, the restlessness and anxiety grew until I couldn't even stay still if I wanted to. I was constantly fidgeting, pacing, finding things to occupy my hands or popping snacks in my mouth just to have something to do.

During our training in the basement of the Howler on the night before the full moon, Xander seemed to sense my restlessness. "Okay, I get it. You're bored."

"What gave it away?" I curled my hands into fists, cutting off the magic.

"I have to admit, you're getting the hang of this faster than I expected. In a few days, you've accomplished what took me months. Though I was a little younger and a little more hormonal."

"I'm sure that's what it was, and not that I'm just better than you," I teased.

"So humble," he said. "Alright. Let's see if you can start to use this. But if you blow us both up, I'm going to be pissed."

Xander walked to the bar and pulled out a few glasses. He lined them up across the top, then stepped back to where I was about ten feet away.

"You saw what I did with the tree. I want you to gather the light in your hand, then you'll scoop it as if catching it, then release it in the direction of the glass. Try to focus on one object at a time. Control is important. It's easier to blow up this whole space than it is to get that light to damage one specific area."

"No pressure," I said.

"You can do this. You're focused. When I went through this training, I was rebellious and angry. My emotions were all over the place, making my control nearly impossible. I see that now, working with you. I don't think it will take you nearly as long as it took me to figure this out."

His comments were reassuring, and also a little sad. I couldn't imagine trying to get control of the thing that had accidentally killed my mother and sister. Every single time he used his powers, he was probably reliving that trauma. No wonder it took him so long to gain control. I wanted to say something comforting, but things felt complicated between me and Xander. I wasn't quite sure if we were friends, or if our goals just happened to be aligned. After everything that happened with Dax, I wasn't going to be quick to trust anyone ever again.

"Go ahead," Xander urged.

Taking steadying breaths, I found the inner calm that I had used as the starting point for calling my magic. I summoned it forward, feeling the warmth fill my palms as I cradled it in my hands. Concentrating on the glass, I called the magic to one hand, until a small ball of light rested there. Using a scooping motion, I pulled it up, and instead of throwing it, I extended my fingers aiming at the glass on the far left.

The magic shot forth from my hand, glowing brighter and more intense than it had in days. I had to squint against the brightness. The light hit like an explosion and the sound of shattering glass echoed through the large empty space as all the glasses Xander had placed along the bar exploded in unison. Quickly, I closed my hand to turn off the magic.

Now that the magic had receded, I could clearly see the damage. Xander was right, pinpointing a specific area was a lot harder than it seemed. Not only were all the glasses shattered, the entire top of the bar was warped and melted by the magic I had sent to it. If I were in a fight, my opponent better be the only thing around, otherwise I was at risk of injuring innocent people. I clenched my jaw in frustration. I knew it would take practice, but there was a part of me that wanted to master this already.

"That's actually not bad. I think you could get it in a few more days. But no training tomorrow because it's the full moon. Dax expects you at the full moon party, and he wants you by his side."

"Dax hasn't even spoken to me in days."

"Missing him?" Xander asked.

I glared daggers at him, and he threw his arms up in mock surrender. "Don't shoot the messenger. But you know what I think about this. It's unheard of for a foundling to rise through the ranks the way you have."

"I didn't rise through the ranks. I'm being used for a deranged madman's power grab."

"That might be the case, but there's a good chance it's still your best option. If Dax gets what he wants, you'll be the most powerful female shifter of all. And if he loses, and the Umbras take over, we're all feral anyway. What do you have to lose?"

"Everything. All I've ever wanted was my freedom. What he's proposing keeps me as pack property. Or his property. It just comes with a fancy new title."

"Here's the thing, Ivy. We are all pack property. Those of us who weren't foundlings, those of us who were born full pack, we only have the illusion of freedom. Sure, we have a few more privileges, but those come at a price. You know that now. You want to be part of the pack, then you have to play the game."

CHAPTER
NINETEEN

ALL OF OUR plans were out the window. Neither Kate nor I expected that Dax would want me at the full moon party after keeping me locked up and away from the rest of the pack since my return. The only other people I'd seen aside from Dax, Xander, and Kate were the elders for a brief moment when I'd been in Dax's house. The memory of the decapitated heads flashed into view and I squeezed my eyes closed, trying to push the thought away. I didn't want to remember that. Especially since there was so much conflict that accompanied it. Knowing Madoc was responsible sent a surge of guilt, but at the same time, I was grateful he'd been able to defend himself. The bond had a way of making me feel like a traitor to the pack, and I wasn't even sure I wanted to be a part of it anymore. It made everything so much more confusing than necessary.

Dax's desire to have me at the full moon party added to the confusion. When I was under the false bond, he had paraded me around and was obvious with his affections. I knew he was telling people that we were still romantically involved, possibly even that we had a mating bond, but he had kept me cloistered away. Add in the guards and it was difficult to see what his intentions were. Did people in the pack seriously think they were guarding me for my own protection? How did they buy that when they never saw us together?

Oh.

That was his game. He needed to remind everyone of our relationship. Fuck me.

"I really thought he'd keep you here until you cracked," Kate said. "Not that I thought you would crack, but his original leverage was me. Do you think he has something else on you?"

Xander's leverage was his mistake with his magic, but that wasn't the same for me. I considered the shifter that I had accidentally killed. I hadn't recognized him, which meant he was either new to the pack or he hadn't come into the Howler regularly. That was far less likely, since most of the adult shifters spent at least some time at the bar. I knew a lot more of the pack members than I realized when I stopped to think about the fact that I had brought them all drinks. That had to be part of the appeal of having me on his arm. I was certain Dax would leverage the *'poor little foundling who rose through the ranks'* angle. The pack might not show me kindness, but they all knew who I was.

I scowled, anger making me squeeze my hands into

fists until my fingernails bit into my palm. I hated that Dax had used me and I hated that he was continuing to do so while I remained locked away here. He was likely spinning some tale about how much he cared for me. It was wrong.

"Ivy, you need to take some deep breaths," Kate warned.

I glanced down at my hands and cursed under my breath. Xander had told me about thinking happy thoughts and trying to stay calm through breathing and visualization, but I hadn't had a reason to use that and it wasn't something we practiced. But I needed it now.

Feeling a little ridiculous, I closed my eyes and pictured the woods with their soothing breeze, clean smell, and the melodic sound of birds chirping. After a few deep breaths, I was feeling more calm.

"Well done," Kate said. "Dax is probably pissed that you've learned how to control it so quickly. I'd be willing to bet he was counting on you frying me so he could use that against you."

That probably had been his plan, which meant he'd come up with some alternative for how he was going to get me to fall into step at the party tonight. "Maybe you should stay here. Pretend that you're sick or something, so Dax can't get his grubby hands on you."

"No way. Since we can't sneak out of here like we intended, you're going to need me as a distraction so you can get to Starlight Hill."

"I'm sure there will be plenty of distractions by

midnight. After a few drinks, Dax probably won't even notice that I've slipped away. He's going to show me off. I'll play his little game and make him feel complacent. Once the party really gets going, it shouldn't be an issue for me to fade into the trees." Honestly, sneaking out from the party should be a lot easier than trying to sneak out from my guarded apartment.

"You're underestimating him. I don't think he's some kind of criminal genius or anything, but he's proven how far he's willing to go to get what he wants. Being able to set up the perfect circumstances for a false bond took a lot of work and a lot of planning. It also shows us he has zero code of ethics. He'll stop at nothing to get what he wants and right now, you're what he wants."

"And I'm going to give it to him. Or at least make him think I have. The last several days, Xander has been saying how he thinks I should take Dax up on his offer. When we first started down this path, he all but told me to run. He's completely changed his mind, and I think it's because he's playing into Dax hands. I'm sure Dax put him up to it, and he probably thought Xander had a chance at convincing me. With his ego, I think it's possible that Dax could truly believe that I would take his side just for the shot at power."

"Then he doesn't know you at all," Kate said.

"No, he doesn't. And that could work to my advantage. Dax only sees power. To him, it's the most important thing there is. I'm counting on the fact that he thinks everyone desires the same." In some ways, I knew I was underestimating Dax. But this was my best play, and I needed Kate not to get involved. She'd already put herself at too much risk by being my friend. Nobody should have to get hurt because of me.

I knew she wouldn't sit it out here if given the choice. Because if the situations were reversed, I'd insist I tag along. My only hope was that they'd make her stay. "If they make you stay here tonight, don't fight them. I can't do this if I'm worried about you."

"You'll be fine. I think they'll want me there, just in case," she said. "It's what I would do if I were an evil genius. I'd probably set some of my best fighters as eyes and ears on my target, AKA me, and then threaten to injure said target if anything didn't go the way I wanted it to."

"Yeah, that's exactly what I'm worried about." She hadn't been injured when Dax held her hostage, but what was to stop him from hurting her now?

"Don't forget, just because I didn't get in as many brawls as you when we were kids, doesn't mean I'm not a solid fighter. I can take care of myself. You need to concentrate on giving him the slip and getting to your mate." She grabbed my hand and gave it a squeeze. "Let me help you. Promise me you won't worry about me. My dad is too high up in the ranks for them to do anything to me. Especially in public. Just focus on getting there by midnight."

I only nodded because I knew I wasn't going to be able to change her mind. Kate was loyal to a fault. I hated that she was at risk because of me, but I knew I'd do the same for her. She was the only one I would put my life on the line for.

The mating bond had to go away. It wasn't just that it was getting stronger, and clouding my judgment, it was also the fact that I knew bad things could happen with an unfulfilled bond.

When the knock sounded on the door, I half expected to see Dax ready to step into the role of doting boyfriend. Instead, it was Xander who had been sent to fetch me and Kate.

As we drove to the woods, Xander reminded me again of the importance of playing the role. I assured him I would. He gave me a suspicious look. "Really? Just like that?"

"I've been thinking about what you said," I told him. "You're right."

"You don't have any plans to do anything crazy tonight? You're going to stay put and play the part?" His brow furrowed.

A spike of anxiety filled my chest, and for a moment, I worried that he *knew*. But how could he know? "Of course."

He shook his head. "I don't know what you're planning, but you should rethink it."

"When I finally say I'm going to do what you've been asking of me, you jump straight to thinking I'm up to something?" I scoffed. "What is it that you want from me, Xander? You want me to continue to defy or do you want me to roll over and submit? You can't have both."

"Just but careful. That's all I'm saying," he said.

THE BONFIRE WAS ALREADY LIT when we arrived, probably because there was still a solid foot of snow on the ground and the air was freezing. I was eager to shift, if only to help me feel warmer.

I felt like everyone was staring at me, which was because they were. Let's face it, when the whole pack thinks you're the alpha's girl, you're going to draw attention. Cold wind rustled the trees and the frozen snow crunched underneath my feet. The scent of smoke and pine mingled with the clear clean sent I'd come to know so well from the woods. Tonight, there was no solace in this place.

It had become a sort of refuge for me during the training sessions with Xander, but tonight it was hard not to feel like that same out-of-place foundling I'd always been. In the weeks before all this had happened, I had started to find myself in terms of who I was in the pack, or at least I thought so. I had a little more confidence than I did right at the moment. But that had been stripped from me so quickly when Dax had shown an interest in me. I knew the false bond was at play, but it was hard not to beat yourself up for falling for someone so blindly.

Xander leaned close to me and whispered, "You have more power in one of your pinkies than any of these shifters have in their entire body. You need to start owning that."

Xander's words were a surprise, especially after the conversation in the car. I suppose I could do both, be powerful and play the part of the alpha's mate at the same time. Wasn't that why Dax insisted on keeping me by his side? He wanted me as a show of his strength.

That wasn't what I wanted, and I was still going to get out of it, but tonight was about breaking my mating bond. Once that was done, I could finally take care of myself and figure out what was best for me. I took a deep breath and rolled my shoulders back, straightening my posture. I didn't owe anyone here a single thing. Not after the way I've been treated my whole life. Why should I care what they thought of me?

"Kate!" Ryan came charging toward us, not waiting for a response from my best friend before he swept her into a massive bear hug. "I've been so worried. I even went to the alpha to report you missing, but he said you were doing some kind of artistic meditation silence thing. I'm so glad you're done with that. I missed you."

I lifted a brow as I stared at the couple. *Artistic meditation silence thing*? Ryan might be beautiful, but there was very little going on in that brain of his. Is that how everyone in this pack was? Whatever the alpha said was truth? How was everyone so blindly following Dax of all shifters? Had it always been this way when Preston was in charge?

I knew there were times we couldn't resist an order

from the alpha and I knew what the alpha said went, but I never took the time to think about just how much it impacted every single aspect of pack life. All these years, we'd been told how much more freedom we had in our pack as opposed to what the Umbra wolves put up with. The more I got to know the details, the fewer differences I saw between us. Both packs were just as controlling, just as dangerous, and just as corrupt.

A chorus of cheers and whoops rose through the gathered shifters and I turned, squinting into the setting sun just in time to see Dax stroll into the clearing. He walked with ease and confidence, a broad smile on his lips. When he caught my eye, he winked before turning his gaze back to the bulk of the gathered group.

My stomach churned with nausea. How was I supposed to do this tonight? They wanted me to play the role of someone madly in love with the alpha. We've had our moments, a time when I thought for sure I was falling for him. But I didn't think I could bring myself anywhere near those emotions to fake this. What if this whole thing was a mistake?

"It's the first full moon of the new year. The first full moon since we lost a great and distinguished alpha, my father, Preston Carver. And while his passing has been difficult for all of us to endure, I know he will be proud of the things coming for our great pack. Tonight, as you run through these woods, take a moment to look toward the sky and howl in memory of our fallen leader. Preston was not just my father, he was like a father to us all."

"Yet you sent away his killer without punishment." A male shifter stepped forward, the crowd making space for him to approach Dax.

"Is that what you all think?" Dax looked around, letting his words hang in the air.

"You dishonor your father's legacy by letting Holden breathe," the wolf shifter accused.

"As alpha, I don't owe anyone an explanation for my actions. But I know how dear you all held my father so I will tell you that the only reason Holden went back to his murderous allies was to make sure that all parties responsible for my father's death would be in the same place when I send them to their ends. We have people on the inside working to see just how deep the corruption goes. Don't you worry. Holden and all his friends will pay."

"So it's true, we're going to war against the Umbras." The male shifter smiled, his sharp canines glinting in the firelight.

I tensed, still uncomfortable with the idea of violence coming too near my mate. I wasn't sure how Madoc had survived the previous attack, but if Dax readied all the fighters our pack had and attacked the Umbras, Madoc was in even more danger. I tried to send away the thoughts. That wasn't what this was about. A war between packs was bigger than my concern over one male. But my stupid heart didn't care. Nobody else's safety seemed to matter.

The bond was getting stronger. Too strong. Midnight couldn't come soon enough.

"Tonight is not about violence or war," Dax said. "But I can assure you, my brother, vengeance and justice are coming for those who have wronged us."

The shifters exploded into a roar of approval. Fists pumped skyward, shifters whooped and howled and hollered. The air seemed charged with a current of anticipation and excitement. Nothing fueled a wolf shifter more than a fight; and war against the Umbras would be a battle unlike anything any of us had seen.

I'd been on the receiving end of blows from that family and I knew how capable they were as fighters. I was sure they had trained the members of their pack even better than our pack had. If they outnumbered us as I had always heard, my pack could inflict damage with the element of surprise, but I wasn't sure it would be enough to win an all-out war. I shouldn't fear for Madoc, I should fear for the Shadow Wolves.

"Let us run!" Dax called over the din.

Shifters stripped their clothes and raced into the woods, some of them already in wolf form. I could feel my own wolf clawing at my chest, eager for a chance to be unleashed. It had been a few days since I'd shifted and she was already anticipating the feel of the ground beneath her paws.

Running as a wolf was thrilling and brought a sense of relief I couldn't get any other way. It cleared my head and helped me think. I was hoping it might bring me some peace before I had to sneak off tonight.

"Did you like my speech?" Dax asked as he walked over to me.

"Riveting, man," Ryan said.

I glanced over at him and wrinkled my nose. I'd forgotten he was there.

"You and Kate should go run. I'd like some time with my mate alone," Dax said.

I clenched my jaw and curled my fingers into a fist. I just needed to get through tonight and I couldn't afford for him to lock me up somewhere where I couldn't escape. Running with Dax wasn't what I was hoping for, but it was expected. The only good news was that we'd likely be back at the bonfire before midnight.

"You lead the way, I'll follow," I told Dax. *Let's get this over with.*

Dax smirked. "Now, that's what I like to hear."

I resisted the urge to roll my eyes. He was so conceited that he didn't seem to care that I was acting out of character. Xander had seen right through it, despite his days of urging me to reconsider. Dax only saw what he wanted. That was going to work to my advantage. If he was complacent about me, it would be easier to sneak off tonight.

Now, I just needed to make it a few more hours before I could sneak away. Everything was depending on it.

CHAPTER
TWENTY

I<small>T WAS EASIER</small> than I thought for my wolf to fall in stride alongside Dax. I knew Kate was out there somewhere, probably running with Ryan. I felt like a jerk for not asking her about him the last few days. I was so focused on breaking the mating bond and figuring out my power that I didn't even think about how the time away from the world was impacting her. She had a life outside of work and our apartment and probably missed the freedom even more than I did. I'd have to apologize to her when we got back for the party.

Dax picked up the pace, taking us uphill faster than we had been before. My breath came out in clouds as I panted, my heart pounding as I matched his pace. It took more concentration and effort, which forced me to be present in the moment, focused on the feel of the cold snow and sharp rocks under my paws. The wind ruffled my fur, but I didn't feel the chill. My wolf was warm from the exertion and the shifter magic that kept out the cold.

I was hoping Dax would be ready to return to the bonfire soon so he could find a distraction that wasn't me. Every time he slowed or changed direction, I worried he was going to shift back into human form and expect the same from me. We were long past the time where I felt anything romantic for him and he had to know that wasn't an option. My plan of keeping him busy until I could sneak off hinged on him keeping his hands to himself.

We splashed through a stream and turned slightly, heading back down a gentle decline. That had to be a good sign that he was tiring of this run and wanted to turn back to the bonfire. For the sake of appearances, the two of us had run together, and I was hoping that was enough for him.

Several times we had passed other wolves, and Dax had greeted them with nods or the occasional howl. Every time he howled this evening, it had resulted in a series of answered calls, reverberating through the woods in an eerie cacophony.

It was probably good that there were no humans near where we lived. Hearing wolves howl one after the other even sent a chill through me despite the fact that I was part of the howling. Last time I had shifted with my pack, there had been one howl and it felt powerful and meaningful. Tonight, it felt more erratic and reactive.

Something tugged in my chest, a sensation urging me to turn around and go the opposite direction. I stopped running as the sensation overwhelmed my senses. The pull intensified, like a silent plea, summoning me elsewhere.

Dax's wolf let out an impatient sound, and I turned back to him, my mind brought back to the present. It took every ounce of willpower to resist the call I was feeling and turned back to follow Dax. I wasn't sure how long we'd been running, or what time it was, but that tug was a connection, something deeper and more meaningful than the desire to run as a wolf with my pack. It had to be my wolf sensing her mate.

She didn't want to keep following Dax. It was difficult to concentrate and drive forward, but I urged her on. I'd be making my way to Madoc soon enough, the thought making my heart heavy.

This was what I knew was coming all along, the moment both of us had been waiting for. It still hurt to think about severing the connection and breaking the bond. I reminded myself that once the deed was done, the pain wouldn't linger. But for now, it felt like I was already splitting my soul to follow Dax in the opposite direction my wolf wanted to go.

To my great relief, I could smell the scent of burning wood in the air and I knew we were approaching the bonfire. I'd never been so overjoyed to shift back into human form, and even my wolf felt like she was willing to make the change tonight. My animal side and my human side both knew what was at stake.

Someone wrapped a blanket around me seconds after I had shifted back into human form. A spark of recognition flickered, and I could almost feel that the person behind me was Xander before I saw him. There was no denying we had some kind of strange connection, probably from our shared heritage. I was curious, and wanted to know more, but I shrugged the feeling away. My mind was still a mass of confusion, but I knew deep down I wasn't going to stay in this pack, which meant getting any closer with Xander would be a mistake.

I glanced around, hoping to catch sight of Kate. Shifters in human form gathered around the campfire, many of them completely naked. Some couples had paired off, making out with very limited cover, while others were wrapped in blankets or pulling on clothes. Our shifter blood kept us warmer in the frigid temperatures, and there was a brilliant bonfire roaring and crackling in the center of the clearing, but there was a chill to the air tonight that even our shifter blood couldn't shake.

Dax leaned closer to me and he slid his hand across my back, pulling my shoulder into his bare chest. I tensed and turned to glare at him. I was grateful for the blanket that prevented my skin from touching his, but it was still closer than I desired. "Don't even think about it."

"Don't worry, my little flower. I'll never force myself on you, but you will play the part. I can wait until you beg me, just as I told you before." He pressed his lips to my forehead in a kiss so fast I didn't have time to push him away before he released me of his own accord.

"I think I need some space," I said.

"Come on, Ivy. There's someone I want you to meet," Xander said.

I turned to look at him for the first time and gave him a nod as a way of saying thank you. Xander might be Dax's right-hand shifter, but he had gotten to know me. He could probably sense that I was closer to breaking the ruse than I intended. I appreciated the effort to keep my interaction with my pretend mate at a minimum.

"Did you run?" My eyes scanned up and down Xander, who was fully clothed in the same outfit he'd worn when we arrived.

"For a bit. But I had other things I had to attend to." He led me around the bonfire and walked up to a small group of female shifters who looked to be about ten years older than me. I recognized most of them as long-time residents who'd at some point or another popped into the bar for a drink.

"Megan, this is the person I was telling you about. Ivy." A woman with fiery red hair and bright green eyes turned away from her companions and locked her gaze on me. She gave me a weak smile before excusing herself from her friends.

"So you're the foundling?" Megan asked.

Her friends were a few yards from us, pretending they weren't listening, but I could feel all of them eavesdropping on every word. I wasn't sure what was going on here, but I didn't think Xander would put me in danger.

"Yeah, I'm a foundling." I glanced at Xander then looked back at the woman. "How do you two know each other?"

"We've got some history. Which is probably why Xander asked me to talk to you. He told me you have an opportunity to dig yourself out of the status us foundlings never seem to be able to shake."

I scowled. "So this is what this is about. Trying to convince me to go along with the plan? I'm sorry for wasting your time, Megan. But I don't think I need to hear this. I've already made my choice."

She set her hand on my upper arm. "Please. As someone who paid off her debt within a year of leaving the foundling house, you need to hear this. I was like you. Single-mindedly focused on becoming a full member of this pack. I sacrificed everything to get there, but I was still not welcome the way that I should have been. That job you had working at the Howler? That was about as good as it was going to get. Trust me on this. There's an order to things in this pack and even when they tell you it's possible to change your stars, you can't."

"You realize this is not at all helping me go along with what Xander wants me to do?" I glanced over at the shifter who I was starting to think of as a friend. How dare he corner me like this? "Telling me there's no way to change my status no matter what I do doesn't help your cause."

"Here's the thing, Ivy. This pack only recognizes power

and authority. And not ours. Not a foundling, and especially not a woman. The only way I gained any sort of respect around here was when I found my mate. I know it's not what you want to hear, and I know it sucks, but that's how we make changes around here."

"Maybe I don't want to make changes around here."

"We both know that's not true. You wouldn't have been working at the Howler, saving every penny, if you didn't want to belong in this pack. Once I married Kane, my whole life changed. It didn't matter that I was a foundling anymore because I took *his* name, I became part of *his* family. I finally found a home and the belonging I always wanted. Don't let your pride take this from you," she said.

"Excuse me, I need to go find my friend." Furious that Xander would set something like this up, I turned away from him and Megan and stormed away.

All it did was solidify my decision that I could never be with Dax and that I could not stay a part of this pack. There had to be more out there, there was so much I didn't know, so much that had been hidden from me. I couldn't stay. I couldn't lose myself just as I was starting to figure out who I was. I had to meet with Madoc and then my life was going to be my own.

On my way over to my abandoned clothing, I stopped someone who was texting and asked them the time. It was already 11:30, which meant I was running out of time.

"Ivy, wait!" Xander called for me, but I didn't turn back to him. I didn't want anything to do with him. I had thought he understood me and maybe we had a shot at being friends. I was wrong.

Storming forward, I was pulled back when Xander's hand grabbed hold of the blanket. Lunging forward, I pulled the blanket from his grasp, careful not to drop it. While I was getting more comfortable being naked when I shifted, it still wasn't something I cared to do if I had other options. He grabbed the blanket again.

"Let me go." I didn't look back. I honestly didn't trust myself. My eyes stung with unshed tears. I felt like Xander had betrayed me, even though he had warned me that he would be loyal to the pack, which meant he would be loyal to Dax. Xander didn't owe me anything and I knew that. It also meant I didn't owe him.

"I needed you to know what your future could be. I didn't want you to do something stupid, something you might regret."

I turned and yanked the blanket out of his grasp. "You act like you know me. But you don't. We spent a few days together. You are my teacher; we're not friends and you don't owe me anything. Not your pity, not your loyalty, not your misguided attempt to protect me. Now either help me find Kate or get out of my way."

Xander's shoulder sagged. "For what it's worth, I'm sorry."

The apology felt heavy and final, far out of proportion compared to what he'd done. I wondered if he was trying to make amends for everything else, all the things Dax had done to me that he'd stood by and silently supported. Even if that was the case, it was too little too late.

I made sure the blanket was still secure around me before going to find my clothes. I needed Kate, and I needed to get out of here. If I couldn't find her in time, she'd know where I went, and she'd cover for me until I could return.

CHAPTER
TWENTY-ONE

Music started, and the crowd grew as shifters returned from their runs to join the party. I weaved through the crowd, searching for Kate. I was running out of time and I knew I should probably just go, but I couldn't leave without saying something to Kate. She'd been locked up because of me, used as a way to keep me compliant. While the two of us had discussed ways to get me to my meeting tonight, we hadn't discussed what would happen if something were to go wrong. I needed to tell her to be safe and to do what she needed to do to make sure she didn't get sucked any deeper into this mess. I also owed her an apology for how selfish I'd been during our captivity.

I dodged a couple so lost in each other's embrace that they nearly ran into me and came face to face with Dax. He grinned, his Cheshire smile sent a chill down my spine. It was as if he'd been standing there waiting for me to run into him, like he wanted me to. I sent the strange thought away and worked to make my expression impassive. "Excuse me." I sidestepped him, but he blocked my path.

"Where are you off to in such a hurry? Are you going to turn into a pumpkin at midnight?" he asked.

"I'm just trying to find Kate. For some reason I get nervous when I can't find her. You wouldn't happen to know the cause of that, would you?" I shot an angry look at him.

Dax held his hands up in mock surrender. "I come in peace. I've told you, I just need you to make this look good. What you do behind closed doors is of no interest of mine. And I haven't touched your friend."

I wasn't sure what he was alluding, but I didn't have time for his games. "Have you seen her around then?"

"I'll help you look." He turned and moved so he was next to me.

I clenched my jaw and sucked in a breath. I did not need him following me around right now and probably should have just fled while I had the chance. Now the minutes were ticking by and every passing second felt like a weight growing heavier on my chest.

I knew Madoc was on his way, maybe even already there, since I had sensed him earlier. It would take me twenty minutes to get to the place I needed to be, and I was wasting precious time. But the last thing I needed was to raise suspicions with Dax. He'd let me out tonight, and it was possible I was on my way to losing the guards around my doors if he thought I was really playing along. I'd need that freedom so I could figure out what I was going to do next.

"I'm sure I can find her on my own," I said. "Don't you have more interesting things to do?"

"More interesting than helping my mate find her best friend? I don't think so. What kind of a boyfriend would I be if I didn't support your deepest desires?" He smirked. Another unsettling shiver ran down my spine. Everything about him was off tonight, or maybe it always had been and I just hadn't seen it before.

"Fine. You can help. Why don't we split up? You go right, I'll go left and we'll meet back at the refreshments table." I suggested.

"No, it's good for us to be seen together at least a little bit." He extended his hand. "Just for the sake of appearances."

Anger seethed and bubbled inside me. I knew he was doing this to get a rise, and I didn't have time for an argument or a scene. The quickest way through was to comply, so I accepted his hand and urged us forward as I continued my search for my friend.

The party was getting wilder, but I didn't even feel the urge to get swept up in the madness. My heart thundered, pounding like a ticking clock, reminding me of the time I was wasting. Kate wasn't in sight, and I wondered if she was still running or if she'd found a quiet place in the woods with Ryan.

Either way, my strategy had shifted from finding her to figuring out a way to get away from Dax. I had to go, or I was going to miss my opportunity to break the bond. Deep sadness and a painful ache made my heart feel heavy. Every step I took felt like a step closer toward my doom. I had to snap myself out of that. Breaking the bond was necessary but it wasn't going to happen if I was still traipsing around the party with Dax's hand gripping mine.

Just when I had given up hope, I caught sight of Kate near the keg. Relieved to see that she was in one piece, I dropped Dax's hand and raced toward her. Her eyes widened as she saw me approach and she closed the distance between us. "Why are you still here?" she hissed.

I inclined my head ever so slightly to where I knew Dax was behind me. She groaned, then lowered her voice to a whisper, "You've got to ditch him."

"Tell me something I don't know." I felt stupid for trying to find her earlier when I had a perfect opportunity to get out of here. Now, I couldn't even tell her the things I wanted to tell her because we had too many witnesses.

"There she is. Kate, Ivy has been so worried about you. Maybe now she'll be less distracted and can join me in some of the fun," Dax said.

I closed my eyes and took a couple of steadying breaths before I turned to face Dax. "I'm not really in the dancing mood, but you should invite someone else to join you."

"You know I only have eyes for you," he said.

Nearby, I heard a female shifter let out a heavy sigh as if Dax's words had been the most romantic thing she had ever heard. All it did was seed the anger even deeper inside me. He was doing this on purpose. He'd ignored me for days, yet now he couldn't keep his eyes off me. I suppose it made sense, since this was the first time he'd let me go out in public. He was probably afraid I would run or that I would say or do something against him.

Kate grabbed my hand and gave it a quick squeeze and then released it. She stepped forward, and I knew she had some kind of plan, but I wasn't sure what she was going to do. Suddenly, she pulled her arm back and punched Dax in the face. "That's for sending my best friend on a dangerous mission!"

Everyone around us rushed forward, forming a crowd. Someone grabbed Kate and pulled her away from Dax. She screamed and kicked. "You could have gotten her killed!"

Nobody was watching me. They were all fixated on the scene unfolding in front of them. I turned and ran.

Please keep Kate safe. I couldn't believe she'd punched Dax. Honestly, I was a little jealous. It was risky and stupid, but as far as a distraction went, it worked.

My chest burned and my thighs screamed as I raced through the woods. There was a chance that someone would follow me once they realized I was gone. I wasn't sure how long Kate's actions would draw a crowd, but I hoped I had at least a few minutes head start.

I reached out with my senses, even though I had not been trained on how to use them. I knew there had to be a way to exploit the shifter and fae magic that flowed through my veins. I didn't feel the presence of anyone else, but that didn't mean anything.

I was worried Xander and Dax would be after me the moment they put it together. As much as I wanted to think badly about Dax, he was going to see right through this as soon as they calmed the crowd.

I continued to run, weaving around trees more than necessary to throw my scent. There wasn't as much time as I hoped and I mostly had to go straight for the meeting place, but there wasn't much I could do about that. Once Kate had shown me where the hill was on the map, I didn't need directions. I knew that site. It was the same place Dax had taken me on my first run. The place where I thought I had started to have feelings for him. It seemed almost too poetic that I would end a true bond in the same location where I'd started a false bond.

Running over the snow made everything more challenging than it should have been. It was taking too long and my progress was too slow. My wolf was eager for release. Desperation and excitement rose up inside me as she responded to the possibility of seeing her mate. As a wolf, I could move so much faster, but it would mean being totally naked when I reached Madoc.

Stumbling over an unseen rock, I landed face first in a snowdrift. Soaked and shivering, I finally gave in. Tossing my clothes aside, I figured they'd at least help throw off my trail. The change came quickly, and I bounded forward, continuing toward the meeting place as a wolf.

Breathless, I reached the top of the hill, overly aware of a cramp in my side. Who knew wolves could get cramps? Cold wind ruffled my fur and my eyes watered. It was freezing up here, even in wolf form. The sooner we got this over with, the better.

CHAPTER
TWENTY-TWO

SOMETHING CALLED MY ATTENTION AWAY, and I turned to face a cluster of trees nearby. It took me back down the hill a bit, but there was no doubt in my mind that the feeling was the pull of the bond.

Cautiously, I moved forward, my paws moving carefully over the snow. The sun melting it during the day mixed with the evening freeze had formed a thin, crunchy layer on top. Sometimes it would hold my weight, other times I would fall through, ending up in snow up to my stomach. The progress was slow going, but I was focused on reaching the cluster of trees ahead.

Part of me rebelled as I moved closer to the more private and enclosed space. If this was an ambush, I'd be defenseless. My inner wolf wanted to release a forlorn howl at the thought of being betrayed by our mate, but I reminded her, and reminded myself, that we didn't know that yet. Just because nobody ever had my back before didn't mean that Madoc was going to turn on us as well. Nevertheless, I was already preparing myself to run if needed. Though, with the mating bond, I knew he'd be able to find me even if I fled. It was worth the risk of a trap to break this bond.

I had to hope this was genuine and that Madoc would make good on his promise to break the bond between us. We both needed that so that we could move forward. Sure, I had no idea what forward looked like, but it wasn't me trapped in my pack or trapped in a bond with someone who didn't want me around.

It was darker under the cover of the evergreens than it had been on the top of the hill, but in my wolf form I could see well enough that I quickly caught the movement of another wolf approaching.

My pulse raced and my heart felt like it was doing somersaults in my chest. The large gray wolf approaching could be none other than my mate. I knew it in my bones; it was as if I would recognize him anywhere. I hated that. I hated the need that coursed through my veins; I hated the urge I felt to run to him; I hated that part of me was crying out to follow him rather than break the bond between us.

Madoc's wolf shuddered, bones snapped and fur receded as he made the change back into human form. Reluctantly, I followed, working through my own change until I stood naked in front of him.

I waited for the flush of embarrassment, the urge to cover myself, but it wasn't there. I stood in front of him, completely exposed and completely at peace. Something was very, very wrong with me.

I was probably too distracted by the gorgeous man in front of me. Every time I saw him, it was like a shock to my system. How could one be so stunningly beautiful and so lethal at the same time?

In the dim light of the moon that filtered through the evergreens, I could make out the sharp edges of his features. His dark hair fell loose, nearly covering his dark eyes. He brushed it back out of the way and took a step toward me. He moved with feline grace, his muscles rippling and moving effortlessly. Every inch of him was chiseled to perfection. He had the shifter gift to help him stay in top form, but this was more than that. This was someone who never missed a workout. And right now, my eyes greedily took in every inch.

My breath hitched as warmth spread all the way to my most intimate places. Resisting him was like resisting breathing. My body wanted to act out the scenes from my dreams, but I balled my hands into fists and tensed my muscles to keep myself rooted in place.

"You figured out that damn poem." He stopped inches from me.

"My roommate did. I'm shit with geography. Never took you for the poetic type," I said.

"I'm not. That was Holden. He figured it might be intercepted. I told him it was a stupid idea," he said.

"Well, I'm here," I said. "So I guess it worked."

He looked around, his brow furrowed as he scanned the landscape.

My adrenaline spiked as I realized what he was doing. "You expecting someone?"

"You're the one who said you told your roommate where we were meeting. I hope she's trustworthy," he said.

"She is. In fact, she's the only person in this whole world I trust. Which brings us to the matter at hand. How do we do this?" My heart ached and to my surprise, I had to fight against rising tears. Facing the loss of the mating bond felt an awful lot like saying a final goodbye to a loved one on their deathbed. Not that I had any experience with that.

"About that... I'm afraid I have some bad news."

"Why am I here then? You told me you could break this. Do you have any idea what I had to risk to get here tonight?" Furious, I started to turn away. I couldn't be here around him unless we were breaking the bond. Me walking away hopefully looked like I was angry when in reality it was self-preservation. Every moment I lingered with him brought me closer to launching myself at him. That was the exact opposite of what we wanted because if the two of us had sex in real life, we'd complete the bond, not destroy it.

"Ivy, turn around." His tone was more pleading and less a command, which sent a strange shiver down my back. He sounded almost as desperate to be together as I felt.

I stopped and turned to look at him for a moment. "If we aren't doing this, I can't risk being here. You have no idea what's at stake for me right now. Not that you care, but my friend sacrificed a lot so that I could be here. I have to get back to her and make sure she's okay."

"You can't go back. I found a way to break this, but we have to visit a witch. We can't do it on our own. The magic is far too complicated. But I did find someone, and she's agreed to complete the spell. You have to go with me; it requires us both there in person," he said.

"You can't be serious. Why bring me all the way out here just to say that? If I go with you, that's it for me. I can't go back home ever again. And my friend will think I completely abandoned her. You have to give people warnings for this kind of shit. Not all of us are set to inherit leadership of the most powerful pack in the world. For us normal shifters, we have obligations, jobs, people who will get hurt if we aren't doing what we're supposed to do. I don't have your freedom," I said.

"You think I have choices? You don't know anything about me. I told you I'd figure out a way to break this bond, and I did. I'm sorry it's not as convenient as you would like it to be, but sometimes we have to make hard choices. If you want this bond broken, and gods know I do, this is the only option we have."

If I went back to town, I could help Kate, and I'd get a chance to say goodbye, but there was risk in that. Once I returned, Dax wasn't going to let me out of his sight. The chances of me getting away again were practically nonexistent. I had sacrificed everything to make this meeting tonight, knowing that I would have consequences to deal with after. But I thought I'd be going back. I thought I had more time.

I wanted to walk away from the Shadow Wolves, but I wasn't ready. Everything I owned was in my apartment, plus Kate was probably currently detained and as much as I hated to admit it, there was a good chance I was the only one who could talk any sense into Dax. He wanted my power, and he wanted me. I could fake it if I had to, if it meant saving my friend.

Kate had attacked the alpha without issuing an alpha challenge. In our pack, that could be seen as an act of treason. I was fairly confident that Dax wouldn't do anything to harm Kate. At least not right away, because he'd want to use her as leverage over me. But I wasn't sure how much time she had, especially if I didn't go back.

"I can't go with you, you're going to have to figure out another way." I turned and started walking away, fighting against the crushing weight in my chest.

"Don't do this Ivy, we both need this bond broken," he said. "It's going to drive us mad if it doesn't drive us together first."

I stopped walking but didn't turn to face him. I knew every time I looked at him it made it harder to walk away. "Everything inside me tells me I should be walking toward you, and that scares the shit out of me. But my whole life, there has been only one person who has had my back, and right now, that person is in danger. I can't walk away from her. Not for you, not for anyone." I continued to walk, emerging through the trees and heading back up the hill, retracing my footsteps to find my way home. Disappointment weighed heavily with each step. At one point, I glanced behind me just to see if he was following. I felt worse when I realized he'd let me go.

The cold bit at my skin and I started to lose feeling in my fingers and toes. Calling to my wolf, I retook that form. Grateful for the warmth of the fur, I shook out my paws and charged forward, eager to get back to the party before it was over. Hopefully, I could get them to pretend that Kate was drunk and have Dax blow it off as a harmless accident.

Just as I reached the base of the hill, I felt a sensation like a string yanking me back. Sudden pain stole my breath, causing me to wince. It receded long enough for me to realize I wasn't feeling my own pain. This was similar to what had happened before, though not quite as intense. My heart raced as I realized Madoc was under attack. Without hesitation, I turned back and ran as hard as I could. I had to reach him; I had to save him. There was no other option. Getting to Madoc was the only thing that filled my mind.

CHAPTER
TWENTY-THREE

I ARRIVED back where I'd left Madoc to a scene of chaos. Teeth and fangs and fur flashed as growling and grunting and whining filled the air. I couldn't tell where one wolf began and another wolf ended in the tangled mess.

There had to be at least six wolves in the fray, meaning somewhere in the midst of the attack was my mate. Anger unlike anything I've ever felt before surged to the forefront. My desire to protect him was so fierce it blurred my vision and clouded my judgment. I charged forward. It didn't matter that I didn't know how to fight in this form, and it didn't matter that we were vastly outnumbered. The only thing that mattered was that I had to protect him, to save him.

I launched myself at a brown wolf, teeth bared. I landed on his back, digging my claws deep into his flesh. The wolf howled then shook in an attempt to throw me, but I held on. Leaning down, I bit into his neck. The wolf batted at me and fell to his side, trying to get me to loosen my grip.

A pair of claws dug into my back and pulled me away, forcing me to release my hold. I yelped as hot pain from the claws brought me back to my senses. I landed in the snow, my breath knocked from my lungs. Whoever had tossed me aside was trying to get me away from the fight rather than trying to cause me harm. I paused for a moment as I righted myself to look at the scene in front of me. Jumping back into the fray was suicide. It would do nothing but get me killed in the process of trying to save Madoc. There had to be another way, but I couldn't see one. I could feel Madoc's pain. He was holding off the other wolves, but he wasn't going to last much longer.

I took a step forward when suddenly a large black wolf blocked my path. He growled, haunches raised. I bared my teeth at Dax. He was preventing me from gaining access to my mate, and that was something I could not let happen. I shifted my weight, and Dax mirrored my movements. He was larger than me, and I knew he knew how to fight. In my other form, I felt I might have a chance against him if the two of us went head-to-head. But like this, I was at a major disadvantage.

An agonized cry shattered the air, and I honed in on it above all the other snarls and growls. My heart felt like it was going to burst as I realized the cry had come from my mate. He wasn't going to last much longer, outnumbered and surrounded. I didn't have a choice. I had to try even if I didn't have the skills.

I feigned to the right, then took off going around Dax's left, charging back into the mess. I was able to swipe my claws on one of Madoc's attackers before I was brought down again.

Dax landed on top of me. His claws were retracted so he wasn't hurting me, but his weight was heavy, keeping me pinned to the ground. I snapped my jaw at him, impatient to get away. He growled a warning, but I didn't care. This wasn't about me and him, this wasn't even about me and Madoc. Aside from the urge to protect my mate, the injustice of the situation seemed to set fire to my insides. This wasn't a fair fight, and I was tired of being surrounded by bullies.

I swiped Dax's face with my claws and he snapped back at me with his teeth barely missing my muzzle. I swiped again, my final warning for asking that he release me. He pushed me harder into the ground, his own claws coming out to dig into my sides. I wiggled, working to break his hold, every movement agonizing as his claws tore into my flesh. Behind us, a horrifying, painful yelp sounded, causing both of us to take notice. Without looking, I knew it wasn't Madoc in danger, but Dax was still looking at the fight.

Using the temporary distraction, I was able to free myself, only to be met by another wolf. This one was dark gray, the scent familiar. I could feel him in a different way than I could feel my mate and my heart broke just a little. I told myself Xander and I had never been real friends, but I didn't think it would come down to this. I didn't want to fight him.

Xander locked his gaze on mine and I hesitated, conflicted about the possibility of harming him. Suddenly, Xander's body began to shiver and bend as he changed from wolf to human. To my horror, my body responded in kind, forcing me into the change despite me urging myself to remain in wolf form.

Xander was on his feet quickly, his hands already lit with the soft glow of his magic.

Panting in a heap on the ground, I looked up at him, not hiding the betrayal in my expression. He'd known. This was why he'd made me talk to Megan and why he'd asked so many questions. He knew the whole time that I had this planned. "How?"

"Go home Ivy," Xander said. "It's not too late. Just go back. We'll take care of this."

"Stop the fighting. Let him go." All I cared about right now was making sure that Madoc was safe. Forcing myself to tear my gaze away from Xander I saw two wolves on the ground and neither of them belonged to my mate. He was still fighting, but he had to be tired and I could feel that he was hurting.

"Stop this and I'll go back."

"Whatever they asked of you, you don't have to deliver. We're your pack. We'll defend you," Xander said. "Go back before you get yourself hurt."

"You don't understand. You have to stop this." Tears streamed down my face.

"It's too late for that. We end this now. He's on our territory and it's our right. When Xander told me you were meeting someone here, I never imagined it would be an Umbra Wolf. You are mine. When are you going to realize that nothing is going to change that?" Dax's words came out almost manic sounding.

I pushed myself to standing and turned to face the alpha. "If you really care about me, you will stop this and you will let him go."

"I told you she fell for one of them while she was away," Dax looked past me to where Xander was standing.

A bolt of pain shot through my chest and I winced as I fell to my knees. "You're killing him, you need to stop. Please, I'm begging you."

"You felt that. You feel his pain, yet you can't connect with your pack," Xander said, his tone stunned.

"What are you talking about?" Dax spat.

"You share the bond, don't you?" Xander stared at me, then turned to Dax. "She's formed a mating bond with this wolf."

"Let him go," I tried one more time.

"It's how she broke out of the false bond with me." Dax moved away from me, turning toward the fight. "It's time to end this. Make sure he suffers when you kill him."

I moved closer to the fight, my hands already glowing with magic. I didn't think. I just moved. Charging forward,

I lifted my hands. Everyone stopped moving. "Release him now or I'll kill you all."

To my surprise, the Shadow Wolves backed away from where Madoc's wolf stood.

"Can she do that?" Dax asked.

"Yeah, she can," Xander replied.

"Don't think I won't do it. I will end all of us if it means I get to take you with me," I said as I stared down Dax.

"Fall back. If she wants to die out here in the woods with him, who am I to stop her?" Dax took a few steps closer to me and I extended one arm toward him while keeping the other pointed toward the shifters surrounding my mate.

"This is where you make a choice, Ivy. You follow through with this, you can never come back. You are dead to me and you are dead to this pack. You better be damn certain his pack is going to welcome you because you have no where else to go." He turned to look away from me and I followed his gaze while keeping my hands in position.

Dax was looking at the remains of the fight. Madoc's wolf had collapsed on the ground, his breathing shallow. He'd put up a hell of a fight, but there was no denying he was gravely injured and would need help. My heart felt like it was shattering into a million pieces. *Please be okay*.

"He's probably dead anyway. And you'll probably die in these woods. Is this your final choice? You'd rather take a dead shifter and your own death over being with me?"

All I wanted to do was help Madoc. I needed to heal

him, comfort him, be there for him. Nothing else mattered. And if my other option was to become Dax's property, then there was no choice. Even if I couldn't be with Madoc, even if his pack cast me out or condemned me to death, it was better than the life that would wait for me in my old pack. I couldn't live like that. I couldn't be what Dax wanted me to be. *I'm so sorry, Kate.*

"If my options are death or being by your side, I welcome death's embrace," I said.

"You heard her. Let's leave her to freeze to death." Dax turned away from me and melted into his wolf form with ease. He ran from the clearing, the other wolves following in his wake.

Xander lingered behind, still in his human form. "I'm sorry. I wish I never figured out that poem. I wish things were different."

"I don't ever want to see your face again." I closed my palms, extinguishing the magic, then covered my chest with my arms.

"I'll make sure Kate is safe," Xander said. "I can at least do that."

The back of my throat burned, and I nodded. Xander and I would never be friends, but if he did this one favor for me, I couldn't consider him an enemy.

"Good luck." Xander shifted, then headed out to follow the rest of the pack.

I raced to Madoc's wolf and dropped to my knees beside him. "It's okay, I'm here. I'm going to help you. But

I need you to shift back because I can't carry you out of here like this." I was pretty sure I couldn't carry him out of here in his human form either, but I was hoping he could walk with some support. I wasn't sure how we were going to pull this off, but I wasn't about to let him die on me.

CHAPTER
TWENTY-FOUR

MADOC'S WOLF was breathing too slowly, but he tried to stand so I knew there was still fight left in him. "Madoc, listen to me. I need you to shift back."

There had to be a car near here somewhere. There was no way he'd run here the whole way in his wolf form. I absentmindedly stroked his fur, trying to ease the anxiety I knew he was feeling. None of it made sense; the way I felt about him didn't make sense. I knew it was the bond connecting us, helping me know what he was feeling.

In the moment when I had called my magic, I literally would have died to save Madoc's life. The only thing I had been concerned about was the thought of my magic harming him. Even as I made the threat, I was working through ways in my head to try to aim the magic enough to keep him safe.

This stupid bond had nearly fully taken hold of me. As much as I wanted to say I chose to leave my pack to prevent a life with Dax, the prospect of getting to have a life with my mate had been the more appealing. But I knew it was impossible. I knew that once I got Madoc taken care of, he would still want to break the bond. As painful as it was, I had to try to keep myself from getting too attached. It seemed like a fucking impossible task, but I was going to get him out of here and save his life so we could break this damn bond.

With a renewed sense of action, I rose to my feet and looked down at the injured wolf. "No more options. You need to shift back now. They left, but there's no reason to believe they can't come back and take both of us out." A flicker of recognition glinted in the wolf's eyes as he met mine. "Yes, that's right. If they come back, they're going to hurt me too." I could tell he was concerned about me the same way I was concerned about him. If I had to use that to get him to safety, I would. "Shift back."

Madoc's wolf seemed to melt away, the fur receding as his body lengthened and stretched until the gorgeous man underneath was revealed. He was bleeding and bruises were already blooming on almost every square inch of his body. His right eye was nearly swollen shut, and I was pretty sure his nose was broken.

His wolf had saved him from most of the damage, but even an alpha would struggle when taking a beating from six other shifters at once. If he were a mere human, he'd be dead.

I offered my hand. "Come on, you need to get up. We have to get out of here."

As I waited for Madoc to move, I noticed how quiet it was. Too quiet. It had been too easy. Dax and his friends had walked away when they were nearly successful in killing their intended target. If they realized who they had against the ropes, there was no way they'd have stopped. If they figured it out, they'd be back to finish the job.

Madoc reached for my hand, and I hoisted him up with all of my strength. He grunted, then hissed as he put weight on his injured limbs.

"I can't carry you, but I can help. Where's your car?" I asked.

"Why did you do this? If they killed me, you'd be free of the bond," he said.

"You're welcome would be nice," I said.

"I had it under control."

"Sure you did, Sugar," I teased.

He chuckled, then moaned in pain. "Everything hurts."

"Stop messing around then, so we can get you some help." I moved next to him and slid my arm around his waist, and guided his other arm over my shoulder. I was a little surprised he didn't resist.

"For real though, why not just let me die?" he asked again.

"We're not having that conversation right now." I didn't trust myself to tell him how he'd suddenly become the most important part of my life. I knew it was the bond making me feel that way, but it didn't change how real it felt.

Madoc turned so he was facing me and with my arm

around his back, and his arm over my shoulder, we ended up in a strange embrace. I could see the pain written all over his expression with every movement, yet he reached for me, brushing a stray lock of hair from my eyes. "Thank you. It's more than I deserved."

I was frozen, locked in his gaze like prey ensnared by a predator. My breath hitched and for a moment, my eyes flicked down to look at his perfect lips. His face was bloody and everything looked like it must hurt terribly. Yet the only thing I wanted in the whole world was to feel his lips pressed against mine.

As if he could read my mind, Madoc lowered his face to mine and gently brushed his lips against mine in the ghost of a kiss. He pulled away quickly, but the sensation lingered, making me feel like my whole body was on fire. I swallowed back the rising desire, and was only able to rein it in because I reminded myself how injured he was and how dangerous it was for the two of us to be standing here naked in the middle of the woods. I adjusted my position so I was next to him again. "Lead the way. I'll help as much as I can."

Madoc started walking. I could tell he was trying not to put his weight on me, but with each step his arm on my shoulder seemed to get a little heavier. We cut through the trees, Madoc seeming to know exactly where he was going. My breath came out in heavy pants. The effort of helping carry his weight was at least keeping me warm, though I had to admit I could no longer feel my feet. Finally, I caught the reflection of something shiny up ahead and I let out a relieved breath as a car came into view.

"I never let anyone drive my car," Madoc said.

I lifted a skeptical brow. "You think you're in the position to drive?"

"I could handle it." He groaned as he stepped away from me to begin walking on his own. He stumbled, and I lunged forward to catch him.

"You're not driving us anywhere. I did not just save your ass to have you kill us now." I continued to guide him toward the car and helped him into the passenger seat. As soon as I closed the door behind him, the hairs on the back of my neck stood on edge.

I glanced back to see a hoard of wolves break through the trees. *Shit.* Dax hadn't just returned, he'd come back with reinforcements. I bolted around the hood of the car and climbed into the driver's seat. Madoc hit the button that started the car and I gunned it, not looking back.

"Your boyfriend is the jealous type," Madoc said.

"Can we not right now?" I gripped the steering wheel as if my life depended on it and weaved between the trees. "Where the fuck is the road?"

"You're going the right way. Keep going north," Madoc said.

I looked in the rear-view mirror and didn't see any wolves behind us, but that didn't mean they weren't on our tail. The car bounced over the uneven terrain and we flew over an incline I hadn't noticed, the bottom of the car scraping the ground as we landed. I winced.

"Shit, you're a terrible driver, you know that?" Madoc asked.

I ignored his comment and purposefully swerved to go over a large fallen branch. Madoc grunted. "That was on purpose."

"It was. Are you going to shut up now?" I snapped.

"Turn here!" he called.

"Where?" We were still in the middle of the woods. There was nowhere to turn.

Madoc grabbed the wheel, nearly sending us right into a huge pine tree. I pulled it back to avoid a collision. "What the fuck?"

I was about to turn to scream at him when I caught sight of a dirt road. Weaving around one more tree, the wheels of the car finally made contact with compressed dirt rather than forest floor. Breathing heavily, I continued to grip the steering wheel for dear life. I looked in the rear-view mirror again and saw no signs of anyone following us. My shoulders eased a little, and I loosened my grip.

"I thought maybe I survived that fight just to die from your driving. What was that you said about me driving?" Madoc asked.

"Are you serious right now?" He was clearly feeling better than he was when I found him. I looked at him quickly and caught the hint of a smile. Rolling my eyes, I returned my focus to the road ahead of us. "We need to get you to a healer."

"I'll be fine," he said.

"You're not fine. You have more injuries than you

should and that wound on your shoulder is still seeping. It's not healing. You need help," I said.

"I didn't know you cared," he said.

"Mating bond, remember? I don't have a choice," I bit out. But the words stung because I cared more than I wanted to and even pretending I didn't hurt.

CHAPTER
TWENTY-FIVE

"You know, you shouldn't have given up your pack for me," Madoc said.

"It wasn't just about you." I kept my eyes straight, focused on the road ahead. We drove in silence for a while and when the chill of the ward ran through me, I gasped in surprise. I hadn't realized we'd been so close to the edge of Shadow Pack territory.

It felt so final as I drove away, knowing I could never return. I had never been welcome in the pack, but it was home. The only thing I was going to miss was spending time with my best friend. My throat tightened and my next breath was difficult. I was never going to see her again. Why had I done that? How had I let myself walk away from her for someone I didn't know? For someone who wanted to break our bond, anyway.

I peeked over at Madoc, who was staring out the window. Longing and desire replaced the sadness I felt for the loss of my friend. With a scowl, I turned away from him. Mating bonds were the worst. Losing Kate shouldn't be so easily overcome. Was she going to be okay? I knew she could get by without me. That wasn't the concern. She had support and love. It was me who always needed her more. The bigger issue was that I'd left her after she'd punched Dax in the face.

I couldn't help but grin at the memory. The look of utter surprise on his face was priceless. I kind of wished I'd been the one to punch him. At least Kate would have that joy to latch on to, assuming Dax didn't do something stupid after I fled. Maybe Xander would make good on his promise to help her. Assuming she didn't punch him in the face when she learned that he'd betrayed me.

Kate was strong, and she'd been accurate when she said her father was important. He was respected and well liked. Even if he had hidden business failures, he was still someone a smart alpha would want on their side. Dax had to know that and he would lose too much support if he did anything to harm Kate. At least, that's what I had to hope.

Why had she been so foolish? I really hoped she was safe. When faced with the with the option of watching my mate die or leaving my pack forever, there had been no choice and I wasn't sure I was capable of changing what I did. My heart would not have allowed any other option. The mating bond was too strong. Besides, going back would have been surrendering to Dax and his plans for me. I couldn't do that. I couldn't spend my whole life as a prisoner, pretending to be something I wasn't.

"Did he find out about the bond? Is that why you broke up with him?" Madoc asked.

Had he known I was thinking about Dax? I shook the thought away. That wasn't possible. "He didn't know about the bond before tonight. And nothing between us was ever real He was using me for... Never mind. It doesn't matter, does it? You don't really care what my life was like or anything else about me. We don't have to do this pretending you care thing."

Internally, I was screaming. I wanted nothing more than to lean into the bond. Fighting it and playing like Madoc wasn't important was physically painful. But it was better than admitting how much I wanted him.

"I'm curious. I've never seen someone walk away from an alpha's affections before. You could have had so much power. He didn't hurt you, did he?"

He hurt me in more ways than I could begin to describe. But admitting how I had fallen for someone after all the abuse he'd put me through in my youth made me feel weak. False bond or no, I should have known better. "Not everyone wants power."

"Not where I come from. It's the only thing that matters in my pack," he said darkly.

"Maybe our packs aren't so different after all," I said.

The dirt road came to an end, and I stopped at the edge of a two lane paved road. "Which way?"

"That depends on where we're going." He was slurring his words a bit, which couldn't be good.

I looked over at the injured shifter. "You need a healer.

I don't know where to find one outside of Shadow Wolf territory. We're on your turf now. Where should I go?"

"My cousin Willow is the best healer I know," Madoc said.

"You sure that's a good idea?" I asked.

"My dad is away with my brothers. We won't risk running into them," he said.

"Can she keep her mouth shut?" Neither of us had said it out loud, but I could feel the understanding between us. We were still moving forward with breaking the bond. It meant my future was a mess, but that's basically where'd I'd been before I burned my bridges.

"She can," he confirmed. "Turn left."

I glanced over at him and noticed that the wound on his shoulder was still bleeding. We didn't have any clothes to use as bandages, so I opened the glove box. It was empty. "You don't keep napkins or tissues in your car?"

His brow furrowed. "Should I?"

I rolled my eyes, then pressed my palm to the cut on his shoulder. He hissed. "That hurts."

"You need pressure on it. It should have stopped bleeding already." I hated how concerned I was about his injury.

"I can do it myself," he said.

He was trying to act like nothing was wrong, but in the short time we'd been driving, his face had gone pale. I kept my hand on his injury as I turned onto the road. "You need to focus on staying awake."

"I told you, I'm fine," he said.

I sighed. "What I wouldn't give for some of Kate's tea now."

"Who's Kate?"

"My friend. Not that I'll ever get to see her again now," I said.

"What kind of tea?" he pressed.

"She used to give me this healing herbal mix her grandmother made. It was supposed to help injuries recover more quickly," I explained.

"You used it a lot?"

"A few times a week. Sometimes daily." I didn't like admitting that. Looking back, I was in a lot of fights. It was amazing I'd survived.

Madoc didn't respond, and I figured he couldn't come up with anything to say. It was kind of pathetic. What kind of wolf shifter gets the shit beat out of them all the time? Thinking about my past brought up far too many negative emotions. Maybe it was good that I was leaving. Except for the whole losing my only friend thing. Maybe I'd make some friends with the feral wolves. That was my only option after breaking this bond. Trying not to wallow in my own self pity, I focused on driving.

After a few minutes of silence, I looked over at Madoc. His head was against the back of the seat and his eyes were closed. *Shit.* That's what I was afraid of. I pushed against the cut on his arm, hating that I was using pain to wake him.

He cried out, then his eyes flew open. "What the fuck?"

"No sleeping. Stay with me," I said.

"I wasn't asleep," he said.

"Liar," I shot back.

"Hey, those butterflies are pretty," Madoc said.

"What butterflies?" I scanned outside, trying to see what he'd found. It was dark, my headlights providing the only light.

"The purple ones are my favorite."

"What purple?" I lifted my hand to check on his injury. My palm was covered in blood and the wound was still oozing. *Fuck*. This was worse than I expected. I pulled over to the side of the road. He was losing too much blood. Why wasn't he healing faster? I had to do something.

"Why'd you stop?" he asked.

What I wouldn't give for any kind of fabric. I looked in the back seat. It was empty. "Do you have anything in your trunk?"

His eyelids were half closed, but fluttered open at my questions. "Hmm?"

"Don't worry about it. I'll check." I headed around to the back of the car and opened the trunk. There was a duffle bag and a spare tire. *Please don't be a head or something equally disturbing.* With a grimace, I opened the bag and blew out a relieved breath when I found gym clothes. Quickly, I pulled one of the large tees over my head then carried the rest of the contents to the passenger side.

When I opened the car door, I noticed another seeping wound on his ribs. This one had a red line traveling from it, down toward his hips. It looked like an infection, but it was too quick for that. *Fuck*. I'd heard of shifters using poison in fights, but I'd never seen it firsthand. Leave it to Dax and his friends to fight dirty.

In the dim light of the car, I noticed a small piece of metal about the size of a thorn stuck in one of the wounds. Carefully, I pulled it out. It burned my fingers and I quickly dropped it on the ground. Whatever that was, it hurt like hell. It had to be doused in whatever was causing the wounds so much pain. Wolfsbane, maybe?

No wonder Dax let us leave without too much trouble. *Shit*. He came back to capture us both. He wanted to bring Madoc in alive. Working quickly, I bandaged him as best I could with torn fabric. I hadn't come this far to lose him now. I refused to let that happen.

"I can feel your concern, you know. You feel like you're fucking terrified," Madoc said, his words slurred.

"Everything's fine. Just making sure you don't keep bleeding." Getting him to a healer was even more important. I wasn't sure how much time we had.

Back in my seat, I tapped on the screen in the console. This car was much nicer and newer than mine, and after a few wrong buttons, I found the GPS. It automatically pulled up a location in the city that was probably the Umbra Estate. "Is that right?" I asked.

"What?" Madoc's eyes were closed again, but he didn't even bother to open them to answer me.

I gently shook him. "Wake up. Look at the map. Is that the right place?"

Groggily, he turned his attention to the screen. "Yeah. That's it."

"Still living with your parents at your age?" I teased, hoping to get a rise from him.

"I have a place. But I don't always go there," he said.

"Probably nicer than my apartment," I said. "Is it in the city?"

"What city?" he mumbled.

Dammit. The GPS told me we still had a half hour to get there. I slammed on the gas, taking the car well beyond the speed limit. I had to keep him awake. "Tell me about your family."

"What do you want to know?" he asked.

"I don't know. Anything? What's your mom like?" I asked.

"She died when I was young."

My face heated. "Sorry."

"It's alright. Actually, my birth mom wasn't my dad's wife. But nobody's supposed to know that. I'd lose the pack if they found out. I have a birth mom but she didn't raise me. I don't even know her name."

My eyes widened. *What. The. Actual. Fuck.* Why was he telling me this? "Oh?"

"Yeah. She was like you. Can't have that in the Umbra bloodline or some bullshit."

"What do you mean, *like me*?" I pressed.

"There was fae blood in her line from way back. Sometime a long time ago. That's what you are, isn't it?" His voice was quiet, his words mumbled.

I had to be hearing him incorrectly. "Are you sure? Part fae?" How many of us could there be around? For a being that wasn't supposed to exist, there sure had been a bunch of them around this part of the world.

"The light you made. I heard about that as a fae gift. But I didn't get that. I got something else."

"What did you get?" I asked.

No response came, and I looked over to see his eyelids closed. *Shit.* "Madoc. Wake up."

I shoved him harder than I probably should have. He didn't budge. *Fuck.* "Madoc!" I screamed. Nothing.

Carefully, I moved my fingers to his neck, feeling for a pulse. It was there, but it was faint. I glanced at the GPS again. We'd picked up some time, but we weren't close enough. "Madoc? Madoc!"

He was out and there wasn't anything I could do but try to get him help before the poison took him away from me.

As I sped down the road, my heart raced and fear like I'd never felt before tightened my chest. I couldn't lose him.

CHAPTER

TWENTY-SIX

As I sped toward the Umbra estate, I continued to check Madoc's pulse. Every time I felt his heartbeat, I released a breath I had been holding. A quick glance at my makeshift bandages told me the bleeding hadn't subsided. He should be healing by now. I thought wolves in an alpha line were stronger than the rest of us, but I guess it was difficult to heal when he'd been attacked so badly. I was grateful he'd been lucid enough to get to the car before losing consciousness.

I slowed down as I exited the freeway and impatiently stopped for red lights as I neared our destination. Anxiety and fear mingled to the point where every inch of my skin felt like it was crawling with restlessness. I was wound as tight as a spring, ready to explode at a moment's notice.

I cursed as I stopped at the gate to the Umbra mansion. I forgot about this part, and I didn't love the idea of having to announce my presence. Madoc needed me, though, so I pushed the button on the intercom.

A fuzzy voice crackled in greeting, "No visitors."

Nice, super friendly. That wasn't making all my anxiety so much worse. "I'm a friend of Willow's. She's expecting me."

"No visitors." The crackling stopped.

I slammed my fist on the button. "Then you can explain to Willow why her order won't be ready on time." I really hoped she was the type who ordered lots of things. Isn't that what rich people did? My instincts were telling me not to reveal that Madoc was injured in the car with me. I was pretty sure I'd be dragged straight to the dungeon if I arrived with their injured future alpha, but if I had to, I would play that card.

"Who is this?" A female voice had replaced the original, and I knew it had to be Willow.

"I'm a friend of Madoc's and Holden's and I have an urgent delivery for you."

There was silence, and just as I was about to slam the button again, the gate opened. I pulled forward, then stopped in front of the massive entry. A burst of light appeared as the doors opened and a thin female form emerged and raced down the steps.

I exited the car, careful to keep my hands where she could see them. "You probably don't remember me, but this is an emergency. He told me you'd be able to help."

Willow didn't waste any time throwing open the

passenger door. "Shit. I can't carry his ass out of here. We're going to need help."

She ran back to the door and called for someone, and then returned to where I stood.

"You can help him, right? He still has a pulse, and I tried to stop the bleeding, but it just won't stop. It just keeps coming." The words spilled out of me in a tangled mess.

A pair of males in dark suits were next to the car now, and Willow ordered them to carry Madoc to her room. Nobody seemed to notice or care that I joined the group. I followed them up the stairs and into a large bedroom, then quickly moved aside as Willow sent the two males away. She closed the door behind them, then instantly got to work removing the bandages and inspecting Madoc's wounds.

"I don't understand why the bleeding won't stop. I think maybe he was poisoned," I said.

Willow crossed the room to a shelf and started pulling down bottles and towels. "If anyone finds you here, they're going to kill you. You probably shouldn't stay." She didn't look up at me as she got to work cleaning and tending to the injuries.

"I need to know he's going to be okay." I approached the bed, and without thinking, I took hold of one of his hands. I couldn't leave and I wasn't sure my heart would allow it. Leaving him while he was in this state might break me in two.

"It's not poison. It's something else, something that

nobody should know about." She looked up at me, her brow furrowed. "Why is he with you? Why did you bring him here?"

"He was attacked, and he told me you could help heal him," I said.

"I need the full truth from you, or I'm calling those guards back and having you hauled to the dungeon until I can figure this out. These aren't normal wounds. Somebody was fighting with iron from the fae realm. How did you know that would hurt him?"

"I'm not the one who hurt him. And I don't know anything about iron from the fae realm. So, whatever you think is going on here, you've got the wrong idea. I'm just trying to help. He was jumped, six against one isn't good odds, and it's not right," I said.

Willow's eyes dropped, and I followed the line of her gaze to where both my hands were clasping his. I hadn't even realized I'd taken hold of him like that.

Willow silently walked back to the shelves full of containers and jars and she grabbed a little box and carried it over. She worked quickly, crushing herbs and applying them to the injuries, not speaking until she had covered every single one of the oozing cuts. It wasn't until she put the box away that she looked at me again. This time, her expression was far calmer than it had been before. "How long have you known?"

Known what? In the last couple of weeks, I had found out a shit ton of information. And considering the fact that she had already threatened to send me to the dungeon, I wasn't about to answer something incorrectly. "You're going to need to be more specific."

"I can see it in your eyes. You care for him. And since there's no possible way the two of you fell for each other while you were being tortured in our dungeon, it must mean you share a mating bond. Which also means that somewhere in your lineage, there's fae blood." She stepped around to the end of the bed, coming closer to me. "So, the question is, did you ask your pack to kill him so you could break the bond?"

My eyes widened in horror at the thought. "Of course not. I would never do such a thing. Besides, if I had, why would I bring him here?"

"That's what I'm trying to figure out. Madoc is my best friend. I will protect him from anything that might cause him harm. And right now, you look pretty fucking harmful."

"Look, I'm not here to cause trouble. He asked me to bring him here. How would I know that? And why would I bother if I wanted him dead? If I wanted him dead, I'd have left him with my pack," I snapped.

"Madoc sent the heads of your coconspirators back to your pack in a crate. Yet you expect me to believe that you suddenly stepped into the role of concerned girlfriend?" She scoffed.

"I never said I was his girlfriend. I'm just trying to help him out of a bad spot." It took more willpower than I expected, but I released Madoc's hand and took a step away from the bed. "Just because I didn't want someone to die doesn't mean there's anything going on between us." She'd already guessed about the mating bond, but I wasn't going to admit it. We couldn't tell anyone if we planned to break it.

"I find it extremely suspicious that he was attacked with the one thing that could cause him irreparable harm. You're dangerous."

"I'm not the one who attacked him, and until our drive here, I had no idea he had any fae blood." I winced, clenching my jaw. I should not have said that. Madoc had told me that in confidence and even though she already seemed to know, I felt guilty for spilling his secret.

A little part of me reminded me that I didn't owe him anything. He had killed members of my pack and he didn't want this mating bond between us. This was temporary, but I still felt bad.

"Nobody knows that. His brothers don't even know. I only found out because we played hide and seek in the dungeon once and got stuck between..."

"The bars," I finished for her. I recalled how they'd hurt my hands when I touched them. Madoc had opened the cell, so he touched those bars too, but it had always been quick. He hadn't lingered.

"Fae iron is rare, but our pack has a long history with those monsters, so we've been trained and we're prepared just in case they return. I just never thought I'd meet one face to face." She took a step closer to me. "Tell me, is that how you convinced him to meet up with you? Fairy magic? Were you able to compel him, make him think you are someone special? You didn't seem all that powerful when you were locked up. Maybe you created a false bond and there is no mating bond."

Anger heated my chest. "I would never do something like that." Even if I had the ability, which I didn't, I knew what it was like to lose that choice. "You are out of line."

I could feel her distrust and sense her fear. Willow was putting on a brave face, but I worried she was seconds away from turning me in. "I didn't mean any harm to anyone and I haven't used any magic on Madoc. If you don't mind, I'll be on my way. I can see he's safe with you."

The last thing I wanted to do was leave, especially since I had nowhere to go. But I wasn't about to be sent back to those cells. I didn't think Cavan would be able to resist tearing me to pieces if he got ahold of me again.

"She's not going anywhere," Madoc's voice was gravelly and quiet, but my heart leaped at the sound of it.

I doubled back and closed the distance between us. "You're awake. Thank the gods."

He pushed himself to sitting, then groaned as he turned and set his legs on the floor.

"Don't you dare. You're not ready to get up yet. You need to rest." I stopped in front of him, my eyes finding his. He gave me a weak smile and my heart flip-flopped. I wanted to resist, to fight against the rising affection, but I was too relieved that he was alive.

"I'm already feeling better," he said.

"She's right, even you need some rest from time to time," Willow said.

"What I need is for the two of you to stop arguing. Ivy didn't hurt me, she saved my life," Madoc said. He looked over at his cousin. "She gave up everything. Her pack, her home. I can never repay what she did."

"Why didn't you just say that?" Willow asked me.

"Would you have believed me?"

"Not even a little." Willow walked over to her cousin and checked on his wounds. "The poultice is working. You should be much better in about 20 minutes."

I let out a long breath of relief, which caught Willow's attention. My face heated, and I knew my cheeks were pink.

"You really do care, don't you?" she asked.

"I told you, six against one isn't right. It doesn't matter who it is." It was mostly true. I'd like to think I'd stand up for anyone, but there were certain shifters I would gladly look the other way for. Dax was first on that list.

"She's my mate," Madoc said.

"Madoc," I hissed.

"She already figured it out, I'm sure. And we can trust her." Madoc leaned back against the pillows and closed his eyes.

"Well, that complicates things," Willow said. "I know your dad was counting on you marrying for an alliance since no one thought you'd ever find a mate."

"How could they be so certain?" Finding a true mate was rare, but it happened often enough.

"It's the fae blood. The chances of him finding a mate were practically nonexistent because he'd have to find someone like you. Someone who was of both realms."

"That does sound like a challenge," I said. "Though, since finding out I was fae, I've met two more with fae blood. Maybe we're not so rare."

"Could be," Willow said. "I wouldn't want to be the one to break it to your father, though."

"We're not telling him," Madoc said. "We're going to break the bond."

A weight settled inside, the disappointment growing every time he mentioned ending our bond.

"Shit, Madoc. That's why you asked about Freya." Willow said. "You sure you want to go through with this? You said she gave up her pack for you."

"It's what's best," Madoc said. "I'll help her settle in here somewhere once it's done. Nobody has to know."

"You want me to stay here? As an Umbra wolf?" I asked.

"Of course. You need a pack. I might intend to break the bond, but I'm not going to abandon you," he said.

I was speechless and overwhelmed with a rush of sensations. I never imagined I'd be part of a pack, even when I was with the Shadow Wolves. It had always been the goal, but it never felt possible. Even when it happened, it was false. This was a chance at the one thing I'd always wanted. But did I want to be part of *this* pack? I heard how awful they were, but was it better or worse than being feral?

It didn't matter yet. We still had to break the bond. I had time to figure it all out.

"Breaking mating bonds is illegal," Willow said.

"I know, but I can't keep this bond and you know that," Madoc said. "This is the only way."

"You think you're going to be able to hide a mating bond from your dad?" She sounded skeptical.

"It'll be gone before he gets a chance to find out," Madoc said.

"I wouldn't bet on that," a rough male voice said.

We all turned to see an older male walk into the room. There was no mistaking the similarities, and I knew instantly we'd been joined by Madoc's father.

TWENTY-SEVEN

Tendrils of dread shivered down my spine.

"I assume there must be some very good reason why I wasn't informed of this news." The alpha closed the door behind him and the distinct click of a lock sent my pulse racing.

Madoc and I seemed to have an understanding, but I had no idea what his father would do when he found out about me. As far as I knew, the easiest and most efficient way to break a bond would be to kill the undesirable member of that bond. Would Erwin's distaste of my pack extend so far as to murder his son's mate?

Madoc pushed himself from the bed, and my fear was replaced by worry. Instantly, I was at his side, offering my support to help steady him.

"She already seems quite devoted to you," Erwin said.

I scrunched up my face as the realization dawned. I shouldn't have been so quick to assist Madoc. It just made us look like we were more of a couple than we were. We hardly knew each other, and we had both agreed that breaking the bond was the best option.

I heard the door open and looked up to see Willow trying to make her escape.

"Not so fast. Close it and come back in here. You two have been thick as thieves since you were small. I should have known if he was hiding something from me that you were involved."

"This has nothing to do with Willow," Madoc said. He shoved me away and took a step closer to his father, and I swallowed down the hurt from his actions. Once again, the bond was reacting for me, giving me responses and emotions I didn't want to feel.

"I've got this under control. For once, just let me take care of something myself. In case you haven't noticed, I haven't been a child in years."

"I walk in here to find you having a conversation about breaking a mating bond and you expect me to look at you with respect? There are few things more sacred than a mating bond."

"They know what she is. What do you think is gonna happen when they find out I have a mating bond with someone with fae blood?" Madoc asked.

His words knocked the wind from my lungs. That's what this was about? This whole time I thought he didn't want the bond because of my pack. But that could have been explained away. Being part fae could not. "That's why you reject me? Because they'll find out that you're not a full wolf?"

Madoc looked at me, his expression cold. All the affection I had felt from him in the past few hours was gone. Now that he was here, and he was safe, he had no use for me. While it had been the intent all along, it hurt to see him go so quickly from seeming to care about me at least a little to having so much hate for what I was. Especially when he carried the same heritage in his veins. "You're a hypocrite."

"No, I'm the future alpha of this pack. If this got out, it would destroy everything."

"You have three younger brothers. The only thing it destroys is your ambition. You'd be sidelined, passed over for the position of alpha, but no one would even bat an eye. Your father wouldn't be the first alpha to take a woman that wasn't his wife." I narrowed my eyes. "You think your pack really doesn't know? That they didn't question that your wife wasn't getting large with child?"

"Enough. Our family secrets have nothing to do with you." Erwin turned to look at his oldest son. "I assume you have a plan for how you're going to break this bond?"

"I found someone who can make it happen."

"And what is she asking for, for keeping her mouth shut?" Erwin asked.

"*She* has a name, and she doesn't want shit from you." I balled my hands into fists. How is it possible that I found someone I hated even more than Dax within the first couple of minutes of meeting him? I know my judgment was clouded from the bond, but Madoc and his father were not the same. They might share physical traits, but I knew they were complete opposites.

"I told her I'd find a space for her in the pack. She gave up hers to help me. I owe her a life debt, which means she's pack now," Madoc said.

"I don't want anything to do with your pack. Or any of you. Once this bond is broken, you won't have to deal with me anymore." I crossed my arms over my chest.

"Good. A new face around here would bring too many questions." Erwin still hadn't looked over at me as if, by not making eye contact with me, he could pretend I already didn't exist. I had an overwhelming urge to punch him in the face.

"Does her pack know about the bond?" Erwin asked.

"Again, I have a name, asshole," I spat.

Erwin looked at me that time, his upper lip curling as he made a low rumbling sound.

"I think a couple of them figured it out." Now Madoc was the one who wouldn't look at me. I felt like I was living in someone's nightmare, because this couldn't be my life.

"I need a list of names. We'll send in a team to take them out," Erwin said.

I lunged forward. "The hell you will. First of all, they don't deserve to die just because the fates dealt me a shit hand. Second, if you go in there and take them out, you're starting a war. Is that really what you want?"

"She was dating their alpha," Willow said. "I'm sure he's pissed he lost his girl to a bond with an Umbra wolf."

"Do they know it was you, or did they just scent our pack?" Erwin asked.

"I'm not sure," Madoc said.

"You leave them alone. I sacrificed my pack to keep your son alive. The least you can do is respect my wishes here. Don't hurt them," I said. While seeing Dax get what he deserved wouldn't bother me, the rest of the wolves attacked at his command. Plus, Kate knew. And I couldn't risk them figuring that out.

"You better back down, girl." Erwin turned his gaze on me. It was cold and unyielding and I could feel his hatred in that look. "You are a complication, but you will not cost this pack its next alpha. One more word from you, and I take the easy way out to ending the bond. The only reason you're still breathing is because I know what happens to a fae when they lose their mate, and I'm not willing to risk that."

"You're a coward and a bully," I hissed. "Maybe it's a good thing that my pack is trying to take you out."

The back of Erwin's hand landed across my cheek, forcing my head to the side. A burst of pain spread from the point of contact and I winced as the sting lingered. In a blur and a growl, Madoc had his arms around me and turned so his body was between me and his father.

He touched my cheek tenderly. "Are you alright?"

Confused, I nodded slowly, unsure of what to say.

Where the hell had that come from? I was more stunned at Madoc's reaction than I was his father's attack.

Madoc turned, keeping a protective arm around me so I was against his back. "I will take care of this. But if you lay a finger on her, it won't just be the truth about me that comes out to this pack. I will unleash all your secrets and I will end any chance of this family maintaining its power."

A low rumbling growl sounded from Erwin. "The only reason I am tolerating this insolence is because I know it's the bond speaking and not you. Get it taken care of. If it's not broken in three days, I'm sending someone after you to break it for you. Consequences be damned."

I couldn't see around Madoc's huge build, but I heard the door open and slam. Breaking this bond just got even more important.

TWENTY-EIGHT

Even though my heart was thumping wildly and my body ached to touch him, I forced myself to move away from Madoc. "We should go see that witch and get this over with."

Madoc's expression hardened. "Let me wash these herbs off and then we can go."

"Ten more minutes, then you can wash it all off and you should be just as good as new," Willow said. "Wait. I'll grab some clothes for your mate."

"Ivy," I said. "My name is Ivy."

"Well, you're small for a shifter, Ivy. But I'll see what I can find." Willow left the room before I could agree, and though I was pretty sure she hated me, I wasn't about to turn down a fresh pair of clothes.

Madoc walked to a chair in the corner and took a seat. He was still completely naked and my eyes dropped right between his legs for a peek at his package. I had to admit;

it was impressive. My gaze moved, exploring his wash-board abs up to his muscular chest, beyond the curve of his shoulders to his strong jaw.

Our eyes met in an intense connection that nearly took my breath away. Checking him out in such an intimate way sent a rush of heat through me. It was dangerous. I tore my eyes away, not trusting what my body might make me do if I stared at his beauty for too long.

I played with the hem of the shirt, which was long enough to be a dress on me. I hated that it smelled like him and that part of me didn't want to take it off. The silence between us was awkward and uncomfortable. In the car, there hadn't been any time to think of anything besides survival. Now that I was alone with him and we weren't running on pure adrenaline, my mind wandered to other things.

There was no denying there was a part of me that wanted to cross the room to him and sit on him in a very particular way, ensuring that I cemented the bond. Another part of me resisted because I knew it wasn't what he wanted.

I wished I was fighting the urge because I felt nothing for him; instead, I felt shame and pain from his rejection. It wasn't even about my pack or the complications that might come with us being from opposing sides. He was rejecting me because of what I was, and that hurt even worse.

I couldn't control who my parents were, and I never asked to be born. That was their choice, and it led me to this place where my mate, who carried at least some of the same fae blood, refused to be with me because of it.

"I know when someone is lying," Madoc said. "That's my gift. Not quite as impressive as yours, but it's something."

"That would have been very helpful for me the last couple of weeks," I said.

"It has its uses. It's why they always have me do interrogations. Even when someone is a good liar, I still know the truth."

I wasn't sure why he was telling me this, unless he wanted me to open up about any powers I might have. "I can't do that."

"My dad said my real mom was probably fifth or sixth generation. The fae blood nearly gone. Most of the time if I touch fae iron it stings, but it doesn't do damage like this. Your whole pack knows about you. They came prepared to hurt you, maybe capture you. It means several of them had tipped their claws with fae iron. They wouldn't have done that to attack a regular wolf."

I stumbled over to the bed in a haze, taking a seat as the information sunk in. He was right. They had come prepared to take me down, but when they found Madoc alone, they'd gone after him instead. My own pack planned to destroy me if Dax couldn't control me.

"I'm amazed he let you go. Whatever you threatened him with, it must be pretty powerful," Madoc said.

The only thing Dax cared about, aside from his power, was his own life. Which meant my reprieve was temporary. I had a feeling Dax would send shifters after me because he wouldn't want my power used by anyone else. He was prepared to let them kill me. Maybe I had been too quick to turn down Erwin's desire to hunt down the members of my pack.

My old pack.

I truly couldn't ever go back.

"That light you make. It's how I knew you were fae. It's how I knew the feelings I had for you were from a bond. Do you remember that, when we first met in the cell? You glowed as soon as I put my hands on you."

I looked over at him as the memory crashed into my mind. I had forgotten all about that, but now it made sense. "You're lucky you're not dead."

"It didn't feel dangerous. It felt like recognition and it scared the hell out of me."

I licked my lips, my mouth suddenly far too dry to speak. Recognition was a good way to put how I felt around him. When we were together, I had this strange sensation, as if I'd known him my whole life.

I wasn't sure why I decided to tell him, but everything starting to spill out. "I didn't know I was fae when we met. I found out a couple of days ago. Consequently, the same day, my power ignited and accidentally killed someone. So yeah, it's pretty powerful."

"I'm sorry," he said, his tone genuine.

"Don't be. It's not your problem," I said.

"It was hard when I learned the truth. I can't imagine

finding out like that," he said. "Do you know what it is or how to use it?"

"I'm working on it. I'm practicing control so that I don't release it accidentally. I haven't mastered it yet, and I've got a long way to go, but it's getting better." I swallowed hard, surprised at the mixture of emotions rising to the surface. It was overwhelming and frustrating. Learning so much at once, while dealing with so much change. It was enough to send anyone over the edge.

"I hate it," I whispered, admitting it out loud for the first time. It was true, though. What I wouldn't give to be a normal wolf shifter.

"I hate everything about it. I hate that it makes me different, I hate that it's so wild and untamed, I hate that the fae part of me draws the wrong people and keeps away the right ones. I'm being punished for what I am. Denied a family, a pack, and now a mate. Simply because one of my parents was different."

Everything inside me felt like it was breaking at my unplanned confession. What would things be like if I didn't have this part of me? Dax would have never paid attention to me. Maybe I'd be joining the Umbra wolves right now and settling into life with my new mate. Then again, without that part of me, Madoc and I couldn't be. All of those thoughts were depressing enough as it was, but the worst thought was about my mother. She'd given me up because of who my father was, abandoning me because being half-fae was dangerous. My own mother was afraid of what I would become.

I had spent my whole life as the underdog. Bullied, beaten, looked down on. Yet, this whole time, I had more power than any of them. Enough for them to fear me if they can't control me.

"You're better than all of them. You're more than I deserve," Madoc said.

I lifted my chin and made a promise to myself to stop feeling sorry for myself. To stop feeling like I wasn't enough. They were right to fear me because, despite it all, I had always taken care of myself and found a way to rise above. I would do it again, and this time it would be on my terms. "I think it's been ten minutes. You should go clean up so we can get out of here."

WHILE MADOC WAS AWAY, I looked through the jars and bottles of Willow's collection. I had never known a wolf shifter with such an array of herbs and concoctions. It reminded me of Kate's house, and the space where her mom kept everything she used for when she worked with magic.

I opened some of the little wooden boxes and smelled the mixtures of herbs. The scents were comforting, reminding me of happy childhood memories when Kate's mom would tell us the names of the plants and what they were used for. It wasn't a skill I invested a lot of time in, and I had forgotten most of it. I picked up a jar and unscrewed the lid and the scent made my eyes widen. It smelled exactly like the tea I had been drinking most of my life.

"Are you familiar with herbs?" Willow asked.

I turned, still holding the glass jar in my hand. Willow approached, a bundle of clothes in her arms.

"My best friend's mom is a witch. This reminds me of her home. I've never seen a shifter with a collection like this," I said.

"When you live with four boys who are constantly putting themselves in danger, you figure out ways to hide the injuries." She set the clothes on the bed, then took the jar from me.

"What is that one? It smells familiar."

She cocked a brow. "You know this one?"

"It reminds me of tea I used to drink," I said. "For healing, right?"

"Not at all. You sure you drank something that smelled like this?" she asked.

I nodded. "I'd know that smell anywhere."

Willow grabbed the lid off the shelf and closed up the jar. "That's a mixture to suppress magic. It's rarely used, because it's not exactly ethical and it's difficult to make. You're sure that's what you were drinking?"

"Are you certain?" I asked.

She nodded.

"Like to make my fae magic not work?" I asked.

"Exactly like that," she said.

I felt lightheaded and unstable. That's why Xander had tossed the tea and told me not to drink it anymore.

That's why he said he thought it would be a few more days before my magic appeared.

Dax said he hadn't known until we got in the ring and then went and looked up my past. But Kate had been giving me this tea for over a decade. Somebody in the pack knew what I was and didn't want it getting out.

I thought back to when I'd stayed the night at Dax's house and he brought me the tea. Kate always made sure I had the tea available, and I drank it at least a few times a week. I thought it was out of kindness, a way to help me heal and recover when I was injured, which, let's face it, was often.

"If you were drinking this stuff regularly, it would make shifting very difficult, almost impossible. And it would definitely eliminate any fae magic. We use this from time to time when we have to be around humans during a full moon just to keep our wolf in check. If you don't use it often, it wears off in about a day. But if you're drinking a lot of it, it could take weeks to get out of your system. They were giving you this?" Willow shook her head. "That's just wrong. It would affect everything. Your ability to heal, your enhanced senses... Everything."

That explained so much, from my late shifting to the fact that I seemed to heal so much slower than everyone else. It explained why my wolf wouldn't come when I had been captured, but why it had no problem shifting in the last several days. Without knowing it, I had detoxed from the herbs while being held by the Umbras, only to be given it again upon my return. But I hadn't had much, so when

Xander tossed it down the sink, it must have gotten out of my system in a few short days.

There was nothing I could do to change the past, but now I knew Kate had been part of keeping my abilities in check. Had she known or had her mom told her it was to help with healing? Her mom had to have known what the drink really did. But why had she done it? Who else knew?

The door opened, and I shook myself from my thoughts. I was going to have to deal with this later.

"Everything alright in here?" Madoc asked.

"Oh, just discovering exactly how fucked up the Shadow Pack is." Willow set the jar on the shelf and walked over to the bed. She patted the pile of clothes. "I brought you some things to pick from. Use whatever you want. Good luck."

She paused in front of Madoc and gave his shoulder a squeeze on her way out the door. The two of us were alone again. I should have my head focused on what we were doing but I was still reeling from the revelation of the tea.

"You look like you just saw a ghost." He strode into the room, his gait confident and relaxed. He was definitely feeling much better.

Clothed in a long sleeve shirt and a pair of jeans that fit him too perfectly, he wandered back to the same chair and took a seat.

"I just found out my pack was suppressing my magic most of my life." There I went again, telling him every- thing as if he cared or as if we mattered to each other. "Forget it. It's my problem, not yours."

"I'm glad you're away from them," Madoc said.

I didn't respond. He was forgetting the fact that I was packless without a penny to my name. But I was done feeling sorry for myself. Somehow, I was going to make my life better than it had been, which wasn't setting the standards too high.

I crossed to the bed and started sorting through the clothes. Willow was nearly a foot taller than me, and broader. I frowned as I wondered if the tea was part of why I was so much smaller than all the other shifters. Settling on some leggings rather than the jeans that I would trip over, I quickly pulled them on and then turned away from Madoc so I could change without him getting a full frontal view. Not that he hadn't already, but being alone in a bedroom was different from standing in the middle of the woods post shift.

There were a few sports bras on the pile and while my chest was smaller than Willow's, they'd offer more support than nothing. I pulled on the smallest one and then tugged on a shirt followed by a hoodie. A thick pair of socks was next, before tugging on a pair of too large tennis shoes.

It wasn't ideal, but I was glad I had something clean to put on. I turned around and put my hands on my hips. "Okay, I'm ready. Where do we find this witch?"

"She's kind of in the middle of nowhere, so we've got a couple hour drive ahead of us. We should get a few hours' sleep before we go. You can stay here. The door locks, and you'll be safe." He stood. "I'll wake you in the morning."

"You sure your dad isn't going to break the bond for you?" I asked.

"He won't. The legends say that fae mating bonds are so strong that if their mate dies, the other goes insane. He'll give us a few days before he risks testing it out to see if that's true," he said. "Sleep well."

With that lovely bit of information, I flopped onto Willow's bed. The more I learned about mating bonds, the more I hated them.

CHAPTER
TWENTY-NINE

"ARE you sure you're healed enough to drive?" I asked again. We'd been driving for over an hour in silence. Even though we'd slept till noon, the injuries I could see didn't look as healed as much as they should.

"I told you, Willow's remedies are solid. I'm fine."

I hated that I was worried about him, but there wasn't much I could do to change that. Not while the bond still thrummed like a current inside me. It seemed impossible, but the connection seemed to be getting stronger by the minute. "How did you find this witch? There can't be a whole lot of people you can ask about breaking a bond."

"You'd be surprised," he said.

"That many? Really? I thought everyone celebrated when they found their true mate," I said.

"We didn't," he said matter-of-factly.

My shoulders slumped. *Thanks for the reminder, asshole.*

"Well, I guess I should be grateful. The sooner we get this done, the better."

"Exactly," he said.

"How does it work? Do you know if it really will work?" I asked.

"It should. I got the info from a reliable source. As far as *how* she does it, I have no idea. I didn't bother to ask. It's not like it would change anything. This is the only way to break the bond," he said.

"Right. Why bother to find out if the witch cuts one of us in half or removes our ability to shift or something equally dark." I sighed. When dealing with magic, it was important to know the details. Even I knew that.

But maybe *he* didn't. "Wait. You don't have witches or other types of shifters around, do you? Only pure wolves. Anyone else isn't welcome. That's why your dad hides you. Shit, how are you even still in the pack? You'd think he'd have sent you and your mom away."

"He probably would have if he'd had his way," Madoc said darkly.

"You can tell me to shut up, but I really don't get how the whole pack doesn't know about you," I said. "It's harder to hide an illegitimate kid when the dad is the one who strayed. Nobody figured out his wife didn't carry you?"

"My dad knocked up his mistress and his wife at the same time. His mistress was hidden away, and they planned to send me to a foundling home. Probably in the Shadow Pack, because my dad found out about his mistress's fae blood while she was pregnant. He wanted nothing to do with her after that," he said.

"How did you end up in his home, then?" I asked.

"Well, my dad's legitimate son was stillborn. My mom, the woman who raised me, was devastated. They worried she'd be unable to carry a healthy child. My dad, being him, was far more concerned about having an heir, so he convinced his mistress to give me up. My birth mom died shortly after and my new mom treated me as her own, so I was raised as the heir to the Umbra family."

"That's heartbreaking," I said. "Your poor mother. Both of them."

"I never met my birth mom, but I guess it was better than going to a foundling house." He winced. "Sorry."

"Don't be. You're lucky. It's not a life I would wish on any child." I took a deep breath and looked out the window. We were racing through endless countryside. Nothing but fields for miles. Silence settled around us and we drove for a while longer, my thoughts in a million different directions. I kept thinking about how different his life was from mine, even though he'd almost shared my fate.

"She must have gone through a lot to keep you around after birthing three more boys," I said, breaking the silence. "Your mom. I imagine your dad would rather have a full wolf as his successor."

"Thankfully for me, I'm seven years older than Cavan. So by the time he was born, everyone already expected me to take over. It would have been too much of a scandal to get rid of me." His grip tightened on the steering wheel. "Anything for appearances."

"Including violating shifter law to break a mating bond," I said.

"Yes, including that," he agreed.

"I'm surprised I'm not dead," I said with a forced laugh. "Even with the risk of insanity, it would be much easier to get rid of me than let us go through with this."

He looked at me, a brief flash of anger in his eyes. "I won't let that happen. I swear to you. Neither of us chose this bond. You shouldn't have to die just because the fates fucked us over."

"You were serious about what you told your dad, weren't you?" My brow furrowed, and I studied him. "You'd tell everyone the truth if he hurt me."

"The truth about my birth isn't even the most scandalous thing my family hides," he said. "And yes, I was serious. If he killed you, I'd burn it all down."

My heart swelled, and a rush of warmth spread through me, making my skin feel hot. He said all the right things, and it was impossible not to feel affection for him. "You're making this harder."

"I know."

"You shouldn't say things like that," I said.

"You deserved the truth. I know what it's like to have everyone keep things from you," he said. "And I know you've had your share of secrets. I won't do that."

"When did you find out?" I asked.

"The day of my first shift. My father pulled me aside

and told me that if I ever showed any signs of having magic, he'd kill me himself," he said.

"Good thing you don't glow like I do," I said.

"I really would be dead if I did," he said.

"Why does your pack hate outsiders so much? My best friend is half-witch, and she's no different than me," I said, though as soon as the words were out, I felt like I had a weight in my stomach. I didn't know if she was aware of what was in the tea. Though, I didn't think her being part witch had anything to do with that. Another shifter could have given me the elixir just as easily. And none of the shifters in my pack had ever shown me kindness.

"I'm not sure," he admitted. "But things will be different when I'm alpha."

"Your work with Holden? It didn't sound different. You were planning to kill the alpha of my pack," I said.

"They're not your pack anymore," he said.

"Thank you for the reminder," I deadpanned.

He hummed. "Yes, I was working with Holden to eliminate your alpha, but I needed more information about his son."

"Dax."

"Yes, your ex," he said.

"Will you stop saying that? We might have a mating bond, but you don't know me. You don't know anything about me," I snapped.

"Then tell me. I told you about my mom," he said.

He had a point, but that didn't mean I wanted to open up about my life. He had been raised in luxury by a family who loved him. Even though his mom wasn't who gave birth to him, he'd made it seem like she'd been kind. I rarely knew kindness.

"What happened between you and him?" he asked gently. "He was frantic when he reached out to get you back. I thought things were serious, but I can see how a mating bond could complicate a relationship."

"You aren't going to let this go, are you?" I asked.

"I'm jealous, okay? I know I have no right, but I want to rip his head off when I think about the fact that he even looked at you in a romantic way."

My eyes widened, and my heart did that stupid flip. *Jealous?* That's what the whole thing was about? It made me feel a little better that it wasn't just me being impacted so strongly by the bond.

I didn't want to revisit things with Dax, but I could sympathize with how Madoc was feeling. "If I tell you this, you're going to want to do worse than rip his head off."

"If you're going to tell me you fucked him, I will most definitely want to do more than rip his head off," Madoc said.

Maybe it was because I wanted to see harm come to Dax. Or maybe it was because there was something so primal and hot about being wanted by a shifter as powerful as Madoc. Either way, I decided I couldn't keep it in any longer.

"Pull over," I said.

"What?"

"I don't want you driving when I tell you this." If he

was telling me about someone who hurt him, I would lose my shit. I wasn't sure how Madoc would react.

He hesitated, but finally pulled over to the side of the road. I looked out the window at a field dotted with cows.

"Tell me what happened," he said. "He didn't force himself on you, did he? Because I really don't need another reason to kill him, but I swear to you, I will make it hurt when I do."

I turned so I was facing Madoc. "My childhood was awful. I was bullied and beaten my whole life. Dax was one of the worst offenders."

His brow furrowed. "I don't understand. How did things change?"

"Have you heard of a false bond?" I asked.

Madoc's expression darkened. "I've heard of it, but I've never heard of it happening. We shift in packs, we run in packs. Every wolf knows this."

"I didn't. I wasn't taught any of that and I wasn't allowed to run with the pack," I said. "And since my shifting was stunted with the magic suppression, I never shifted on my own. He timed it all correctly to make it happen, then he kept me from shifting again so he could keep the bond between us longer."

"I'm going to tear his dick off and feed it to him before I kill him," Madoc said. He tightened his hands into fists and I could feel anger flowing around us. It filled the car, making the air seem to crackle with heat and electricity.

I set my hand on top of Madoc's. My own embarrassment and anger were nothing compared to the urge I had

244

to ease his pain. It was as if knowing the emotional mess I'd gone through directly injured him. The connection between us was intense, and I understood how they said a mating bond was like two halves of the same soul. He was feeling what I felt.

"You broke it," I told him. "Meeting you let me see more clearly, and by the time I got back to my pack, the bond was nearly gone."

Madoc reached for me, resting his large palm on my cheek. "Nobody hurts you and lives. Do you understand me?"

His touch made my breath shaky and all the hurt I'd felt at the hands of my former alpha dissolved. Madoc staring into my eyes was everything I needed. Nothing else existed besides us. Without realizing what I was doing, I leaned closer to him and he met me, our lips crashing together.

He slid his hand around the back of my head, fingers tangling into my hair, as he pulled me closer. I unbuckled my seatbelt without taking my lips from his. I needed to feel his body against mine the same way I needed oxygen.

We deepened the kiss, a clash of lips and teeth and tongue. It was hungry and violent. His stubble scraped across my cheeks and my hip bumped into the center console. I didn't care. I needed closer. I need more.

I needed him.

Somehow, I ended up on top of him, the steering wheel against my back. He lowered the seat down and the two of us went down with it, never breaking the kiss. His hard length was against my center, the cloth of our pants the only thing keeping us from making this bond permanent. In the back of my mind, a warning sounded, reminding me that this was dangerous. I broke away from the kiss and looked down at him.

Panting and full of need, I stared at the man under me. His eyes were heavy with lust, his lips swollen from our kisses, and the edge of his shirt was bunched up, revealing his lower abs. My body was screaming in protest. I was on fire, and only he could put it out. But this was wrong. It was the bond, not a choice. And we were going to break it. Neither of us wanted this. "We shouldn't."

He toyed with a lock of my hair. "You're right."

Fuck it. I lowered my face to his, and he grabbed the back of my head. Our lips collided again, as if we'd never stopped. One of his large hands slipped under the hem of my tee and I sucked in a breath. His touch was like magic on my skin, sending tingles of pleasure in its wake.

"Pants stay on," I managed between kisses.

I felt his lips curve, then he sucked my lower lip into his mouth. I moaned in response, feeling reason and logic leave. I wasn't sure I had any willpower left. I felt like I was coming undone at the seams. Without thinking, I reached lower, my fingers resting on his waistband.

He pulled away. "Pants stay on."

His words knocked just enough sense back into me. "Yes."

"Just pants." He sat up enough to pull his shirt over his

head, tossing it in the back seat. I grinned and followed his lead.

He stared at me as he took me in and instead of feeling self-conscious of my scars; I felt powerful. Desirable. Wanted.

"You are so fucking beautiful." He said the words like a prayer, then softly dragged his fingertips from my neck, over my breasts and down to my stomach.

He lingered there, his fingers dangerously close to my waistband. My breath hitched, and I drank him in, my eyes scanning every perfect inch of his bare skin. I noticed he had his own share of scars but instead of finding them unsightly, as I feared mine would be, I wanted to kiss each and every one.

Slowly, I leaned forward and pressed my lips to a scar on his chest. He caught my chin, then guided me back to his mouth. Our kiss was different this time, slower and softer. It was as gentle as the first had been violent. Yet somehow, this kiss was more intense. Wetness pooled between my thighs and I moved my hips against his hardness, trying to appease the building heat.

He groaned, his hands grasping my ass, guiding my movements and encouraging me to grind against him. We were both panting between kisses, and the air around us felt charged and thick. His mouth moved to my neck, lips and teeth brushing against the sensitive skin. Hands cupped and caressed my breasts, fingers played with my taught nipples. I gasped, letting my eyes flutter closed as the sensations built.

"Gods, you're gorgeous. I really don't deserve you." Madoc's voice was raspy and gruff. He cupped the side of my face, his thumb caressing my cheek.

I shivered and stopped the movement of my hips. There was so much heat built up and I was desperate for release, but this was too much. This wasn't just sex, this was personal.

It hadn't been like this with Dax. There was no connection there. This was dangerous.

With shaky breaths, I set my hand on top of his. "This isn't real. It's the bond."

His jaw tensed, and a vein in his forehead flickered. "Bonds are supposed to be real."

"Ours can't be." That's what *he* kept telling me, wasn't it? I climbed off him and reached for my shirt. If I didn't stop this now, I wasn't going to be able to stop.

My heart shattered. I was broken. Ripped in two as I resisted the urge to go back to him, but I had to. He couldn't be with me. Even if we changed our minds, we couldn't be together if he was going to lead the Umbras. His father would kill me or I'd have to make him abandon everything he'd worked for. He was connected to his pack. It would devastate him. I couldn't do that to him, even if every part of me wanted him.

Madoc was silent as he dressed and righted the seat. We didn't speak as he started the car and resumed our drive.

I stopped us to prevent him from making a terrible mistake. Why did I feel like I made the wrong choice?

CHAPTER

THIRTY

WE STOPPED for food and gas as the sun dipped lower into the horizon. All conversations were polite and muted. Every time we spoke, my heart broke a little more. I'd hurt him when I stopped us, but I knew if I hadn't, we'd have completed the bond.

"We're almost there," Madoc said.

"Good." I kept my eyes out the window, unwilling to get caught in his gaze. My chest tightened, and it hurt to think that the connection between us would be severed so soon.

Vivid pinks and dark purples lingered in the sky after the sun was below the mountains. It was a beautiful sunset, the colors so alive and intense. They were a brutal reminder of how dark and fractured I felt.

A sound like a miniature explosion broke through the air, and Madoc swerved. I turned, checking on him before looking out the window. The flopping sound of a flat tire was followed by another immediate popping explosive sound. I tensed. One flat tire was a coincidence. Two was an attack. I looked over at Madoc. His nostrils flared and his jaw was clenched. "Stay in the car."

"I can fight." My wolf had no idea how to fight, but I could already feel the magic flowing through me and it was taking all my concentration to keep it contained rather than release it right here in the car. I knew it was still a risk to use it, but I had some practice at controlling it, and at the very least, it could be used to defend us if needed.

"But I can't if I'm worried about you," he said.

I swallowed over a lump in my throat. Why did he have to say things like that? It was just making what we were doing so much harder. He exited the car, leaving me stunned by his comment. After hours of silence, it felt like a declaration of how he was really feeling. Part of me wanted to celebrate that he cared. I squashed it down. It didn't matter. We were still on our way to break the bond.

I might be conflicted on how I felt about him, but I wasn't a damsel in distress and I sure as hell wasn't going to let anyone hurt him. My wolf clawed at my insides as I opened the door. She wanted out. She wanted to defend her mate. *We're not going to let anything happen to him.*

The wolf side of me seemed to relax a little when I joined Madoc.

"I told you to stay in the car." Madoc said with a growl.

"I just gave up everything to save your ass. Do you

FORBIDDEN SIN

really think I'm going to let someone kill you now?" I snapped.

"Don't die on me." He didn't get a chance to say anything else because several large figures emerged from the trees, closing in around us.

The hair on the back of my neck stood on end. I glanced around, doing a quick count as the wolves approached us from all sides. The last time Madoc had been outnumbered, I couldn't protect him. Charging into the fight would have resulted in both of us dying, and using my magic was too risky with him in the middle of the fray. This time, he wasn't being attacked yet, and I wasn't going to wait.

The desire to protect him welled up inside me like a rush of anger meeting something ancient and temperamental. It was the feeling of my magic building from my chest, expanding outward until it reached my hands. I worked to contain it, keeping the magic simmering right at my fingertips. I moved carefully, maintaining my focus so I didn't have an accident as I moved in front of Madoc. I wasn't going to let them have him.

"What are you doing?" he hissed.

"Stay out of my way. I don't want to hurt you."

"I'm supposed to be protecting you," he said.

"Keep your archaic male protector stereotypes to yourself," I snapped. "I can take them all out, but I can't if you're out there with them."

"It has nothing to do with stereotypes," Madoc said. "It has everything to do with you."

"Please stop talking," I managed, my throat tight. He had to stop doing that. He had to stop speaking to me as if I was something he cherished. We both knew it wasn't going to last.

Then again, maybe we'd both be dead soon anyway and this stupid bond wouldn't matter.

Fuck that noise. Neither of us was going to die. I raised my hands. "Turn around. You don't want to mess with us."

The wolves approached slower now, a couple of them hesitating as they looked at my hands. I could almost feel their apprehension, or maybe that was just the tension in the air. I lifted my arms, letting the light expand from my fingertips. "Back down. This is your only warning."

A large wolf with reddish brown fur took a step forward before his body began to break and crack. I kept my hands up, willing myself to hold the magic without releasing it. It was exhausting, and I wasn't sure how much longer I could control it before I needed to either close it off or let it go, but I couldn't let them know that.

"Stay on guard," Madoc said as he moved closer to me.

"Behind me," I said. "I don't want to hurt you."

"You won't," he said. "Focus on him. He's probably coming to negotiate."

I nodded and kept my eyes locked on the naked man walking toward us. He had long blonde hair and a lean, long build. He moved with grace and ease, unconcerned with the fact that I was threatening him with magic. "Put that away. We would never harm one of our own."

He glanced back. "Return to your patrol. She's not our enemy."

The wolves turned around and melted back into the woods around us. I felt my magic falter, but I didn't close it off. Not yet.

"She travels with one of *them*," a female voice came from behind us. She approached from the side and stopped next to the male. She had dark hair and brown skin. Like her companion, she was long and lean. Both of them had a very different build than the shifters I'd grown up around, but I could sense their strength. I knew not to lower my guard.

I could almost feel the tension and anger directed toward Madoc and before I realized what I was doing, I moved in front of him again. It felt good to have the power to protect someone I cared about after all those years of not even being able to protect myself. "You harm him, I will kill you."

"Nobody is going to harm anybody. Just close off your magic before someone gets hurt," the male said.

"He can't be allowed passage. Not after everything *they* have done," the female said through gritted teeth.

I was feeling lightheaded, and I knew I had used more magic than I was used to and it was taking a toll on me. Rather than showing weakness or losing control, I closed my hands, turning off the magic. "Explain yourselves. Why did you blow our tires?"

"You crossed into our territory with a member of the

Umbra Pack. You can't blame us for shooting first," the male said.

"We did nothing to justify that," I said. "So yeah, I can blame you for that."

"After everything those Umbras have done, you should both be dead," the female sneered.

"I don't know what your beef is with the Umbras, but we're just passing through," Madoc said.

"Who are you?" If they were Shadow Wolves, I would know them. Madoc clearly didn't know them either. Which meant they were either feral, or they belonged to one of the other packs. There was a lot of unclaimed land, and I knew the borders were constantly changing. It wouldn't be unheard of for a major pack to expand or for feral wolves to have claimed formerly neutral territory.

"What I wanna know is why someone with fae blood is willingly in the presence of one of the murderous Umbra Wolves? You don't seem like you're his prisoner, yet I've never seen one of their kind allow one of ours to live." The male crossed his arms over his chest and narrowed his eyes as if studying something he'd never seen before.

"I'm not his prisoner," I said.

"We're here to visit a friend who lives nearby," Madoc said.

The male smirked. "You're here to see the witch, aren't you? You Umbras hate magic unless it can do something for you."

"What we're doing here is our business," Madoc said. "It has nothing to do with any of the packs."

"She can pass," the woman said. "But not you."

"We both need passage," I said.

"Will you vouch for him?" the male asked.

"Of course," I said.

A vicious smirk spread on the female's face. "Oh, good. Then we get to kill both of you as soon as he steps out of line."

"That's not going to happen," I assured her. "Once our business is complete, we'll leave."

"After we find a way to fix two blown tires," Madoc mumbled.

The male shifter approached. "How did you hear of Freya?"

I tensed as I recalled hearing that name before.

"A friend," Madoc said.

"Named?" the naked shifter pressed.

"Willow," he said.

Now I knew how Willow knew so much about herbs. The Umbras despised magic, yet Willow was learning from a witch. They really did have a lot of secrets in that family.

"I'm Lucian. I'm one of the elders in these parts. We might be feral, but we're not monsters." The male shifter extended his hand.

Madoc tensed and I knew it was because he couldn't share his name. I stepped closer to Lucian. "I'm Ivy, this is Mal."

Lucian shook my hand, then reached for Madoc. "Nice to meet you both. You can wait at our camp until Freya returns."

"Returns? Where is she?" Madoc asked.

"You're not the only ones who need her services," the female hissed.

"She'll be back soon. She is helping another shifter," Lucian explained.

My trust had been betrayed more times than I could count, but my instincts made me feel like Lucian was genuine. I glanced over at Madoc. "We can't go back. I think we should go with them."

Madoc's whole body was still tense, as if preparing for a fight. He didn't seem to want to back down.

I set my hand on his arm and he flinched, but I could feel some of his tension melting away. "We can't stay out here. My pack is going to be looking for me and we can't go back to yours."

"Your people have caused my pack nothing but trouble. Why should I trust you now?" Madoc asked Lucian.

"They have shielded the truth from you well. We have never attacked anyone. But we do defend our territory, and we will fight when threatened. As long as you keep the peace, you have nothing to fear from us."

I lowered my voice, hoping that only Madoc could hear me, "Your father will kill me if we go back, and you know we can't call them for help. My pack will kill us if we go there. These shifters have no quarrel with us. Our car isn't going to take us anywhere, so if they wanted us dead, they could just follow us."

"That's not reassuring."

I grinned. "Well, if they try to hurt us, I'll protect you."

He smirked. "Or maybe I'll protect you."

"We'll take care of each other," I agreed.

Madoc took hold of my hand, closing his fingers around mine in a gesture that felt far too intimate. He took a step toward Lucian. "Thank you for your hospitality."

Lucian inclined his head, then gestured for us to follow. The female scowled at us, shaking her head as she matched pace with the elder. Madoc and I followed the pair, still clasping hands.

"Does your promise of peace extend to all the shifters here?" Madoc glanced toward the broody female shifter.

"Yeah, yeah. I'm not going to hurt you. Though I'm a little flattered that you think I could," she said. "There's not a whole lot we can do against that magic your girl-friend weilds."

"She's not my..."

"My mistake," the female shifter said. "You two seemed... close. I suppose I read your vibration wrong."

"Ignore Tasha, she skipped lunch." Lucian parted the boughs of a pair of evergreen trees, revealing a path. "I get what she's saying though. I thought I sensed a connection between the two of you. And our gifts are rarely wrong."

"Should you really be sharing that information with these strangers?" Tasha asked.

"We already know her magic, and they are here to see Freya. They're going to find out," Lucian said.

"You have gifts?" Madoc asked. "What kind of gifts?"

"Not as strong as your *friend's*; none of us have magic

that strong. But most of us here have something that makes us unique. Though for most of us, our fae blood is so diluted, the gifts might not even be noticed. Most of our members have something small, like enhanced strength, or better eyesight. Things that we wouldn't pick up on if we were part of a normal pack."

"Your pack made sure that wasn't an option for any of us. Hunted us down, took us to the brink of extinction," Tasha said.

"I have no idea what you're talking about," Madoc said.

"You are an Umbra wolf, correct? You smell like one. Perhaps only those in the ruling family know of their treachery and deceit," Tasha said.

Madoc squeezed my hand, and I could tell this information rattled him. I squeezed back, trying to be reassuring. Mostly, I was grateful I had used a false name for him.

"They're the reason we're here, in hiding. Cast out from the rest of the packs. It happened long ago. Very few were alive during the great purge, but we share with the younger wolves so they know the risks," Lucian said.

"So you all have fae blood?" Little flutters of excitement filled my chest. I had so many questions and if these shifters were like me, maybe I could learn.

"That's how it started. But we expanded. We take in anyone the other packs won't have. The outcasts, and those who don't want to conform," Lucian said.

"Lucian, I don't think we should be sharing all of this," Tasha said.

"Why not? She's one of us. There's a reason you're here to see Freya. That's not my business. But if you're here to ask her to remove your powers, that's the one thing she can't do." Lucian turned and lifted another pair of tree boughs, revealing another path.

In the dim light of twilight, it was nearly impossible to see the trail. Even though there was a worn path underfoot, it practically blended in with the surrounding landscape. With human eyes, it would look like a forest floor.

"When will she return? Freya, I mean," Madoc asked.

That sinking feeling in my gut returned, a sensation of disappointment that came every time I had to face the fact that the bond was going away.

"Not sure. Could be tonight, could be tomorrow," Lucian said.

"How can you not know?" Madoc asked. I could feel his anxiety spiking, his unease growing as we went deeper into the woods. He was worried and I could understand why, but for some reason, I wasn't getting those same emotional responses myself. I shouldn't feel safe around these two strangers, but I felt more comfortable around them than I had around members of my own pack.

"Babies don't come at a scheduled time," Tasha said.

"We're spread out. We live in small groups just in case any of your people come to attack us. It's not safe for us to be in large numbers. Freya travels where she's needed and returns here in between. We are the heart of the feral wolves, she must return to us, so she will," Lucian said.

So we were on our way to the primary home of the

feral wolves. Lucian had called himself an elder, after all. Based on the elders of my pack, that should be enough to make me nervous, but he seemed the opposite of all the shifters I've grown up with. I couldn't explain it, but he felt like sunshine and chamomile tea; whereas the shifters in my pack felt more like gasoline near a lit match.

The trail narrowed, forcing us to single file. Madoc dropped my hand, then moved behind, wrapping a possessive arm around my waist. I hated how much I enjoyed his presence. I knew I should push him away, that every second spent getting closer to him was going to make things more difficult, but I couldn't do it. I wanted to be near him. I wanted to soak up as much of him as I could before I would lose him forever.

Lucian paused in front of another pair of trees and lifted the boughs. I expected to see another turn in our path, but this time I saw the flickering of campfires and a clearing dotted with canvas tents on raised platforms. It was a small community, maybe thirty tents in all, but there was a warmth that surged through me as we crossed into the space. Something about this place felt like home.

THIRTY-ONE

LAST TIME I had been around a group of shifters and a bonfire, the scene had been one of debauchery. This was the absolute opposite. People sat on benches having quiet conversations, others spread out on blankets, laying back with their faces toward the sky. A few kids ran around engaged in a game of tag, and I caught the scent of roasting meat and spices.

Everything was so different, yet the whole place felt familiar. Something in particular was giving off that energy and I moved toward it, drawn in like a moth to flame. Pulling away from Madoc, I headed away from the fire.

"Where are you going?" Madoc called.

"I'm not sure," I said.

"Maybe you shouldn't then," he said.

"No, there's something over there." I continued,

moving toward a cluster of trees that didn't look like anything special.

"Lucian," Tasha said, a note of warning in her tone.

"Let her go," he said.

All of their conversations seemed so far away, and nothing that they said was going to stop my progress. Whatever was in the woods was calling me. Its pull greater than that of the bond I felt with Madoc.

Stepping into the dark woods, I moved with ease. The moonlight barely cut through the dense canopy, but I knew where I was going. Each step was purposeful and driven by something beyond me. I embraced it, letting it take over.

Footsteps crunched through the underbrush behind me. I heard someone stumble and curse, but I couldn't stop. I had to know what this was.

Ahead, another clearing emerged. Soft grass was dotted with red flowers. A ring of aspen trees full of bright green leaves surrounded the clearing in a perfect circle. My brow furrowed. Flowers shouldn't be blooming at this time of year, and the trees should be bare. Unlike the woods I'd walked through, there was no sign of snow. The feral camp was muddy and well worn, the snow gone due to walking and the heat from the fire.

This space looked like perpetual spring. As if snow couldn't penetrate the circle. I took a deep breath and passed the trees, stepping among the flowers. My magic flared in my chest, pure and strong. I gasped, over-whelmed by the sensation.

Light exploded from me, bathing the circle in a warm glow. My pulse raced, and the magic intensified. It rolled through me, and I felt lighter than air. Then, pain and agony crashed into me, as if I was feeling the suffering of hundreds of people all at once. I cried out, my body buckling under enormous pressure. Tears streamed down my face.

Suddenly, Madoc crashed into me, wrapping me in his arms. "It's okay. You're okay."

The pain eased, and the glow faded, leaving us in the moonlight. Shaking and confused, I took a few deep breaths before I realized what he'd just done. My magic flared and Madoc was holding me.

"What did you do that for?" I pulled away from his embrace. "I could have hurt you. I could have killed you."

He stepped forward, taking my hands in his. "You needed me."

"I don't understand," I said.

"We can't harm each other, remember?" He smoothed back my hair with his hands.

Relief wasn't a strong enough word for how I felt at that reminder. The magic I had was deadly, and I spent so much time concerned about harming those I cared about. But that was impossible with him. I could be myself with him, without worry.

"You lit up like the sun," he said as he wiped the tears from my cheeks. "Then there was pain. So much pain. I could feel everything you were feeling. Are you alright?"

"I'm okay now. I don't know what that was," I said. "Something awful happened here."

"Well, fuck me," Tasha said. "You're holding back, girl. I haven't seen someone react to this circle like that ever."

"You're like a firefly," Lucian said. "I haven't seen magic like that in decades. I've seen the sparks in the hands, but never the whole body. Not even inside the circle. If you're not full fae, you're really damn close."

"They told me my dad was fae," I admitted.

"Probably one of the only fae still wandering our realm," Lucian said.

I tried to ignore the comment. I didn't want to linger on the fact that my dad might be out there somewhere. There was too much on my plate already to deal with unprocessed parental issues. "What is this place?" I asked.

"It used to be a portal to the other realm," he said. "But it's been locked down for more than twenty years."

"The magic still lingers," Tasha said.

"What happened here?" I asked. "I felt so much pain."

"There was a massacre here long ago. Shifters and fae at war. We used to come and go between the realms, but that was centuries ago. They locked us out from their side after the war, but they could still visit. For a while, we got the occasional fae visitor, but we lost the ability to go to them," Lucian explained.

"Nobody gets through anymore," Tasha said darkly.

"That's true. The Umbra wolves figured out a way to lock it from our side about twenty years ago. About the same time, they wiped out most of us."

"No, they wouldn't do that," Madoc said. "They don't bother with anything outside our territory."

"Your kind carries a lot of secrets," Tasha said.

"See if they're lying," I suggested.

"They aren't," he whispered. "I just don't want to believe it."

Tasha narrowed her eyes. "You're fae. Holy shit. I thought maybe my magic was messing with me, but it's not. You two have more than just a connection. You have a bond. A strong one at that."

"No, of course not," I said, mostly so I wouldn't have to feel the hurt of Madoc denying it first.

"So that's what you're here for," Lucian said. "I can't say I agree, but you must have a damn good reason to give something up something so rare."

"It's complicated," I said.

"It always is," Lucian said. "The gods wouldn't give us a mate that didn't help us become who we are meant to be."

I considered his words and tried to think of a good excuse for why we were breaking the bond. Moving forward with it would change nothing for me. I had nothing else to lose. No pack, no family, no home. If I completed the bond with Madoc, he would be all I had, and that was truly terrifying.

I wanted to be able to take care of myself since it was mostly what I'd always done. Sure, things didn't always work out the way I wanted them to, but at the end of the day, I had always only been able to count on myself. Kate had been there to support me, but finding out about the tea changed the way I viewed my friendship with her. I didn't know who I could trust, which just went to show me that the only one I could trust was myself.

Madoc still had options. I was already screwed. There was no sense in both of us losing everything. "Sometimes the fates give you a hand you just can't play," I said.

"Maybe," Lucian said. "We've got a couple of spare tents set up for newcomers or visitors. Let's get you to some dinner and you can get some rest. Hopefully, Freya will be back by the morning."

I couldn't even look at Madoc as we exited the fairy circle. He hadn't said anything about us either keeping or removing our bond. I probably shouldn't think on it too much. It wasn't going to change anything either way.

Navigating back to the camp was a little more difficult because the lingering twilight we'd had on the walk in was completely gone. Or maybe it felt worse because Madoc was still silent. In the circle, he'd felt my pain, the same way I'd felt his. And the fact that he could withstand my magic was difficult to ignore. Mating bonds were powerful, and I found myself resenting the fates. Why give us something so incredible when it was impossible?

There were three fires burning now, all of them smaller and more contained than the massive bonfires of my pack's full moon parties. They seemed more functional, designed to provide warmth for those sitting around them or used as a way to cook their food.

"You hungry?" Tasha asked.

"I could eat," I said.

"They caught some rabbits and fish, so there's plenty of food tonight. This way."

I followed her, though I could have just as easily followed the scent of cooking meat. Still resisting the urge to turn around, I wondered what Madoc was thinking. Had he changed his mind? My heart did the annoying flip-flop thing, and I clenched my jaw, reining in the fleeting sense of hope. It wasn't possible, even if we wanted to be together. I didn't want to live with the threat of my mate's father hunting me down for the rest of my life.

Curious gazes settled on us as we made our way toward the farthest campfire where a group of shifters were cooking meat on a metal grate over the flames. The shifters we encountered were friendly and welcoming, quickly filling plates with food for both me and Madoc. He took a seat on a bench and I was invited to join a pair of female shifters at a picnic table.

Every so often, I glanced over to see how he was doing. It warmed my heart to see him smiling and easily conversing with the other shifters around him. The feral wolves were curious about me and asked questions, but I noticed they didn't ask anything too personal. I got the sense that they understood the importance of protecting your past. To my surprise, I enjoyed the company and the food.

The feral wolves seemed a peaceful bunch, unburdened by the politics and ambition of the pack I'd grown up in. We'd always been told that going feral was the worst thing possible, yet the shifters here seemed happy. That was more than could be said for most of the shifters I brought drinks to on Friday nights at the Howler.

"Are all the feral communities like yours?" I asked between bites of freshly caught fish.

"Not all. Just like the major packs, we have things that make us different. Really, the only thing that makes a shifter feral is they aren't part of one of the official packs. We form our own small packs, outside shifter law. We're too small for them to care, which is exactly how we like it," Paula, the shifter sitting across from me, explained.

"How do you stay out of it? Don't they try to rein you in?" I asked.

"As long as we stay away from their settlements, they don't care what we do," Paula said with a shrug.

"I'm honestly surprised there's not more of you. Growing up, there was always gossip about shifters leaving our town to go feral. Either because they were kicked out, or they ran out of money, or they simply had enough of the drama," I said.

"Oh, there are plenty of us. We keep in touch, and respect each other enough even if we're not part of the same pack. It's safer in smaller numbers, so that's another way we stay off their radar," she said.

That was basically what Lucian had told us, but I pictured just a few small settlements like this one, which still wouldn't be very many shifters. If they had larger settlements or a ton of these little ones, they would easily outnumber the shifters in my pack and Madoc's. Maybe they did. It was possible there were more of them than there were of the two packs combined.

I finished my food and cleaned up my dishes, pausing to watch Madoc juggle for a group of kids. Seeing how playful and sweet he could be was melting my heart. I knew so little about him, yet the glimmers I got showed me that he could be kind, even if he came from a pack with a bad reputation. He had decapitated members of my pack, but what did any of us do when threatened?

When I thought about it, our packs weren't all that different. Shadow, Umbra, we were both considered ruthless. There were just different reasons for the reputations. While being a Shadow Wolf carried its own preconceptions, Madoc had it worse being the next alpha. I knew he got his hands dirty, and I knew he could be violent and dangerous, but right then he was none of those things.

Two of the rocks he was juggling fell on the ground, one landing on his toe. He cursed, then hopped; the children bursting into laughter as he grabbed his injured foot.

I bit down on my lip, keeping myself from laughing out loud. It made everything harder to see this side of him. Since I'd known him, I'd mostly seen the protective and compassionate side. The murderous side, the part of him that decapitated members of my pack, seemed to exist when I wasn't around. I had to remind myself of that or I would never let myself break this bond.

"Whose idea was it?" Tasha's voice came from behind. She stopped next to me, her arms crossed over her chest. "Well, you gotta give me something. It gets very boring around here. A couple with powerful fae magic coming to break a mating bond is pretty fucking juicy. So, whose idea was it? Yours or his?"

Neither of us wanted the bond, but he was the one who had come up with the idea to break it. It didn't feel right to throw him under the bus when I agreed to it so readily. "It's what's best for both of us. That's all that matters."

"It's not the only thing that matters. The way you feel right now? You're going to remember that. When the bond is broken, you're going to feel all that fondness and it's gonna hurt like hell. Just because the bond is gone doesn't mean that what you're feeling will go away."

"Why are you telling me this?" I asked.

"Because those of us with fae blood very rarely find a mate. When we do, it's celebrated. It's the most amazing and terrible thing someone can experience. That kind of love is on a whole other level. Some of us know what it feels like to love someone with that kind of intensity. And I can tell you, when that is ripped away from you, you'll experience pain that makes you wish you were dead." Her jaw tensed.

"I'm sorry for your loss," I said. "But sometimes there are other things beyond our control and we can't change our stars."

"They say the ancient fae, the first ones to come through that portal into this realm, are the ones who created the stars." She dropped her hands to her side and walked away.

I felt numb as I said a stunted goodnight to Madoc. It was the only way I was going to get through this. I had to shut it all off. I couldn't let myself feel anything or I might break. Alone on a cot in a strange tent, I curled up on my side and wished I could let myself cry. But I knew once I opened the floodgates, I wasn't going to be able to stop. For now, I needed to build a wall to protect myself and close myself off. After this was finished, and I was far away from Madoc, I could let myself cry.

CHAPTER
THIRTY-TWO

I woke to the smell of coffee and my first thought was that Kate was up early. Reality hit hard, reminding me that I wasn't home and that things with Kate were complicated.

With a groan, I rolled off the cot, sending positive thoughts to the gods. Not that they ever listened to me before. Regardless of what Kate's part was in the tea, I wanted her to be safe. She had created that diversion so I could leave, and that counted for something.

"Ivy, you awake?" Madoc called. The tent flap fluttered, and I tensed, the rest of reality crashing in around me. Madoc. The bond.

"Yeah, come in," I said on reflex, instantly regretting it.

He stepped into the tent, having to duck a little to keep from hitting the top. I guess that was a perk to being short. The tent had plenty of head clearance for me.

"Mind if I join you?" He gestured to the cot.

I scooted to the end, shoving the pillow out of my way.

He took the other end. "How'd you sleep?"

"Fine," I said.

"Good," he said.

The silence between us was uncomfortable. I was still trying to keep myself shut down, afraid of opening up around him like I had in the past.

I was failing.

Every part of me was crying out internally to go to him. My inner wolf was beside herself, clawing and whining and begging. She was furious that I was resisting our mate.

I hated everything about it.

All I wanted to do was to embrace the bond and tear Madoc's clothes off right here. But I couldn't. As I sat there in awkward tension, I realized it was because my feelings for him had grown too deeply. I cared about him too much to allow us to go forward with the bond. Doing so would cost him his family and his pack. I couldn't do that to him.

"I came here to thank you for not telling them who I really am," he said.

"Of course," I replied.

"It was quick thinking on your part," he said.

"Well, I'm a nobody. You're not," I said.

"That's not true," he said.

I chuckled. "It really is, and I'm okay with it. It's not a dig against me, it's just life for most of us. I'm sure you can only name a few shifters in my pack, and probably not a whole lot more in yours."

"Sometimes I wish that was my life," he confessed.

"Everything has been planned out for me. There was never a time someone asked me what I wanted to be when I grew up. They just knew."

"Same for me, but different," I said. "Nobody cared enough to ask me and nobody expected me to do anything important."

Madoc's hands were holding mine before I could react to his movement. "Say the words and I'll call the whole thing off. Maybe the feral wolves are right. Maybe our bond shouldn't be broken."

"And then what?" I asked. "We build ourselves a tent and learn how to hunt rabbits?"

"Why not?" he asked.

He sounded sincere, but I could feel his apprehension. I could also feel something else that felt an awful lot like deep loss. Giving up Kate just about killed me. I still wasn't sure how I was going to deal with that, even with the confusion I was facing. He had brothers and Willow. He'd never be satisfied here.

"Your life isn't here," I said. "You want to change things. Hopefully, for the better."

"I do," he said. "No more division. No more black market deals and men running things from behind the curtain."

"That's good," I said. "Your pack needs you. Shit, all the packs need that. The corruption and greed have lingered too long. They need the younger wolves to step up and change things."

His thumb brushed over mine, his touch soothing. I wanted this, but if he was even a little better than his father, he would help so many.

"Ivy?" A female voice called seconds before the curtain was pulled back. Tasha lifted a brow. "Did you two change your minds?"

I hopped up from the cot. "No, of course not."

She hummed. "Well, Freya arrived late last night. She's ready to see you now."

FREYA'S TENT was in the center of the camp. It was the only tent with any exterior decorations, making it stand out among the other plain tents. Colorful strips of fabric were sewn along the canvas, washing her tent in vibrant colors.

An old woman smoking a pipe stepped out as we approached. She had white hair and her face was lined. She looked ancient, and I was a little surprised she'd traveled to another camp alone. Many wolf shifters lived well beyond human years, but I wasn't sure if witches were the same.

She blew a ring of smoke at us, then narrowed her tiny eyes, making them almost disappear into the wrinkles on her tan skin. "You're Willow's friend?"

"Yes, Mal, nice to meet you," Madoc said.

"Hmm, fake name. Not even original." She took another pull on her pipe, then blew it out in a cloud. The smoke was sweet and earthy. It didn't have the scent of anything I'd smelled before.

"Thank you for seeing us," I said.

"Well, when you're as old as me, you never know when your time will expire, so we might as well move on with this." She ducked into her tent.

I glanced at Madoc. He shrugged, then followed her inside. I went in after him.

The tent was small and crowded. Her cot extended along the back, and spread in front of it was a large ornate rug. Spindly tables lined the left and right sides of the tent. They were topped with jars of herbs, wooden boxes, and canvas bags. It reminded me of Willow's collection.

Freya settled on her bed. "Have a seat on the rug. I don't sit on the ground anymore. The gods are going to have to forgive my insolence or not."

Madoc and I sat, and I noticed that he looked as uncomfortable as I felt.

"Tasha tells me you have a bond you want to break. That is not something I see often. Of course, when I was young, bonds were more common. It wasn't as rare to see them broken." She took another puff of her pipe, then blew the smoke above us. It made the tent hazy as it settled.

"What do we need to do to break this?" I asked.

"It's simple enough," she said.

"So you can break it?" Madoc asked.

"Of course I can." She sounded insulted.

"Thank you," I added quickly, hoping she wasn't going to turn us away because we upset her.

"First, I must know this is what you both want. This can't be undone. You must be certain," she said. "Do you wish to sever your bond?'

I couldn't find my voice, but I nodded. Madoc must have nodded because Freya inclined her head in acknowledgement.

"You should know, all magic comes at a price. And this is no exception," she said.

"What kind of price?" Madoc asked.

Freya pushed herself to standing with a grunt. Madoc jumped to his feet. "Can I help you?"

"Aren't you sweet?" Freya accepted his elbow, and they moved to the side of the tent. "If I were younger, I might see if you were interested in a rebound after you ditch your mate."

"I'm flattered," Madoc said.

My face heated. I shouldn't be jealous of her, but I was. Fucking bond.

Freya picked up a small glass bottle about the size of a tube of lipstick and then gestured for Madoc to help her back to the bed. Once she was settled again, Madoc rejoined me on the floor.

"This is what you need. It'll break the bond within twenty-four hours of use." Freya held up the bottle. "Only one of you needs to take it, and then you wait. As long as you don't do anything to override it while it's kicking in, the bond will break."

"What do you mean, override it?" I asked.

"Sex, of course," she said with a cackle. "Once the bond has been complete, this is useless. I assume you haven't consummated the bond? I should have asked that first, but typically couples aren't willing to break it once they reach that point. Unless the sex is really, really bad." She scanned Madoc. "And I get the feeling you know your way around a woman."

What the fuck? Is she hitting on him? I bit down on the inside of my cheek to keep from shouting at her. She was just a harmless old woman, and she was helping us. I needed to keep my shit together.

"That sounds easy enough," Madoc said.

"The difficult part is deciding who will take the potion," she said. "All magic has a price, and this one can be a doozy."

"I'll take it," Madoc said. "You gave up your pack for me. I should do this for you."

"We don't even know what it does." I looked up at Freya. "What is the price?"

"Magic for magic. Whoever takes this will likely never shift, or use any other kind of magic, again," she said.

I swallowed hard. That was a big cost. I had just gained my magic. Both shifting and fae. I wasn't even sure what I was capable of yet, and I had to admit that I liked how powerful I felt.

"I can do it," Madoc said.

"Hell no, you won't." The words came out as pure reaction. "Absolutely not."

I wanted to keep shifting; I wanted to keep my fae magic, but I was already without a pack. My wolf felt like she was going to shred me into pieces, but I pressed on. "If I lose my magic, I can just go live with humans. I can't go home anyway, and I've only shifted a handful of times. It's no loss for me."

It was a loss. A major loss. But I wasn't about to tell him that. I'd adapt. It was what I did. If he couldn't shift, he couldn't be an alpha. It would make this whole process moot. We might as well not even break the bond at all.

My wolf rejoiced at that thought, but I reined her in. *We're doing this for our mate.* It was the only option.

"No, we'll figure something else out," he said.

"The longer you wait, the harder it will be," Freya said. "You should do this or complete the bond."

"That's it?" I asked. "One of us drinks what's in that vial and then it's done?"

She nodded.

Madoc shook his head. "It's not worth it."

My stomach twisted into knots. I knew what I had to do, and I hoped I was fast enough. I couldn't let Madoc beat me to it. "Alright," I told him. "We'll find another way."

He blew out a breath and his shoulders dropped as he released some of his tension.

It was now or never. I reached for the potion, grabbing it out of Freya's hand. Quickly, I popped the cork, then I tossed it back. Nearly gagging, I choked down the putrid mixture. It was thick and earthy, but not in a good way. Like a drinking pure sludge kind of way.

"Ivy!" Madoc threw me to the ground as he batted the bottle out of my hand.

It was too late.

"It is done," Freya said. "Now you wait."

CHAPTER
THIRTY-THREE

Madoc was on top of me, his legs straddling my hips, his arms bracketing my head. "Why did you do that?"

I wriggled out from under him, then pushed myself to standing. There wasn't anything to say. He knew exactly why I did it, and if I was being honest, I'd do it again if I had to. To prevent him from losing everything, I'd give up anything. I picked up the discarded bottle and handed it to Freya. She took it, then nodded.

"Ivy, talk to me!" Madoc sounded frantic and the tent suddenly felt suffocating. As if it was full of a flurry of chaotic emotions pressing in around us.

I didn't want to look at him, because my inner wolf was pacing restlessly inside and I was pretty sure I was never going to be able to reassemble the shattered pieces of my heart. But I reminded myself this was the only option. This was what was best. Forcing myself to hold my chin high, I turned to face him. "One of us had to. And like I said, you can't be an alpha if you can't shift."

The back of my throat burned and I couldn't risk breaking down in tears in front of him, so I left the tent and walked without direction. I couldn't feel him following me, which was both a relief and soul crushing. I wanted his comfort, even though he was the one person I should be avoiding. This wasn't done yet, and I had to get through today without giving in to the tangled feelings I had for him.

I felt my wolf settle, as if resigning to her fate. That sensation of giving up was what finally brought the tears forth. I wiped them off my cheek, uncomfortable with anyone seeing me cry. In the Shadow Pack, we learned any kind of weakness was an entry point for pain. I learned to lock down my tears years ago, and I rarely cried. But since meeting Madoc, my emotions had been more intense and difficult to command.

I supposed that was a benefit of breaking this bond. I could go back into locking everyone out and locking everything I felt away. Emotions and attachments made me vulnerable, and I had learned my lesson too many times to count.

I was standing in the woods, facing the ring of aspen trees around the fairy circle. My legs had carried me here without thought and grief washed over me as I considered what I had just given up. That new power inside me was just starting to blossom. It was part of me as much as my wolf was, yet neither skill got the attention or time it deserved.

I hesitated, knowing that if I entered, I would feel my magic surge, which might cause me more pain. But I recalled the warmth that had come from that space once I'd gotten over the initial shock of the memories of the pain that had happened here. This was a place of great and terrible loss, and also a place of mystical energy and peace. It was difficult to comprehend how one place could have so much conflicting energy, but that about matched how I felt. I was grateful I could make this sacrifice for Madoc, but I had also never felt this level of despair. Somehow, I knew I would overcome this and time would ease this pain.

I crossed the circle of trees, sucking in a deep breath as I prepared for the crushing memories of the destruction and loss that occurred in the sacred space. This time, it didn't come. Nothing came. My magic didn't flare. I didn't feel the energy or the connection I had before. The emptiness was almost worse.

I sank to my knees, already feeling like I'd lost a part of myself. The ground here was soft, the earth warm. It was such a wonderful contrast to the muddy, wet remains of the last snowfall. If nothing else, this was a good place to wait. Crunching sounded and I turned to see Madoc just beyond the ring of aspen trees.

"I had a feeling you'd come here." He stepped into the space and walked over to me, joining me on the grass. "You should not have done that."

"I didn't have a choice, and you know that." I looked at my hands and focused on keeping my emotions in check.

"I told you we didn't have to go through with this before we went and visited her, and then in the tent I told you we could find another way," he said.

"That's the bond talking. You don't even know me and I'm not letting you risk your pack and your family for some foundling," I said.

"Don't talk about yourself that way. You're not any different than me or any other shifter. What happened to you could have just as easily happened to anyone. It almost happened to me. It should have happened to me," he said. "You aren't any less because of your path in life."

Gods dammit, why did he have to say things like that? His pretty words were part of why I had to do this. He'd have gone through with it, giving up everything for a shifter he didn't even know. I didn't deserve such pure love. He deserved someone who wasn't broken.

I sucked in a breath and steadied myself. He needed to go. Having him here was too painful. "Listen, you don't need to sit here with me and try to make me feel better. I'm fine. I already told you this actually helps solve some of my problems. I didn't have anywhere to go. Now I have the entire human world as an option. I'll get a job some-where and just blend in."

It was basically all I ever wanted. I wanted to be a part of my pack simply so I could be like everyone else. It seemed ridiculous now. Who sets a goal of just existing? What kind of life is that? I ran my fingers through the blades of grass, then touched the petals of one of the red flowers. When I stopped to think about it, my past life had been quite pathetic. Maybe this was a chance for me to start over, maybe I could do something more than simply existing. I could build a good life for myself, maybe find a passion or a hobby. Back in the Shadows, all I had time for was work. I wasn't even sure who I was.

"That doesn't sound like a good life," he said.

"It's what I want," I said.

"There are other ways to accomplish that. Plenty of shifters live in human cities. They don't belong to packs, they blend in with them every day, but they don't have to give up their magic to do that. If that was what you wanted, you didn't have to sacrifice half your soul for it."

I had no idea what it was going to feel like when my wolf was inaccessible to me, which was what he was referring to by the half my soul comment. He had no idea that the part I was more concerned about losing was the part of my soul that was connected to him. And that scared the shit out of me.

"Stop worrying about me. Go home. Tell your dad it's done. Go back to your parties and your vicious brothers and your plans." I took a deep breath and looked up at the sky. Sitting here in this grass staring at the cloudless blue expanse made it feel like spring had finally come. I was tired of winter, and this was a wonderful reprieve. I would miss this space and I wondered if I should find a human city somewhere warmer, somewhere where it was spring all the time.

"You know I can't do that," he said.

"Sure you can. It's not like I can betray you and take this back. You heard Freya, it's done," I said.

"I still don't understand why you did it. Do you think so little of me? You're just like everyone else, aren't you? All you see is my father and the actions of those around me. I opened up to you, but you couldn't wait to be free of me," he said.

"Are you serious?" How could he say something like that? I gave up my pack for him. I gave up my magic for him. How could he not see that everything I did was for him?

Madoc stood. "I understand. I'm the monster who sent the heads of your friends. Let me tell you something. I will always protect myself, my family, and those I care about. But I am not like them and when I'm alpha, things will change."

I jumped to my feet, anger surging through me. My emotions came in a torrent, unleashing everything I had worked so hard to bottle up. "How can you be so stupid? Why do you think I did this? If I thought you were going to be the same tyrant that your father is, that all the alphas I've ever known were, I would have insisted you drink the potion and put an end to it. I did this because there's a chance that you might be better than your father."

"I'm nothing like my father. I would have completed the bond with you or drank that potion just to keep you from this. How do you not see that I care about you? It's not just the bond, you don't see how incredible you are and that's infuriating," he said.

"When the bond is broken, you won't feel that way anymore. You can go marry whatever girl is going to strengthen the alliance in your pack and you can forget about me. Live a long happy life, bring peace to the packs and whatever you're going to do, you get to do it because we broke this bond. If you stayed with me, none of that would be possible. You'd lose everything," I said.

"Well, aren't you altruistic," he snapped.

"I don't know why you're so mad at me. You win. You get everything you want."

"Not everything," he said.

"You'll find someone else. Someone you can choose rather than the fates choosing for you," I said.

"Why did you really do it?" he asked softly.

"I told you why. Lots of reasons why. Now, please go. I want to be alone." I turned my back on him as the tears forced their way out.

"I know you're lying."

Damn his fae gift. I balled my hands into fists. This was so much harder than I thought it would be.

"Everything you said makes you look like a hero, but none of it's the truth. Why did you really do this?" he asked.

Something seemed to explode in my chest, a surge of emotions so intense I felt like I was spiraling out of control. I spun around, tears streaming down my cheeks.

"I did it because I care about you, you idiot. Now get the fuck out of here before I do something stupid."

He smirked. "There you are. There's that strong woman who stood up to her alpha. I knew you were still in there."

"How dare you!" I shouted. "You were trying to piss me off."

"Can't you just accept that maybe this bond is for real?" He closed the distance between us, our bodies nearly touching. I stared up into his dark eyes, my mind and body at war. He was too close to me; I was too close to him. I could feel his warm breath on my face, and I swear I could sense his arousal. Or maybe that was mine.

"Tell me you don't want this and I will walk away," he said.

My lower lip trembled, and I tried to wrap my mind around his words. I should push him away, tell him to go, finish what we started. But I couldn't do it. My body and my soul seemed to beg for him. He truly was my other half, the missing piece. "Are you sure?"

"I've never been more sure of anything in my life. I know there's a reason the fates put us together."

"Your father won't allow it. He'll disown you or kill me," I said.

"We'll figure it out. Together." He lowered his head so his forehead touched mine. I closed my eyes, breathing him in. He smelled like fresh snow, cedar, and a touch of something floral. It was intoxicating and comforting, and familiar.

When his lips found mine, the kiss gentle and tenuous. There was hesitation in his movements as if he thought I might push him away, but all the fight was gone from me. I wanted this. I wanted him. Like he said, we'd figure it out.

I tangled my fingers in his dark hair and deepened the kiss. That was all it took for him to know he had my answer. In an instant, the tenderness was gone, replaced by a sense of urgency as we devoured each other.

CHAPTER
THIRTY-FOUR

MY BODY HEATED, and I was vaguely aware of the fact that I was glowing, but it didn't seem to bother Madoc. In a frantic dance of teeth and tongues, we kissed as if it were the last time we would ever be able to touch each other. Somehow, it was even more intense than our kisses in the car.

My chest felt full, and I felt more alive than I ever had, but I realized I was still holding back. I gave in, and a burst of light exploded from me, the brilliance causing us to break the kiss. Still wrapped in each other's embrace, the two of us looked around.

"What was that?" Madoc asked.

"I'm not sure," I said.

The aspen trees were glowing, each of the little green leaves had turned a vibrant gold, emitting their own beams of light like drops of sunshine. The whole circle was bathed in the warm light, even though my skin was no longer glowing.

"I don't know what that means, but it has to be a good sign," Madoc said.

"The only thing I want to know is why you stopped kissing me," I teased.

Glowing magic should impress me, but hunger roared deep inside, begging for release. Madoc was the only thing that could satisfy my craving.

He growled and scooped me up in his arms. I wrapped my legs around his waist as he folded to the ground. I was on his lap now, His hardness pressing between my thighs. Our clothing was the only thing that prevented us from what we both wanted. Almost as if Madoc could read my mind, he tugged the hoodie up over my head and threw it aside. He made a low rumbling sound deep in his throat when he saw the additional layer of clothing preventing access. Quickly, he grabbed hold of the collar of my shirt and easily ripped it in two. My pulse raced, and wetness grew between my legs. I reached for his shirt, pulling it over him and tossing it aside. Eager and desperate, I pressed my palms against his skin. "You're like a work of art."

"So are you." His hands moved up and down my arms, leaving a trail of sparks in their wake.

My fingers trailed down his perfectly sculpted chest and this time when I reached his waistband to work the buttons, he didn't stop me. I climbed off of him and the two of us abandoned all of our clothes before ending up tangled together on the soft grass.

It wasn't the first time we'd seen each other naked, but it was the first time I truly let myself enjoy his body. He was all hard muscle and warm skin and feeling his body pressed against mine was like a taste of heaven. Our hands explored each other, touching and caressing. I traced my fingers down past his hips, around his ass, and up his back. Madoc's hands worked their way across my stomach to the curve of my breasts. There was a sense of awe from both of us as we simply touched and explored.

Madoc lowered his face to mine, trailing kisses along my jaw before moving lower. He kissed his way down my neck to my breasts. Using his fingers and his mouth, he teased and licked and sucked. I dug my fingers into his back as he continued to lavish his tongue and lips across the sensitive skin. One of his huge hands dipped down between my thighs, his thumb finding the sensitive nub. I gasped as he teased, the sensations mingling from his mouth and his hand, driving me crazy.

His lips found mine again, colliding in a passionate kiss as he slipped a finger inside me. A second one joined, and he curled them just right, thrusting in and out. I moaned into the kiss, my hips lifting and lowering of their own accord to meet the rhythm of his hand. All reason left me as he drew forth the coiling sensation of a building orgasm. I closed my eyes and gripped the earth for support as tension built.

Without warning, he bit down on my lower lip and the

quick burst of pain sent me over the edge. With a gasp and a cry, I shook under his expert touch as a climax rolled through me. When I opened my eyes, Madoc was staring down at me with a self-satisfied smirk on his face. "You're even more beautiful when you come."

He traced lazy circles on my stomach, his hand going lower and lower with each movement. I wanted more, but I wanted to give him the same kind of release he had given me. I was unfamiliar with pretty much everything in regards to sex, but I understood the concepts well enough to give it a go. Rising to my knees, I pushed him down to his back. "Your turn."

He lifted his brows. "What did you have in mind, sugar?"

I grinned, finding the nickname playful instead of condescending. Who knew I'd be here with this cocky wolf? I recalled the first night we met. The pull to him had existed before I even saw his face. Our bond was so intense, it overwhelmed everything else. He'd stepped in to protect me, without even knowing who I was or why he felt the urge to keep me safe.

A flicker of a reminder popped into my head. It wasn't too late. If I didn't want this, I could still walk away. I moved closer to Madoc and rested my hand on his stomach and let my eyes drift to his. I could feel him, completely vulnerable, yet completely at ease. The connection thrummed between us, a warm and comforting thread that bound us to each other.

I didn't want to break it.

We'd figure it out. Neither of us were where we were supposed to be. Our lives had been complicated by those around us, and we both deserved to find happiness. That was what Madoc was to me, a chance to be happy. Even if there was a part of me that didn't believe I could have the same kind of happiness as others, I believed *he* could. And completing the bond would help bring him that. It was odd, caring about someone else with such ferocity. Giving in to him required a level of trust I'd never experienced. It made sense that I would be cautious, but when I tried to find excuses to walk away, I came up empty.

He reached for my face, his brow furrowing. "Is everything alright?"

I closed my eyes, leaning into the warmth of his hand on my cheek. In Freya's tent, the only solution seemed to be to drink the potion. Now, the only solution seemed to be to complete the bond. It was crazy and irrational, but it felt right.

Opening my eyes, I nodded. Then I took hold of his hand, lowering it to his chest. I bit down on my lower lip, feeling a little nervous at what I was about to do. Not because I was uncomfortable around him, but because I wanted to do it right. "I've never done this before," I confessed. "But I wanna try it."

Madoc lifted a curious brow as I lowered my head. He opened his mouth as if to speak, but went silent the second I closed my lips around his cock. The only sound he made was a groan of pleasure. I used my tongue and bobbed up and down. Based on the bucking of Madoc's hips and the sounds he made, I got the sense I was doing it right. He threaded his fingers into my hair, helping guide my head as I continued to work my mouth.

"You're going to make me come if you don't stop," he said, his voice breathy.

I released him from my mouth. "Isn't that the point?"

"Sometimes, yes. But not today. Today, I need all of you." He guided me to the ground, his hips settling between my thighs.

My breath hitched and I reached for him, pulling him closer to me. I wanted to feel his body against mine. I kissed him, then gripped his biceps, bracing myself. Anticipation and desire built as I waited for him to complete our bond. "I'm ready."

"I really don't deserve you," he said.

"Maybe I'm the one who doesn't deserve you," I said. "I'm the nobody. You're basically a prince."

"You're not a nobody; you are my everything." He leaned down, pressing his lips to mine once again. I felt him at my entrance, poised and ready. He pulled away, so his lips hovered above mine. "Are you sure this is what you want?"

"I want you." I reached for his hips and urged him forward. He got the message, and he thrust into me in one forceful movement.

I gasped as I stretched to accommodate him. He was larger than Dax, and at first, it was uncomfortable. I adjusted quickly, and we found a rhythm as he thrust in and out. The initial discomfort gave way to pleasure as the two of us moved in unison. My hips lifted to meet his thrusts, and our hands explored each other's bodies. I gripped his shoulders, holding on to him for leverage as his pace quickened.

Heat built, and everything tightened as each thrust brought me closer to release. Suddenly, Madoc lifted my thighs and his thrusts went deeper. I cried out, over and over, as he pounded into me. I dug my fingernails into the grass as my breathing grew more rapid and my eyes rolled into the back of my head. Gasping for air, I reached a crescendo as a climax exploded through me. I cried out his name over and over as waves of pleasure crashed through my body. The sensations rolled together, ebbing and flowing. He wasn't done with me and my body responded, giving me more pleasure than I thought possible.

He released my legs and leaned down, so we were pressed together. Still inside me, he moved slower, letting me catch my breath. He took his time as he ran his fingers through my hair and kissed every inch of me. Suddenly, Madoc scooped me up in his arms, moving us so he was sitting and I was straddling him. With his hands on my hips, he guided me and I found my rhythm, rolling and lifting as I rode him. Tension coiled low in my belly as another orgasm built. I continued on, getting lost in the sensation of Madoc's touch. His tongue played with the sensitive peaks of my nipples, driving me closer to the edge. Just as I thought I couldn't take much more, his finger found my clit, pushing me to the breaking point. Tossing my head back, I grabbed hold of him for support.

My whole body shuddered as my release crashed through me. Madoc tensed, his fingers biting into my back as he came.

His hand guided my head to him, and our lips met again. There was something different now, a change between us, amplified by our kiss. I realized the thread I'd felt before wasn't just a thread anymore. I couldn't sense where my body began and his ended. We truly felt like we two halves of the same whole. I wasn't just kissing Madoc Umbra; I was kissing my mate. I wasn't sure when the change happened, and I couldn't explain it, but it was there.

Between the lingering effects of my orgasms and the knowledge of our completed bond, I was breathless. "Did you feel that?"

He grinned. "I felt it. You are mine."

His words sent a shiver down my spine. He traced his thumb over my lower lip. "And I am yours."

WE DOZED in the fairy circle, enjoying the warmth from the magic and the weak winter sun. When I woke, the gold had faded from the leaves and the sun was low in the sky. We'd slept for hours, content in each other's embrace.

"You're awake," Madoc said.

"Do you think we could get away with just staying here forever?" I teased.

"I think we'd both be bored with that," he said.

"I can think of plenty of things to keep us entertained." I dragged my fingers down his chest and grabbed his length.

"On second thought, you make an excellent point," he said.

My stomach growled. "But there's no snacks."

Madoc laughed, then helped me up. "Let's find you some food."

Dressed and still in the afterglow of consummating our bond, the two of us headed back to camp.

We arrived in the midst of a frenzy of activity. Half the tents were gone, and the others were in the act of being dismantled. Shifters were loading up backpacks and several pickup trucks were parked near the remains of last night's bonfires. The feral wolves were hard at work, racing around to load the trucks.

They were leaving.

"What's happening?" Madoc asked.

Quickly, I scanned the area, looking for a familiar face. Lucian was carrying a bundle toward one of the trucks. "Over there."

Madoc and I and ran toward him. "What happened? Why are you leaving?"

"The Shadows attacked the Umbras, and we aren't going to get in the middle of their war," Lucian said. "We fixed your tires, and you're welcome to join our convoy. We'll ride out the war away from their territory."

"You should go with them," Madoc said. "You'll be safer with them."

"You're going to fight my pack," I said. "I mean, the Shadows." It was still difficult to not view them as my pack, even after everything I'd been through.

"You're an Umbra Wolf now," he said. "Your old pack isn't going to hurt you ever again."

That was how it worked when someone found their mate. The female joined the male's pack, but I hadn't thought about that because it really wasn't an option for us. "Your father isn't going to let me join."

"Once we settle this mess with the Shadows, we'll figure that out," he said.

"I can fight, I can help," I said.

"I can't fight if I'm worried about you," he said. "Besides, my father thinks we broke the bond. I need time to figure that part out, but you've got to trust me."

Part of me wanted him to stay with me, but that wasn't the right call. I took the potion so he'd be free to live his life. I wanted him to be able to go back to his pack and lead as he should, but now that he was my mate, I didn't want to leave his side. This was a new kind of pain that I wasn't prepared for.

Swallowing hard, I set aside my desires. This wasn't about me. Madoc was a strong fighter, and even Dax had his doubts about beating the Umbras. They hadn't seemed prepared for war when I'd left, which made me think Dax was acting on emotions. Maybe I could help, but not in the way I wanted. "Dax wants revenge. He's emotional, and he's immature. The elders don't support war, and they can be bought. That's your ticket out of this."

Madoc kissed me. "Thank you. I'll see you soon."

I hated staying behind like a damsel in distress. I wanted to be with Madoc and help him, but his father had to think we'd broken the bond.

Watching Madoc walk away from camp nearly broke me.

"You're welcome to stay with us as long as you like," Lucian said.

I looked at the older shifter, and I caught the sympathy in his expression. He meant well, and I did think I'd be safe with him, but I couldn't do it. I had so few good things in my life and I wasn't about to give up Madoc.

"Thank you, but I can't stay," I said.

"Of course you can't, but the offer stands if you need it," he said.

I nodded, then I ran to catch up to Madoc. "Wait!"

He turned. "Miss me already?"

"I'm going with you," I said.

His jaw tightened, and I waited for him to tell me that he didn't need me. I expected him to disappoint me, the same way everyone always did. Instead, he extended his hand.

I wasn't sure what we were going to do when we reached his pack, but we were going to have to figure it out. Together.

THANK you for reading Forbidden Sin! What will happen when Ivy and Madoc return to the Umbras? Find out in Feral Queen!

Want to keep in touch? Sign up for Alexis's newsletter for updates on new releases and information about current works!

About the Author

Alexis Calder writes sassy heroines and sexy heroes with a sprinkle of sarcasm. She lives in the Rockies and drinks far too much coffee and just the right amount of wine.

Also by Alexis Calder

Moon Cursed Series

Wolf Marked

Wolf Untamed

Wolf Chosen

Royal Mates Series

Shifter Claimed

Shifter Fated

Shifter Rising

Academy of Elites Series

Academy of Elites: Untamed Magic

Academy of Elites: Broken Magic

Academy of Elites: Fated Magic

Academy of Elites: Unbound Magic

Brimstone Academy Series

Brimstone Academy: Semester One

Brimstone Academy: Semester Two

Bloodfire Academy Series

Bloodfire Academy: Cursed Magic

Romcom books published under Lexi Calder:

In Hate With My Boss

Love to Hate You

Made in the USA
Las Vegas, NV
25 February 2022

44552343R00184